CHRISTMAS IN DREAM VALLEY

S J CRABB

Copyright © S J Crabb 2021

S J Crabb has asserted her rights under the Copyright, Designs and Patents Act 1988 to be identified as the Author of this work.

This book is a work of fiction and except in the case of historical fact, any resemblance to actual persons, living or dead, is purely coincidental.

All rights reserved. No part of this book may be reproduced or transmitted in any form without written permission of the author, except by a reviewer who may quote brief passages for review purposes only.

NB: This book uses UK spelling.

MORE BOOKS BY S J CRABB

<u>The Diary of Madison Brown</u>

My Perfect Life at Cornish Cottage

My Christmas Boyfriend

Jetsetters

More from Life

A Special Kind of Advent

Fooling in love

Will You

Holly Island

Aunt Daisy's Letter

The Wedding at the Castle of Dreams

My Christmas Romance

Escape to Happy Ever After

Cruising in Love

Coming Home to Dream Valley

Christmas in Dream Valley

New Beginnings in Dream Valley

sjcrabb.com

CHRISTMAS IN DREAM VALLEY

Settle down in a magical place that time forgot, where the snow glistens on the frosty ground, the fairy-lights glow like magical stars in the trees and romance blossoms against all the odds.

When the new vicar and his family move to Dream Valley just before Christmas, they need a lot of help.

Local playboy, the gorgeous Brad Hudson, takes one look at the vicar's daughter and, he is the first in line.

He will do anything to win Dolly's heart, but having heard of his reputation, her father has other ideas and does everything in his power to tear them apart.

Unused to having to work for love Brad tries his best but he has never come up against a protective father quite like Scott Macmillan.

Ex-special forces soldier turned military vicar; he proves a tough adversary.

Brad is determined to make Dolly fall in love with him and rises to the challenge until her father reveals his trump card, leaving Brad and Dolly battling to stay together.

Will love blossom under the starry skies of winter or will the vicar have his prayers answered and keep his daughter's heart safe?

CHAPTER 1

My breath collides with the icy air and offers me a brief moment of warmth as I wrap my arms around my body in the hope of getting some heat inside. I lost all feeling in my feet a while ago and as I attempt to wiggle my toes, it hurts.

A sigh of frustration makes its way into the frozen atmosphere and once again I try desperately to coax the little car back to life, to no avail.

The sound of a dying car is not a pleasant one and the tears sting as I swallow the lump in my throat at the realisation this is the end of my pride and joy only one year after I got her. That's the trouble with second-hand cars and I suppose we always knew her time was limited. The fact we were given the car from one of dad's parishioners whose mother had died makes it all the more poignant because it appears the car didn't want to carry on without her rightful owner, anyway.

Sighing, I peer through the windscreen and in normal circumstances would be more than excited about the view. Gentle rolling hills covered with a light dusting of snow. A bright blue sky with the rather wispy clouds scurrying along on their business. Frozen fields empty of life as the usual wildlife snuggle in their burrows and wait for the first sign of Spring and the frozen puddles that remind me why I'm in this mess in the first place.

It's one of them that made my little car skid to the verge and as she stalled, she decided life wasn't worth living and just gave up on me. Once again, the tears build and I sigh inside because what on earth am I going to do now? My phone has no power in this undulating landscape because the signal can't reach me. There is no life for miles because Dream Valley is the land that time forgot. A sleepy town that has barely made it out of village status and my frustration is growing as I contemplate living here for however long my father has got.

The pile of leaflets on the seat beside me reminds me I have an important job to do and I suppose they may come to my rescue because I am on my way to Dream Valley town to post as many of them as possible to encourage the locals to come and help make Christmas special.

Sighing, I lift the pile in my frozen fingers and leave my dying car to be retrieved later and start the torturous walk towards what passes as civilisation around here.

Despite the fact any heat left my body ages ago, I try to enjoy the view. Maybe the exercise will warm me up and chase away the bite of the cold. I certainly hope so because until I get a signal, it's my only shot at surviving this twist of fate that could be serious if I don't reach a warm fire or a hot bath soon.

With one eye on the signal bars on my phone and one hand gripping the leaflets tightly, I set off at a brisk pace, trying not to let my frozen limbs scream in protest. At least I'm wearing a coat that would draw a Yeti's admiration before eating me alive for being so foolish and the faux-fur hat that felt so fashionable and snug on my head is a welcome addition to any degree of warmth my body can scrape together.

Grateful of the sheepskin gloves that were a present from my mother last Christmas and the sunglasses that keep the glare of the sun from hurting my eyes, the only thing I'm unhappy about are the sheepskin boots that seemed so perfect when I selected them but are slightly too small and are now pinching my toes. In fact, it's painful to put one foot in front of the other and I wonder how long I must endure this torture for.

Lifting my eyes to the heavens, I mutter a silent prayer to God to deliver me from this evil because I want to get this over with and join the rest of my family around the inglenook fire, sipping the amazing soup that was boiling on the stove when I left.

As I head towards the town, I try anything to keep my

mind off the predicament I'm in now, namely my fight for survival, because I'm in no doubt I'm facing one now. The town could be hours away and I may not have that long because my feet are screaming they will give up at any second and my hands are turning blue inside my gloves. I want to cry so badly but I can't resist the tears freezing on my cheeks and so with a determination that has been drilled into me from an early age, I walk as briskly as my feet will allow in the direction I hope leads me to Dream Valley town.

Maybe it's been fifteen minutes, possibly half an hour later, I hear the welcome sound of life on the road behind me.

A car!

Lifting my eyes to God, I offer a silent prayer of thanks because surely I am saved. The fact it may be dangerous doesn't even enter my head because I'm in survival mode right now and as I see a large camper van heading my way, I wave my frozen arms as I step out from the side of the road.

The van passes and my heart sinks, but as it slides to a stop a few feet away, my heart lifts and my soul sings because I'm saved.

As quickly as possible I run towards it, my feet slipping slightly on the frozen ground and as I reach the window, it rolls down and I see a young man inside, looking at me with curiosity.

"You ok, darling?"

"I'm sorry but…" My voice sounds weak and slightly breathless as I try to get it to work and my throat hurts as the icy wind enters my mouth and takes away any warmth I was holding onto.

"Um, my car broke down and I could use a lift to town. I'm sorry to ask but…"

"It's fine, jump in, I'm heading that way."

Ignoring the warning that has been drummed into me

from an early age, that under no circumstances to ever accept a lift from strangers, I jump up into that van as if my life depended on it and, to be honest, I think it does.

Sighing with relief, I feel so happy to be in a warm place at last and the fact I'm with a stranger doesn't seem to matter.

He pulls away from the side of the verge and says cheerily, "You must be new around here. I'm Brad Hudson, local heartthrob and all-round great guy."

His laugh has a wicked edge to it and despite myself, I smile. "Dolly Macmillan."

"Nice name."

"If you say so." I grin and note how easy on the eye this saviour is. An open, friendly face with a slightly wicked smile and the bluest blue eyes sparkling with mischief. He is wearing a warm hat and appears as wrapped up as I am, and certainly doesn't look like the sort of man my parents warned me about.

"So, Dolly, what brings you Dream Valley?"

"God."

I giggle at the look on his face as he faces the fact he may have offered a mad stranger a lift and, taking pity on him, I say brightly. "My father's the new vicar, Scott Macmillan. We moved in a couple of days ago and I've been sent out to spread the word."

Lifting one of the leaflets, I sigh. "My mission, whether I chose to accept it or not, was to post these flyers around town inviting the volunteers to save Christmas. We don't have long either because if we are to spread peace and love, we only have a few weeks left."

Brad laughs and as my toes begin to warm up, opening up with a sigh to the warm air on my feet, a sweet Christmas carol plays out from the stereo.

"So, Dolly, what do you do when you're not on a heavenly mission? Do you work?"

He seems interested and has a genuine smile that makes me comfortable with him. In fact, he's the first person I've spoken to since we arrived, outside of my own family, and it's good to talk to someone new. Maybe it's because he's incredibly handsome as an added bonus, and he seems sweet enough, which makes me relax so I shrug.

"I finished university in the summer and have been helping my parents until I work out what I want to do."

"What did you study?"

"Theology, sadly."

Brad laughs and shakes his head. "So, you want to be a nun, shame."

"Good God, no." I stare at him in horror and he raises his eyes. "Are you allowed to say that?"

"Only when my father's not listening and in the company of people who couldn't give a damn."

I grin as he laughs out loud, "Can you even say that too? You're a wicked woman Dolly Macmillan."

"What about you, do you work?" I'm curious about a man who appears to have been sent to me by God and he shakes his head. "Not really. Like you, I'm in between careers and deciding what I want to do with my life."

"What are you thinking?" I'm curious because I could use any suggestions myself because nothing really appeals to me and he sighs. "I want to travel - a lot. See the world and have experiences."

"That sounds… expensive."

"It can be, but I'm kind of thinking of doing it with my van and hitting the road and seeing where it takes me."

"And that sounds… scary."

Just thinking of taking off without a plan goes against everything I've ever practised in life because I plan absolutely everything and he says with curiosity, "So, you're not one for adventure, Dolly."

"Not really."

Looking out at the landscape flashing past, I sigh. "I've had more than enough adventure to last me a lifetime. You see, we've moved around a lot and never really settled anywhere. I suppose I'm hoping to find somewhere to call home. To make a life in and set down roots. Build a future I always imagined having and forming lasting friendships that I've never really had before."

I sound pathetic even though it's true. I do want that. I want to feel as if I belong somewhere and not just passing through on a wing and a prayer.

For a while there's silence and I expect Brad has moved on already. We are so different that's obvious and as we pull into civilisation, I feel a little disappointed the moment has passed.

"So, here we are, Dream Valley metropolis. What's your plan?"

"I suppose to start at one end of the high street and work my way along. Then I'll call my father to come and get me."

I sigh and, turning to face him, smile brightly. "Thank you so much for rescuing me. I really appreciate it, Brad."

"Anytime, angel."

A soft shiver passes through me at the way he smiles and stares at me with a gentle look, the endearment dripping from his tongue and wrapping me in interest. Brad Hudson appears to be my dream man and I'm reluctant to leave the warmth being around him creates, not just physically, either.

Tearing my eyes away, I make to leave and he says quickly, "Why don't I buy you a hot coffee or something? I wouldn't consider I've rescued you properly unless I restore warmth to every part of your body."

He grins cheekily and for some reason my face flushes as

I feel a little heated and nod shyly, "I'd like that, but please, let me pay as a thank you for the lift. I really do appreciate it."

He nods toward a sweet little coffee shop with 'The Cosy Kettle' in bold lettering above the door.

"We'll argue about who's paying later. Come on, let me introduce you to the finest hot chocolate in the world."

As we leave the warmth of the van and the icy wind whips around my face, I no longer register it because deep inside me an inner glow is growing by the second because of him. Brad Hudson. My rescuer, saviour, and the hottest man I think I have ever met. I always knew there was a God and I should know, my father works for him.

CHAPTER 2

I almost whimper with delight when we cross the threshold of the warm and cosy coffee shop. Fairy lights are draped around Christmas decorations and the intoxicating scent of spice and cinnamon wafts towards me like the purest form of temptation.

Brad appears to be well known here because I immediately notice that almost every eye in the place is drawn to him and many wave a cheery greeting as he chats to them as we pass.

A smiling woman looks out from behind the counter and I don't miss the curious look she throws my way.

"Hey, Brad, your usual?"

"Not this time, Miranda. I'd like two of your most decadent hot chocolates for me and my frozen friend."

The woman's eyes swing to me and she smiles with a warmth I could bask in all day.

"You must be new around here. I'm Miranda."

"Dolly."

I smile and she looks between us as if trying to work out our connection and Brad obliges by saying, "I found this damsel in distress walking here from the church. Her car broke down and she was struggling."

"You have my sympathy sweetie, both for your car trouble and the fact it was Brad who found you."

She laughs and Brad rolls his eyes and grins. "She loves me really."

There aren't many empty tables, but Brad points to a couple vacating one by the steamed-up window.

"Grab that table, angel and I'll pay."

"Oh, I couldn't…"

Frantically, I reach into my bag and he shakes his head. "You can get them next time." He winks and turns away as my heart skips a beat. *Next time.*

Somehow, I like the sound of that and as I make my way to the table, the couple pulling on their gloves and scarves look at me with friendly curiosity.

"Good morning." The woman smiles, and the man stares at me a little too hard and I say shyly, "Hi. I can't believe how cold I am. I'm Dolly."

The couple share an amused grin, and the woman says in a friendly voice, "Hi, I'm Scarlett and this is Mark. Welcome to Dream Valley. Where are you living?"

"The church." They share a look and I grin. "Well, the vicarage behind it but close enough."

"You must be the new vicar's…"

"Daughter." I finish the sentence because I could tell Scarlett was a little unsure of my connection.

For some reason the couple share an amused look and I see the woman glance across at Brad who is leaning on the counter chatting to Miranda.

My eyes drag after him a little too long and Scarlett whispers, "Just a word of warning where it concerns Brad Hudson, Dolly."

"Oh, why?"

I look back quickly and she raises her eyes. "Listen, he's a great guy. They all are really, but you would be well advised to keep him at arm's length." She leans even closer. "He has a reputation around here as a bit of a player. I don't think there's many young women who haven't enjoyed a ride in his camper van, if you know what I mean?"

I swallow - hard.

Mark laughs. "Scarlett's right, honey, and we should know. We run the Dream Valley caravan park and Brad's van is a regular. Not to mention spending most nights parked up at Pineland Forest with another willing companion to keep him warm."

My heart sinks like a burst balloon and Scarlett says kindly, "Like I said, he's nice enough and extremely easy on the eye, but a little promiscuous. I'm pretty certain your parents wouldn't approve, so, well, just a friendly word of advice, no harm intended."

They smile as Brad heads our way, and he says cheerily, "Hey, my favourite campsite dwellers, it's unusual to see you both in town – together."

"Hey, mate." Mark nods at him and smiles. "Not much going on at the moment, out of season, you know. You should swing by for a few beers before Christmas. It would be good to catch up."

"Sure, I'll take you up on that."

"How's your mum?" Scarlett smiles at him warmly and I notice a slight softening in Brad's eyes as he says happily, "Good thanks. She's relishing all the organisation that goes into Christmas. Are you coming to our usual Christmas party this year?"

"Wouldn't miss it for the world."

Scarlett looks at her watch. "Come on Mark, we still have some Christmas shopping to do and I think parking will be a nightmare in Riverton. We've left it too long already."

Mark groans and pulls a face. "Do we have to?"

"Yes, let's get this over with."

They grin as they head off, and the blast of icy air from the open door makes me shiver.

Brad points to the newly vacated seat and smiles. "Tuck yourself in there. The drinks won't be long and I've taken the liberty of ordering some nice hot crumpets to take the edge off."

He is being so kind and yet Scarlett's' warning is fresh in my mind and I feel a little disappointed about that.

I'm not one for paying attention to gossip, but if she's right and Brad Hudson is a little free with his favours, there is no way possible I could entertain any thoughts outside of friendship with him. Then I feel foolish because he's only being friendly and probably wouldn't be interested in me anyway, so I smile my thanks. "You're a lifesaver, and I'm pretty sure you will get your reward in heaven."

"Well…" he leans forward until his mouth is inches from mine and a prickle of danger passes through me as he whispers, "I was kind of hoping I wouldn't have to wait that long."

Leaning back, he smiles his megawatt smile at Miranda as she heads our way with two steaming mugs of hot chocolate, containing more cream than is good for me and two plates of hot buttery crumpets that are making my stomach growl.

"Here you go, lovelies, nice and warm."

I almost fall on them before she even leaves because I am so desperate to thaw out and Brad laughs. "See, I told you I was a lifesaver."

I look at him between narrowed eyes as I chew on the delicious treat and find him watching me with the type of look my father always warned me about. I would say mother but she would more than approve of Brad Hudson because she likes to live her life a lot closer to the edge than me and for a moment as I think of my incorrigible mother,

CHRISTMAS IN DREAM VALLEY

my heart settles and Brad says with interest, "What are you thinking?"

"About my mother, actually."

"Tell me about her."

He seems interested and I laugh. "I couldn't possibly describe somebody you would need to meet to enjoy the full experience of. I'll let you make up your own mind about my mother, but if you ever meet my father, you are well advised just to listen and keep conversation to a minimum."

"If?" He leans back in his chair with a smirk. "Not if, Dolly, *when* I meet your father because you need volunteers and I am the first in line."

"Excuse me." I stare at him in surprise and he laughs. "Isn't that what this mission is about, to get people up to the church to help out? Well, you can consider me your first recruit because I have time on my hands which is lucky for you, and would love to help out."

"You would?" I'm surprised because Brad Hudson doesn't seem the type to loiter around churches, and he grins. "Consider me at your disposal night and day." He winks, causing a blush to creep across my face before I can stop it.

His eyes twinkle as he leans forward and whispers, "Only if I can work with you, though. That's my one condition."

I feel a little flustered because from the look on his face, he is interested in more than helping out and Scarlett's warning is sounding loud in my mind as I struggle to distance myself from this obvious player.

"Um, thanks, you're very kind but don't jump too soon, you don't know what's involved yet."

Taking a sip of my drink, I try to regain some form of self-control and he shrugs. "I can kind of guess. My mother has volunteered over the years and sometimes I help out when she needs some muscle. It's fine, we'll soon have Christmas organised and everyone will be happy."

"Your mother?" As I set the mug down, he laughs softly and leans forward and before I know what's happening, reaches out and wipes his thumb across my lips. I almost jump from my seat as he gazes into my eyes with an intimacy that makes me shiver. I immediately chase the feeling away as he says softly, "Cream."

"Sorry."

"You had cream on your lips."

"Oh… um, thank you."

I am now a nervous, anxious mess and he leans back and looks at me with a considered expression.

"So, do you agree to my terms, angel? Can I be your partner in crime and help save Christmas?"

My head is screaming no, but my heart is strangely jumping for joy. After all, why wouldn't I want to spend the next few weeks in his company? He's good at it and I haven't had so much fun in ages but Scarlett's warning is bellowing loud in my mind and so I smile and lean back in my seat and say dismissively, "Well, any help would be greatly appreciated but I won't hold you to it. See how you get on first."

Once again I fall on my hot chocolate and try to regain some of my composure because now I've been warned off the intoxicating Brad Hudson, I am setting the barriers in place around my heart because I will not be another conquest for him to boast about and if I'm sure of anything it's that.

CHAPTER 3

A screeching of tyres makes us look up and my heart sinks when I see the huge Toyota Hilux squeal into a parking place outside.

Oh no.

Brad peers out and says with admiration, "Wow, I'd love one of those."

As I stare out in utter mortification, I wonder if he's talking about the car or the occupant, because my mother is certainly eye-catching. Looking as if she's just stepped off the slopes in Aspen, she slams the door shut and flicks the alarm on. The fact she's wearing a huge white padded ski jacket, mirror shades and a Cossack style white fur hat makes her look like a movie star. Her tight black velvet leggings are tucked into huge white furry snow boots and she slings her designer handbag over one shoulder and looks at her phone.

Now I'm afraid.

With a gasp, I pull out my own phone and see the six missed calls and several texts that I must have missed and I look at Brad guiltily. "They've found me."

"Who?" He looks worried and I sigh.

"I'm sorry about what happens next, Brad. Please forgive me for not checking my god-damned phone."

He raises his eyes with a smirk as the door bursts open and the chill of winter accompanies my mother inside. As she stares around the quaint little tea room, her eyes settle on me and she gasps, "Oh thank God, babe, your father's doing his nut back there."

I squirm in my seat as every eye in the place turns to view this encounter, and I wish the ground would open up and swallow me as she heads our way.

I only have a brief moment to throw Brad an apologetic look before she reaches us and her razor-sharp stare zones in on him immediately.

"Wow, babe, who's the hunk?"

Looking slightly shocked, Brad says hesitantly, "Um, Brad Hudson, Mrs…"

"Call me Tina, everyone else does."

She tears off her hat and shrugs out of her coat and grabs a spare chair from the nearby table with a smile of thanks. I notice that the couple watching her with their mouths open just nod as if in a daze, as she sinks down into it and taps out a text with a flourish.

"There you go, problem solved. I've called off the dogs."

"I take it you're referring to dad."

"Obviously."

She grins. "Although we don't have long, because he's currently fiddling with your car in a bid to resuscitate her. We've got to pick him up on the way back and either tow the baby home or meet him there."

Praying for the latter, I see the look she throws Brad's way and says with interest, "So, what happened and why didn't you answer your phone?"

"Um…" I swallow – hard. "My car died, and I started walking to town. Brad stopped by and…"

"Don't tell me you…"

"Sorry, mum."

She shakes her head. "Maybe it's best we don't tell your dad you hitchhiked; you'd never hear the end of it."

"So." She turns her attention to Brad. "I suppose you're the brave rescuer who stopped and took care of my girl. I need to know everything about you, including your name, address and star sign."

"Mum please." I can't believe this is happening, as she shrugs and grins. "I'm the least of your problems, Dolly babe. Just be grateful he can't resist a motor in distress and despatched me as the advance party. Anyway, you can tell me all about it on the ride home."

Spying the leaflets nestling on the table beside me, she rolls her eyes. "For God's sake, those bloody leaflets. I told your father not to bother and that all we needed was a post on the parish page on Facebook, but he's old school and now look what happened. You scared the living daylights out of us when we saw you had stopped."

"Saw?" Brad looks confused and I die a slow death inside.

"Tracker, baby. Scott insists on tracking every move we make. It's just lucky we were, um, otherwise occupied, otherwise he would have been here sooner."

Brad looks at me with an open mouth and if the shock of meeting my mother doesn't kill him, my father will finish the job.

"Yes, babe, we like to know where we all are. So, Scott insists on a tracker. Well, you can imagine the fuss when he saw Dolly's car was stationary and there was no sign of her. It's only when we picked up the signal, we saw she was here. You know, I think I may offer the vicarage up to the signal company to rent them a mast because the signal around here is shocking."

Brad looks a little worried as my mum lowers her voice.

"Word of advice, babe. Dolly is the apple of her father's eye and he's a little overprotective of her. It may be best not to mention the hitchhiking incident. I don't want you to lose that pretty face of yours."

"Mum, please, there's nothing to tell. Brad saved me from an icy death if you must know, so if anything, you both owe him your thanks not, well, you know."

"Oh yes, Dolly, I do know. The fact you were alone in a car with a strange man will get his protective juices flowing. He won't be interested in anything but the fact you endangered yourself. No, best to say you made it town and leave it at that."

"I won't lie."

Mum shrugs. "Then on your head be it, don't say I didn't warn you."

She studies her fingernails and winces. "I don't suppose you know of a nearby nail technician, honey. I could sure use a manicure."

"There's my brother's girlfriend. She runs Beauty To Go and I could drop her your number if you like."

Mum's smile brightens as she nods. "Perfect. Here."

She slips her card across the table and I inwardly groan as his eyes widen at the script on the card in bold letters before he smirks.

"For Christ's Sake. That sounds interesting."

"Yes, it is. It's my brand, babe. You should look me up on YouTube. Lots of tips and tricks to keep you on your toes. I'm on Instagram, Snapchat, Tiktok and Facebook. Whew…" She laughs softly. "It certainly keeps me busy, but I love this whole influencer business. It keeps me sane."

Brad looks as if he disagrees with that and I have to join him because my mother is one step away from being certified.

Her phone rings and I know who's calling as my father's

distinctive ring tone of Elvis's Jailhouse Rock blares out in the Cosy Kettle.

"Hey, babe, found her."

She rolls her eyes as she listens and then says, "Keep your hair on, she's safe and well and enjoying a hot drink with one of the locals."

She holds the phone away from her ear as she studies her chipped nail polish and then sighs as she says, "On our way."

Reaching for her hat, she spies the leaflets and groans. "We'll have to do this tomorrow. He wants us back inside of ten minutes."

Brad says quickly, "I can distribute them around town if you like."

Mum laughs softly and looks between us, before saying sweetly, "You're a god send. Thanks, babe, I'll put in a good word for you."

Knowing she means with my father and not God, I gaze at him apologetically as I grab my own belongings. "Thanks for the rescue mission. I really owe you."

Mum taps her foot on the floor and I know she is eager to get going and Brad just smiles sweetly, "It was nice meeting you, Dolly, thanks for your company."

My heart sinks as I sense his interest in me fading as quickly as it came, which is probably a very good thing for everyone concerned.

CHAPTER 4

I take my seat beside mum and she glances behind before reversing out of the space like a stuntman in a car chase.

"So, the hunk. He seems nice. I want to know everything."

"There's nothing to tell. He found me walking to town almost frozen like Elsa and offered me a lift. Then as soon as we got here, he offered to help me thaw out in the coffee shop before helping me with the leaflets. He was really nice actually."

I conveniently leave out the warning I received because my mother definitely doesn't need to know that, and she nods. "Well, if it was up to me, I'd say go for it, honey. You could use a little excitement in your life, but well, it's not that easy, is it?"

"No, it isn't."

My heart sinks when I think about the reason why my life is definitely not easy, and I wonder if it will ever change.

It doesn't take long before we reach my abandoned car and an extremely cross looking father in every sense of the word.

He is wrapped up in a huge military issue padded jacket with a sheepskin hat and ski gloves, his combat trousers tucked into army issue boots.

Like my mother, he wears his polarised sunglasses with panache to guard against the glare of the snow and for some reason it brings a tear to my eye as I breathe a sigh of relief at the always comforting presence of my father.

Mum squeals to a handbrake turn beside him and winds the window down.

"Safe and well babe, how's the casualty?"

"Not good." He peers into the car with an anxious look and then grins. "You almost sent me to meet my boss, princess. Why didn't you call?"

"Signal." I shrug and he nods, looking at his own phone in disgust. "We'll have to sort that. I'll make a few calls, get some masts erected and make sure the blind spot in our operation is dealt with."

Mum shakes her head because this is so typical of my father. Everything is approached with a military mind and seen as a problem to be solved despite any obstacles in our way. He's always been the same and despite how fierce he is, I absolutely idolise my father and I know the feeling is definitely mutual. In fact, we all do. Mum is besotted by him as she is fond of telling everyone and my brother Beau is trying his best to follow in his boot prints. Currently enjoying life as a member of the special forces, trying everything possible to live up to the legend that is Scott Macmillan.

He wasn't always a military vicar. He started life out as a soldier and progressed to special forces himself. Maybe the nature of his job made him stop and think because one day he gave it all up for religion. Became a military vicar and never looked back. The trouble is, old habits die hard, and he still operates like a military mastermind which can be a little overbearing at times. Like today, for instance. No normal person reacts like this, but then again, I know it's coming from a very good place, so I forgive his overprotectiveness and just try to accommodate it as best I can.

"We need to tow her home and get her looked at by a professional. It may not be good though, princess, so we'll have to formulate a contingency plan."

Mum claps her glove encased hands. "A new car. That would be so exciting. I'll start researching them right away. You never know, we may even be able to use it as a company car and you can drive around advertising my business. I can see it now, 'For Christ's Sake,' emblazoned on the side in bold pink glittery lettering. Leave it with me, babe, I'll make it happen."

My horrified expression connects with my father's and he shakes his head and looks at my mother fondly. "We'll talk about that later, honey."

The look they share always fills my heart with warmth because I have never met a couple so embarrassingly in love in my life. My parents are both besotted with one another and it can be quite uncomfortable at times. The fact they took so long to notice my situation today tells me they were wrapped up in each other and I sigh inside. It can be quite awkward at times living with them and it's only when I returned from university that I noticed it at all.

My thoughts turn weirdly to Brad Hudson, and I bat them away as quickly as they came. No, stranger danger indeed where it concerns him because it's obvious that man would be extremely bad for my health.

By the time we have attached the tow rope to my car and made the short journey to St Thomas's, I feel quite weary with it all. As missions go, this one was a failure. Or was it? At least I got out and met some of the locals, although maybe one of them is best forgotten and as we sweep into the driveway of the vicarage that nestles behind the sweet old church, I am just looking forward to sitting in front of the fire with a good book.

Leaving my father to fuss with my car, I follow mum inside and as we shrug out of our warm coats and boots, she says cheerily, "Go and sit by the fire and I'll make us a brew. I think the mission can wait awhile."

She laughs as we head off to the slightly antiquated kitchen that looks like something out of a turn of the century period drama. The old iron range powers out some serious heat, offsetting the cool flagstones that require footwear at all times.

As I take a seat in one of the rocking chairs by the fireplace, a warm furry body joins me.

"Squirrel." Our little Westie jumps onto my lap and lifts her paw for a tickle and I sigh with relief. I'm home. Safe, warm and surrounded by people who love me and my toes now feel as if they may survive and actually work again.

The door opens and dad stamps his feet on the mat and exhales sharply. "It's like a freezer out there. Thank God for log fires and medicinal brandy."

"I'll chuck one in your coffee if you like love." Mum calls across and he nods gratefully. "Thanks."

He peels away the layers of protective clothing and sits opposite me in the other chair by the fire.

"So, bad morning?" He raises his eyes quizzically.

"Not really."

"Why?" His eyes narrow and I shake my head with a sigh. "Ok, it was bad the car breaking down and the fact I had no signal. However, luck was on my side and..."

"Here you go."

Mum interrupts and flashes me a warning look as she hands us both a steaming mug of coffee.

Shaking my head, I go against what she thinks and say

bravely, "So, luckily, a kind local stopped and gave me a lift to town."

The silence hangs in the air like an interested spectator as I stare at my father with a defiant look in my eye. I think mum stands frozen to the spot as her eyes swing between us and from the looks of her, she's not even breathing right now.

My father grips his mug tightly and only the slight narrowing of his eyes tells me he's struggling with this. I lean back and as the fire crackles in the grate, I wait for this to blow up in my face.

"This person." He leans forward and fixes me with his interrogator's eyes. "Male or female, old or young?"

"Male. Young."

Outwardly I appear brave, foolish I know, but inwardly I'm cowering waiting for the explosion to wreck my safe world.

"Male and young. Does he have a name?"

"Brad, um, Hudson, I believe."

Mum looks wildly around as if hoping for a miracle and even Squirrel is watching the scene with interest.

"So, let me get this right. You left the safety of your vehicle and started walking in an unfamiliar landscape towards a town you have never been to when your home was even closer. Then you accept a lift from a complete stranger, who could have been absolutely anyone, I might add, and your safety was compromised. Then you take tea with this potential murderer and don't even think it prudent to snap the number plate before you get into the vehicle and send it to me to get checked out. You ignore your phone and blatantly disregard every measure we have put in place for your own safety because you thought it would be ok."

"Um, yes."

I feel myself quaking inside as I wait for an outburst of

epic proportions and yet he just fixes me with a steely gaze that has me on the edge of confessing every secret I ever had in fear.

Mum says nervously, "I thought he seemed nice."

My dad turns and looks at her for a very long moment and to her credit, mum just shrugs. "Well, I did. Quite easy on the eye, pleasant personality and not weird at all. In fact, we owe him two favours now because he promised to distribute those bloody leaflets. Maybe I should invite him to tea by way of thanks."

Dad looks thoughtful and my heart sinks.

"That sounds like a very good idea. Leave it with me, I'll search him out and issue the invitation – personally."

He sinks back in his chair and I can tell he's still angry. The fact he has gone to a faraway place in his head tells me he is plotting the blackest revenge against my knight in shining armour.

Mum throws me a reassuring smile but I'm not convinced because inadvertently she has thrown him the ammunition he needs because any amount of delving into the character of Brad Hudson is likely to have my father heading down the warpath. I almost pity Brad because being on my father's naughty list is much worse than being on Santa's and even one black mark against any man's character is liable to send my father feral.

CHAPTER 5

*L*uckily, we have more than enough to occupy our time and spend the rest of the afternoon unpacking and trying to arrange our belongings in the unfamiliar space. As rectories go, this one is smaller than most but has a sweetness to it that I immediately fell in love with. I have my own gorgeous little bedroom under the eaves and I love the slightly uneven floors and the chipped paint on the walls. This house bleeds history and I wonder how many occupants have lived here before us.

I even love the sweet chintz curtains that hang proudly at the leaded window, but my mother obviously doesn't share my admiration because she heads inside with yet another box marked 'Dolly' and sighs.

"Here you go, I think that's the last of them."

Looking around her critically, she shakes her head. "I'm sorry, love, but those curtains have got to go. We need to perform a serious makeover on this room and fast."

She looks around thoughtfully. "I'm thinking sage green and cream. A few pink accent colours and a pretty chandelier hanging above the bed. Possibly a mirrored side table and some gorgeous flower prints in silver frames. Yes, perhaps shutters would be good, or a handmade blind for the window. A couple of bedside lamps and some floral displays to bring some life into the room. Yes, leave it with me and I'll feature it as a 'before and after' on my channel. Church chic I'll call it, or sleeping with the clergy, something along those lines."

From nowhere, she whips out her phone and starts dictating a shopping list and website ideas and I feel a buzzing noise in my ears that always seems to surface when she's in one of her moods.

"But I like..." She holds up her hand. "Don't thank me, Dolly, it's what mothers are for. I'll get your father to organise a painter and decorator. I'm sure they'll be quiet at this time of the year, anyway. There must be a local one we could use."

Before I protest, she is off and as I hear her footsteps against the bare boards, I look around the sweet little room in dismay.

The trouble is, I knew this would happen. She loves a good makeover and I can already see the before and after pictures on Instagram. Mum has two hundred thousand followers and is on there several times a day. I know there is no use protesting because she will do it with or without my consent and my father will back her up every time.

I wonder what that feels like. To have someone batting in your corner, whatever shot you take. Having your back and accommodating your wishes despite how mad they are. My father adores my mother so much he indulges her every whim and fantasy. I hope I meet a man like that. Someone who loves me with every bone in his body and every beat of his heart. Someone I love just as hard and want to please. A team. A friendship and a romance that never dies. My mum found my dad, but is that really a thing? Are all couples like them? I doubt it, many are far from the fantasy and through my dad's work I have seen the flip side of the coin when couples argue, fall apart and subsequently divorce.

I want the dream and I won't settle for anything less, but will I find that here in Dream Valley? Even thinking of Brad Hudson is a bad idea, but somehow, he is not far away and is lingering in the forefront of my mind.

His easy-going nature, his cheeky grin, and those astonishing blue eyes. The gentle way about him that put me at ease immediately and the fact he was so kind in offering to help and buy me some very welcome food.

Yes, Brad Hudson could be that man, but for one thing. His reputation.

I'm not a girl to ignore a warning, and the one I heard was enough to send me running. I don't need a man like that in my life and I must resist at all costs because if I relent and push any doubts away, my father is right behind me to deal with the matter personally.

I sometimes worry that I'll never meet anyone because nobody can ever measure up to my father's plan for my future husband. I've even had those dreaded thoughts of always living at home and being *that* girl who never finds anyone. Stuck with her parents and becoming their carer in later life. I can almost see that happening, which is why from time to time, I rebel against this and part of me is interested to see if Brad is worth rebelling for.

A knock at the front door drags my attention back to normality and I hear my mother shout excitedly, "Come in, darling. I can't believe you came already."

Feeling intrigued, I head down the slightly rickety staircase and see a pretty girl standing in the kitchen, carrying a suitcase, of all things. It looks to be the kind that make-up artists or hairdressers use, and she smiles as I catch her eye.

"Hi, I'm Florrie. Brad told me you needed a nail technician, and I was passing the door and thought I'd drop in my card."

"Well," Mum looks at her nails critically. "It's a bit of an emergency, love, I don't suppose you have time now."

"I do as it happens." Florrie smiles and I find myself studying the pretty stranger with interest. Her hair is a soft caramel colour and her eyes a striking shade of green. She looks to be around my own age and I'm glad that someone is at least. Taking the seat by the fire, I watch as she sets up on the scrubbed wooden farmhouse table and mum says politely, "Can I get you a tea, coffee or something with a bit of a kick."

"Tea would be lovely, thank you."

As mum turns away, she looks at me with curiosity. "You must be Dolly. Brad told me he met you earlier."

"Yes." I smile and she grins, showing a perfect set of whitened teeth.

"I'm pleased to meet you. Brad said you were pretty and now I can see why he was so enthusiastic."

I feel a little uncomfortable and laugh with embarrassment. "He was very kind. He rescued me from a near death experience and brought me back to life by way of hot chocolate and crumpets."

Florrie laughs. "That sounds like Brad."

"He said you were seeing his brother." I remember him talking about her and she nods. "Jake Hudson. We live at Valley House, not far from here, with the rest of the Hudson family. You should come and meet them. I could arrange it if you like."

Mum turns, looking interested, and I shrink a little lower in my seat. "Um, yes, sounds great."

For some reason, all roads lead to Brad Hudson in Dream Valley and I'm not sure I should be travelling on them at all. Just the thought of fending off an amorous player, only to be tossed aside as soon as the next pretty face swims into view, doesn't sound like a good idea at all.

Then, to make matters worse, my father heads inside and grins. "Hey, that was quick. Tina only chipped that polish a few hours ago and the rescue mission is in place already." He holds out his hand and flashes Florrie a smile that could turn a thousand nun's heads. "Scott Macmillan, newest vicar in town and the most fortunate man alive."

He shakes Florrie's hand and smiles at mum. "You've met my better half Tina and Florrie, my number one daughter."

"Yes, pleased to meet you all and welcome to Dream Valley. It's a special place."

My heart sinks further as dad drags out a chair and says, "So, Florrie, have you lived here long?"

"A few months. I met my boyfriend when I was on holiday and he persuaded me to a fresh start here along with my best friend."

"Interesting." Dad looks curious and mum says quickly, "Scott, Florrie is living with Jake Hudson at Valley House. I think that was its name."

I groan inwardly as they share a look and dad says thoughtfully, "Hudson, hey, any relation to Brad."

"Oh, you know him." Florrie smiles. "Yes, Brad's his brother. There are four of them, actually. Marcus, Dom, Brad, and Jake. Marcus married my friend a few months ago and I'm with Jake."

"They move fast, these Hudson boys."

Florrie laughs as she starts work on mum's nails. "You could say that, although they're not so bad, unless you count Brad, that is. Boy, does he make up for the rest of them."

I wish the ground would open up and swallow me whole as my father looks at me with a sharp warning in his expression.

"So, he's a bit of a player then?"

Florrie looks worried. "I'm sorry that sounded bad. Don't get me wrong, Brad may be popular with the local girls, but he has a heart of gold. He's funny, has a kind heart and a wicked sense of humour. You know, he is the most likeable man you could ever meet and …"

She tails off because you can't miss the immediate tension in the room as she tries desperately hard to cover her tracks and my father appears to have formed his own conclusions and says, "He sounds like someone I would love to meet."

Squirrel decides to seize the moment and starts scratching at the door and I say hastily, "I'll take her out."

Mum nods and smiles with a reassurance I know is false and I say politely, "It was nice meeting you, Florrie."

"You too, Dolly."

Quickly pulling on my coat and boots, I grab the lead and thank God for Squirrel and her natural urges.

CHAPTER 6

Once again, I'm out in the cold and shiver as the last of the sun's rays dip behind a cloud and the icy blast of air destroys all the heat from the fire in a nanosecond.

Shivering against the icy wind, I head down the cobbled path towards the graveyard. St Thomas's Church sits in the centre on a slight hill and as the wind whips around me, I shiver, wishing I was tucked up warm inside. Squirrel sniffs the gravestones as I read the inscriptions and wonder about the people who have their final resting place here. Did they live in Dream Valley their entire lives, or was it just the place they exited from?

Heading towards the large oak door of the church, I'm grateful to step inside the portico and ease the door gently open. Squirrel runs inside and proceeds to sniff every pew and I stare around at the pretty country church that is obviously centuries old.

As churches go, it's not the biggest one we've been in. In fact, it could be classed as one of the smallest, yet it's definitely the prettiest.

As I wander down the aisle, I take comfort in the peace

this space gives me and the thinking time needed to reset my mind.

The polished wood of the pews and the pulpit look lovingly cared for. The holly and ivy arrangements describe the season despite the cold and the perfectly tapestried kneelers crafted with love and care from grateful parishioners, offer a splash of colour against the enchanting stained-glass window that overlooks the congregation.

I wonder if we will stay here.

Having moved around for as long as I can remember, I'm well aware of the danger of dreaming. Falling in love with a place and wishing I could stay there. Forming attachments and feeling my heart break when we leave. Friends, special friends and romance take second place to my father's job and before the last box is unpacked, we are usually packing up again.

Squirrel starts barking and scratching at a door in the corner and I sigh.

"Not today, little one. We'll explore another day. Come on, let's go and freeze again and try to wear you out."

We head outside and I close the door carefully behind me. My father always leaves the church door unlocked, just in case a weary parishioner needs comfort at any time of the day or night.

As we walk down the path towards the stile leading to the neighbouring field, I wonder how long I've got before the light goes.

Deciding one trip around the field will suffice, I pull my leg over the stile and head into new territory.

Squirrel appears to love this place as she spies a bunny heading to its burrow for the night and as she shoots off, I laugh to myself when I see her fat little legs heading at speed across the frozen ground.

A soft chuckle makes me jump as a familiar voice says close to my ear, "We meet again."

Spinning around, my heart rate increases when I see Brad standing behind me. "But…"

He laughs. "Don't panic. I'm not some crazy stalker or anything like that."

He holds up the leaflets.

"I was going to drop these in on my way home and I saw you in the distance. I could keep them, but I thought you might need them. If you like, we could head out tomorrow and finish the job and wallpaper Dream Valley in them."

"I'm not really…" I am struggling for words because more than anything I want to say yes, but the thought of explaining this to my father is not a pleasant one and so I sigh.

"I would like to, but I may be needed here. I think my father's intending on decorating the church tomorrow. The tree's been propped up against the stone wall for weeks already and we need to get a move on if we are to offer the full number of services for the locals."

"I could help."

He looks so keen standing there and I feel like the biggest bitch alive as I knock him down. "No, it's fine. We'll be fine, you've done enough already."

He looks a little wounded and I try to ignore it because he may not think it now but I'm saving him from a whole lot of trouble and my heart flutters as he steps closer and I feel his warm breath on my face as he whispers, "I want to help."

To refuse would be cruel and more than anything I would welcome his company, so I sigh. "The thing is, well, it's my father."

"The vicar."

"Yes. He's annoyed that I accepted a lift from a stranger and, well, I'm sorry for whatever he says when he meets you for the first time. He's a little over protective and it may not be a pleasant experience. To be honest, I'm saving you back because one good turn deserves another."

I laugh nervously. "Trust me, I'm doing you a favour here."

"And you, what do you think?"

"About…"

He steps even closer. "Me."

He is so close now it wouldn't take much to touch my frozen lips to his and as I stare into those bold blue eyes, I feel myself falling into a situation I am struggling to get out of.

"I, well…" I lick my lips because God help me, I am falling into something I should avoid like the plague and so with the greatest effort of my life, I look away.

"I would like you to leave."

He steps back.

"Ok."

My heart sinks.

As he turns away, I feel the icy chill of regret twisting my heart at what could have been a bit of fun to brighten my boring life and as he heads off, I am aching to run after him and tell him I didn't mean any of it and of course I'd welcome his help.

However, I stand firmly rooted to the spot watching him go and then he turns and says as an aside, "I won't give up you know."

My heart starts beating even faster as he says with a slight edge to his voice. "Don't always believe the rumours, Dolly. There is good in everyone with the right person."

Then he turns and leaves as quickly as he came, leaving me feeling like the biggest bitch alive.

Squirrel is charging around the field like lightning, and yet I can't even laugh at my mad friend for once in my life. Telling myself it was for the best and that it probably wouldn't have gone anywhere, I turn for home and wish things had happened differently today.

From the moment my car broke down to now, every encounter has been followed by a problem and just thinking of the battle Brad will have with my father if he asks me out on a date, tells me I did the right thing.

No, Brad Hudson is just a delicious dream for when I'm alone because nothing is worth engaging my father's attention and it's always been that way.

Thinking back on the boys, then men who tried, makes me smile a little. Usually, sons of soldiers and then young soldiers themselves. Local boys that accompanied their families to church who showed an interest, only to come up against the wrath of my father.

Nothing was worth the interrogation, mind manipulation and threats he dished out like prayers, and soon they kept a wide berth away from me out of fear of recriminations.

My father has always had a threatening edge to him that he puts to good use and so Brad should continue as quits because he doesn't know it yet, but I have just saved him from a whole heap of trouble that he can definitely do without.

CHAPTER 7

The next morning dawns with a bright blue sky and frost covered ground. I even think there is frost forming on the inside of my windows and I shiver as I make the mad dash to the shower.

By the time I make it to breakfast, I'm pleased to see the fire has been lit and the smell of bacon frying makes my stomach growl.

Mum and dad are waiting in the cosy kitchen and my father smiles. "Morning princess, I hope you slept well. It's going to be a busy day today."

"Why?"

Slipping into the seat opposite him, I reach for the ever-warming pot of tea that rests underneath the knitted cosy that mum loves so much.

"We must decorate the church and then I have a few calls to make in between."

Mum slaps a cooked breakfast in front of him. "You know, Scott, I hope we get a few volunteers at least. I'm not sure we can manage everything with just the three of us. I mean, I must video the whole thing, of course, and that takes time. How long have we got exactly?"

"Just today because I have a service tomorrow and it's the first one since my predecessor left. We need to make a good impression."

Mum nods. "Leave it with me, honey, I'll make you proud."

She turns to dish up my own breakfast and my father catches my eye and winks as I roll my eyes. We both know what today will involve with my mother filming the whole experience. Neither of us mind, though. We both indulge her every whim because underneath it all, she has a heart of gold and does everything for the right reason.

As I tuck into my own breakfast, I think about their lives. They met at a young age and mum gave up everything to travel with him as much as she could. A military wife is not a happy one because they never had the opportunity to put down roots before they were sent to the next base and the next country. Beau and I were dragged along with them and there were many houses and many countries, different schools and new friends every couple of years. I used to envy those kids that had a permanent place to stay. A history of a place they grew up in. Memories to cherish and an extended family to share their lives.

Our grandparents made do with snatched visits and occasional holidays together. As much as I loved travelling, there's always been a yearning deep inside me for a permanent home. Somewhere like Dream Valley perhaps; it could happen.

Then, for some reason, my thoughts turn to Brad Hudson and his own yearning for travel. Another reason to steer well clear of him because we obviously want different things, anyway. He may not be interested after yesterday's disastrous encounter, but I could definitely see myself with a man like him, just maybe not Brad Hudson himself.

"Florrie was nice." Mum takes her own seat and reaches for the ketchup.

"Sweet girl." Dad nods and looks at me sharply. "I'm not sure about the company she keeps, though. That brother of her boyfriend sounds like someone you should avoid, princess."

"You don't even know him, dad and you always said we should give everyone a chance and not let first impressions be the only impression."

Mum laughs. "Yes, you do say that, Scott, you can't deny it."

"It's true most of the time, but I have a bad feeling about this one and I want to check him out first before I trust my pride and joy with him."

"I'm not a possession, dad. I can make up my own mind who I see as *friends*."

I emphasise the last word because since when is Brad even that. My father is overreacting as usual, and I need to make a stand. He can't continue to run my life like he does. I need freedom to make my own choices and for once I'm going to do what I want, regardless of what he thinks.

I note the look they share and don't care that for once I've bitten back because I'm an adult now and will make my own mistakes in life and they had better get used to it.

"Why is it so cold?"

I shiver under the copious layers I dressed in as we head to the church to start transforming it into a festive paradise.

"Maybe there's a heater we can use, I'll check the cupboards."

Dad heads off and mum groans. "I wish Christmas was in the summer. You know, Australia has the right idea.

Christmas on the beach in a bikini sounds extremely attractive right now."

She looks around and sighs. "Do you think anyone will come?"

"Maybe, we can only hope."

Almost as if they heard us, we jump as the church door opens and my heart sinks when I see the first person through it and quickly look for my dad, who, luckily, is still searching for the heater.

"Hey, help has arrived."

Brad grins and mum nudges me sharply before saying brightly, "Brad, honey, you're a godsend."

"I don't know about that." He chuckles and I look behind him as a woman heads inside, dressed head to toe in what appears to be ski wear.

"Good morning, it's certainly a cold one. You must be the new vicar's family."

I look in surprise at a woman who appears to be related to Brad due to the similarities. She has the same twinkling blue eyes and friendly grin and must be his mother due to the fond look he throws her as he drags her beside him.

"This is my mother."

"Camilla Hudson, pleased to be of service."

She steps forward and smiles brightly and mum grins. "Pleased to meet you. I must say, I'm glad we have some help at least. For a moment there I thought I'd be filming alone today."

"Filming?" Camilla looks confused and my heart sinks as mum says brightly, "For my YouTube channel, darling. It's called For Christ's Sake and its mission in life is to take the cold out of the church and replace it with cool."

Camilla looks astounded, and Brad grins as we all shiver in our boots. "I'll look forward to losing the cold bit, it's freezing in here."

CHRISTMAS IN DREAM VALLEY

Mum nods. "Don't worry, honey, Scott's dealing with that. Anyway, let's make a start, it may warm us up." She turns to me and says slyly, "Dolly, babe, why don't you and Brad go hunting for festive foliage. I think there's some fir in the woods and maybe some holly. Take some gloves though and a bin bag. Don't be long though, we need it back here in record time."

I look up sharply and she winks before turning to Camilla. "Why don't we make a start on the tree and I'll show you what's involved in filming a YouTube video. You can be my assistant; it will be such fun."

I squirm with embarrassment but Camilla just looks interested and Brad whispers, "This is right up mum's street. Chances are she'll have a channel of her own by the end of the day. Maybe this wasn't such a good idea."

Mum says loudly, "Hurry up guys, you don't have long."

I know exactly what she's doing and for a moment, I take time to appreciate that. The only time restriction we have is that my dad is due back at any second and so I say impulsively, "Come on, we should get going."

As we step outside, the wind whips around my face and causes me to shiver and Brad says quickly, "Come on, we can take the van. There's lots of what we need at Valley House and I don't think mum would mind if we raided the gardens in the name of St Thomas's."

I'm just grateful for the warmth of the heater as I climb into Brad's camper van and sigh with relief.

"You know that's twice now you've saved my life."

He laughs softly. "It's my pleasure."

As we head off, I'm grateful for a moment's distance from the church. It's nice being with my parents but sometimes I like my own space and some different company. It can get quite lonely sometimes and so I push away any doubts and decide to give Brad a chance. I mean, everyone deserves that at least.

CHAPTER 8

We head up a sweeping driveway and my mouth drops open. "Is that where you live?" I blink as if to reconfirm the fact I've arrived at a place I thought only existed in story books.

"Yes, she's a beauty, isn't she?"

I can only nod because Valley House is the stuff of dreams. A large stone-faced home of grandeur and opulence. Tidy grounds and neatly tended hedges dress a place that is probably just as well cared for inside. I'm not even sure how many rooms must be hidden away inside and Brad says proudly, "It's been the Hudson family home for centuries. My father passed away not long ago and so the title of home-owner fell to my oldest brother, Marcus. He lives here with Sammy Jo, his new wife, along with the rest of us.

"Do you have a large family?"

"Three brothers and mum. Obviously, the usual aunts and uncles, but mainly it's just us."

"Tell me about them."

"Well, Marcus is the eldest and runs his property empire from an office above a shop in town. He's about to build a new community not too far away called Dream Valley Heights."

"That sounds impressive and a little bit scary." I smile as he chuckles. "Then it suits him because Marcus is just that – scary."

He pulls to a stop outside the huge wooden front door and says impulsively, "I'll show you around if you like."

The curiosity is burning away any reservations I have and I say eagerly, "I'd love that."

I can't get out of the car fast enough because this is right up my street, spying on how the other half live. What's not to love about that.

We head inside and the first thing that strikes me is how warm it is, and I sigh with delight.

"There *is* heat in Dream Valley." I grin and he looks concerned. "You are always cold, Dolly, that can't be good for you."

A prickle of pleasure flutters through me as I see the concern in his eyes, and it feels good.

Brad helps me off with my coat and says casually, "Come on, let's see if Mrs Jenkins is still here. I'm sure she could point us in the direction of a couple of hot drinks and some snacks."

"Who's Mrs Jenkins?"

"Our lady that does." He winks, and I giggle as he shrugs. "Actually, I think mum employs her as an alternative to speaking with Alexa. They were the only female company she had for a long time until Sammy Jo and Florrie moved in. Now it's unbearable being a man in this house because the women have taken over. I mean, look at that, case in point."

He shakes his head at a beautiful flower arrangement set beside a burning scented candle.

"What's wrong with that?"

"Nothing, it's just they're everywhere. Little feminine

touches and articles of clothing a man should really never see. It's torture living here."

He points to a heap of clothing waiting to go upstairs in a basket and I see various items of lingerie spilling over the edge.

He growls, "All they talk about at breakfast is beauty products and the latest reality show. It's driving me crazy."

"What do you normally talk about then?"

"Cars mainly and… well, men's stuff."

He turns away and I can only imagine what Brad Hudson likes to talk about and I remind myself he's not to be trusted with my heart. We can be friends though. He seems nice enough, so I follow him to an amazing kitchen that takes my breath away.

Wooden units are topped by granite and a huge island dominates the centre of the room. It feels as if the whole of the vicarage could fit inside this room and my mouth drops open at the super clean tiled floor and gleaming surfaces. Even the chrome of the taps and ovens gleam against the sun that touches the darkest corners with its warming rays. I fall instantly in love with this room alone, but Brad sighs.

"Damn, she's gone already. Sorry, Dolly, you'll have to make do with my attempts instead."

He pulls out a stool for me and says sweetly, "Take a seat and I'll fix us a drink."

I watch as he lifts a glass dome off a cake stand and grabs a plate from the rack on the wall. "At least she left us some shortbread. Have as much as you like, I always do."

He winks and sets about tinkering with a scary looking coffee machine and I sigh inside. This is all so perfect. I could never imagine a life like this and it reminds me of how much I want to start one of my own, but where and doing what?

I chew on the biscuit and watch Brad work, and it's not

hard to admire a man who obviously takes good care of himself.

From his slightly messy light brown hair with streaks of blonde, to the sparkling blue eyes that twinkle when he looks at me. He is broad shouldered and stands around 6ft tall and I can see why he's so lucky with the ladies in this town, because there is absolutely nothing not to like about Brad Hudson.

"So, Dolly, tell me about your dad. From the sounds of it, he's a scary man and I know a lot about living with one of those."

"Really." I'm sad about that because from the bite of the words as he spoke, I'm guessing it's not a happy memory.

"My father." He sighs as he holds the mug to what appears to be a steady stream of frothy milk.

"He was quite overbearing, hard to live with, and difficult to please. A monster really who had no shame."

"In what way?"

Brad sighs. "You've met my mother, who is a saint among women everywhere for putting up with him all those years. He treated her terribly and didn't care what anyone thought either."

I'm not liking the sound of Brad's father at all and he shakes his head. "He was unfaithful to my mother and a hard man to love. I don't want to be like him; none of us do, but sometimes I worry I could be."

He turns to hand me the drink and I stare at him with compassion because gone is the happy-go-lucky, warm and friendly guy and behind the mask is a man trying to deal with his own demons.

"Then don't be." Just thinking of his reputation is a warning flag because he may not want to be like his father, but he is following in his footsteps in one way at least.

He takes his seat beside me and stares into his coffee as if the answers all lie there and sighs.

"The thing is, I'm a young guy with a lot of options. Lots of temptation and lots of opportunity to indulge it. If you haven't heard the rumours already, you soon will and they're all true."

My heart crashes and burns as he admits something I already knew but hoped was different.

"The reason I'm like it is because of him – my father."

Now I'm confused, and he says with an edge to his voice, "I thought I'd get it out of my system. Sow my wild oats, as they say, and overindulge, so I don't face temptation in the future. I want to make sure that when I finally settle down, it's with the right person and for all the right reasons. I'm young though and want it all. I want to travel, see the world and yet part of me yearns for somebody to share that with me. A friend, a companion, as well as a lover. If I sound selfish, I'm sorry about that but one thing you should know about me is I'm a man of extremes and when I fall in love, it will be no different."

"What are you saying?" I'm a little confused, and he smiles. "I'm not really sure, but it matters what you think of me. I don't know why but it does. I just want to spend time with you as a friend, and I suppose I'm asking for that chance at least."

"You may not like what that involves."

"In what way?"

I sigh heavily. "My father. He won't make it easy being my friend because he thinks men have only thing on their minds at all times if you believe his account. He won't understand that two people can hang out together as friends and will make your life a living nightmare. To be honest, it's a little stifling, infuriating and wrong on every level, but he's my father and only has my best interests at heart. I suppose what

I'm saying is, I would love to have a friend around here. I would love it to be you, but you may find being my friend isn't worth the trouble it will cause."

Brad shakes his head. "He sounds like my father - controlling."

"A little, but it's coming from a good place. He cares and has seen some terrible things and doesn't want that for his family. He is overprotective for a reason, and it's done through wanting to protect us from the harsh realities of life. Unlike you, I adore my father. In fact, I love my parents so hard and I've always tried to be the model daughter. The trouble is…" I smile into his eyes. "I need to be set free at some point in life and I'm starting to realise that could be now."

For a moment, we just sip our drinks and fall silent as we think about our conversation. I was a little surprised that Brad opened up to me and I wonder if it was just a line he has cast many times before, hoping to reel someone in with his boyish grin and lost little boy act. Then again, I saw the emotion in his eyes and I wonder if he's just as lost as I am. Maybe we could help each other. It could even be fun. Perhaps we should give it a go on a strictly friendship basis.

As we head outside to the garden, I try to push away the doubts and just enjoy the moment because it's likely we will move on soon, anyway. And if we don't, Brad will.

CHAPTER 9

Armed with bags of holly and sprigs of fir, we head back to the church in good spirits. Brad is great company and kept me giggling for most of the two hours we've been away. There were no loaded looks or flirtatious comments, just an easygoing friendship that I certainly need right now.

As we burst through the church door, I look around in delighted surprise when I see the tall tree being gaily festooned with colourful decorations hanging amid glittering fairy lights.

"There you are, Dolly. What do you think?"

Mum is standing on a ladder and Camilla is handing her the decorations she needs.

"It's beautiful, mum."

"We've had such fun, darling." Camilla smiles at us both. "I must say, I never knew how delightful it would be to film a video. Your mum is a natural in front of the camera and she has made some very good points in demonstrating how to decorate a tree. I've subscribed to her channel on my phone already and am looking forward to watching past episodes as soon as I get a minute."

"Oh, Camilla, honey, you are so kind." Mum laughs as she topples precariously on the ladder and Brad rushes over to either steady it, or catch her if she falls, I'm not sure which.

"Where's, dad?" I look around me with concern because no doubt he will have something to say about our mission and mum giggles. "Relax, he's gone to see a local woman about a wedding. Someone wants to book the date, and he thought he'd call in on a few parishioners along the way. Apparently, there's a Mrs Judd he needs to see who plays the organ and not very well either, if Camilla is right."

"Shame really." Camilla shakes her head. "She only knows a handful of tunes and hyperventilates if someone asks her to play anything else. I think she should give it up but what can you do? She loves fiddling with an organ, it keeps her young."

I resist looking at Brad but I can feel his laughter from here as he listens to his mother and mum says lightly, "Go and make us a cuppa, babe, it's bloody freezing in here."

"Ok, shall I let Squirrel out?"

"Bring her with you, she's been cooped up all morning, poor little lamb."

I feel Brad's eyes follow me as I leave and for some reason, my heart is pounding inside me. I'm not sure why he affects me this much, but he does. He's working his way into my mind and heart and there is nothing I can do about that because I like him. His company, his easy-going personality and I'm attracted to him. Maybe I should get out more and join a few clubs because I obviously need to broaden my horizons.

* * *

WHEN I RETURN WITH SQUIRREL, there are a few more volunteers merrily helping out. Brad has been detailed with sorting out the boxes of decorations and Camilla is erecting the nativity scene in the manger. A pretty girl smiles at me as I make my way in with the tray and says in a friendly voice, "Hi, I'm Sammy Jo, Florrie's friend."

"Hi." I smile shyly because I recognise the name and know she is married to one of Brad's brothers - the scary one, apparently.

I hand mum and Camilla their tea and then head across to help Sammy Jo decorate the stone window ledges.

"It's Dolly, isn't it?" She smiles with curiosity, and I nod. "Yes, for my sins."

"Sweet name."

"To some." I laugh. "If it was up to my dad, he would have called me Priscilla after Priscilla Presley because he's a huge Elvis fan. Mum's always been a Dolly Parton fan and threatened to shorten my name to Silly Macmillan if he got his way and so, as always, mum's choice won."

Sammy laughs. "The sign of a good marriage."

Feeling curious, I know she's recently married and I say with interest, "Brad told me you are married to his brother. It must be nice to have found love and be settled."

Her eyes take on that dreamy look of the besotted, and she smiles. "It is. I can't believe how happy I am."

"That's nice." I feel so envious of this pretty woman because she has everything I want for myself.

Love. To belong and a man who puts a smile on my face.

She lowers her voice and whispers, "You know, I had to come and help, Dolly and meet the girl who Brad hasn't stopped talking about since he returned home last night."

"Really." I stare at her in surprise as she grins.

"He's a funny one, you know. Always off in that camper van of his, but never really discusses the details – until last night. I don't think there was any other topic of conversation at dinner and it was quite amusing to watch the usual closed book opening up a little and reading out loud."

"What do you mean?" I feel on edge and she smiles. "Just don't let him have everything his own way. He's always found it easy and needs to learn that not everything in life comes so effortlessly."

"Oh no. You've got it wrong, we're, well, we're just friends."

"Of course." She seems to find something amusing and carries on to the next window sill and I can feel a certain man's eyes burning into my back as I follow her.

Suddenly, we hear a loud, "Who owns the camper van blocking the entrance?"

My heart sinks when I see my father looking irritated as he scans the room. I know Brad isn't blocking anything and guess already it's dad's way of 'having a word.'

I shoot him a warning look and he shrugs as Brad races over with his keys at the ready.

"I'm sorry sir, that's my van."

I want to curl up and die at the look my dad gives him. He stares with a scowl and a look of 'leave my daughter alone' and Sammy exhales sharply. "Wow, is that your father?"

"Yes." I sigh and she shoots me a sympathetic look.

"I wouldn't want to be in Brad's shoes right now."

Neither would I because as Brad scurries past him, my father turns and marches swiftly behind and I know that look on his face. He's about to make Brad's life hell just for the fun of it.

More people turn up and I watch my mother in her element, guiding people to piles of decorations and instructing them where to hang them. Mainly I work with Sammy Jo who is pleasant company indeed. Her tales of the Hudson's make me giggle, and I envy her just about everything she has. If only my life was so easy, but it's doubtful that will change anytime soon.

Sammy appears to know everyone here and points to a rosy cheeked woman who is tying red bows around flower sprigs.

"That's Mrs Bevan. She works in the village market store. Her husband Garry, with two rrs is a volunteer firefighter in his spare time. Over there arranging hymn books is Harriet Marshall. She owns the gift shop and has never married, to my knowledge. They're all lovely people who will make your family very welcome."

"They all sound nice."

Sammy lowers her voice. "Mind you, just one word of advice. If you ever need a taxi in this place, don't call Jim Burrows."

"Why not?"

Sammy laughs. "He's the local farmer and moonlights as a taxi driver at night. The trouble is, he thinks he's still driving his tractor and he may as well be because you could run faster than he can drive."

"Is he here?"

Sammy shakes her head. "No, he's probably still on his way."

We dissolve into fits of giggles, which is where my mum finds us and she looks at me fondly. "Hey, babe, things are shaping up nicely. I think we'll be done soon at this rate and I was just telling Camilla I'd love to invite her family to dinner."

I stare at her in shock and she winks before turning to Sammy Jo. "You'll come, won't you, darling? Bring your new husband so I can approve of your choice – or disapprove, you never know."

Sammy grins. "I'll enjoy seeing what you make of him. When were you thinking of?"

"Sunday, perhaps, after the morning service. Scott loves an early roast dinner and would be so happy to have company."

I raise my eyes and my mum pretends not to notice and just claps her hands. "So, it's decided then. All to ours after prayers and we can get to know one another properly."

She heads off and I sink wearily against the wall and wish my parents weren't quite so hospitable sometimes, and Sammy looks at me in concern.

"What's the matter?"

"Everything."

"Why?" She smiles, looking curious, and I sigh. "Mum loves to entertain, she always has, dad not so much. The trouble is, wherever we go, she invites everyone around for Sunday roast without thinking of the practicalities. Firstly, we don't have enough chairs and so the guests are forced to eat on their laps in the sitting room. Then she never has enough plates and we end up serving things on anything close to that. I've even known her to serve Sunday lunch to the guests in the church pews because they were the only available seats. She even raids the communion wine and, quite honestly, the clearing up is monstrous afterwards. Dad has a go about it and she ends up arguing with him and then later on that evening they retire early to 'make up'."

Sammy laughs out loud. "I love your mum."

Grinning, I shake my head. "Once was enough, but every time we move to a new area it's the same routine."

"Have you moved a lot?"

"All my life. To be honest, I'm growing weary of it all and want nothing more than to put down roots and see if I'll actually grow up for once. It's hard being the protected daughter of a military vicar; my life sucks sometimes."

"Then maybe I can help."

She smiles sweetly, "Leave it with me, Dolly and I'll see what I can do."

Our attention is drawn back to the door of the church as it opens, letting in a gust of icy wind and with it Brad, closely followed by my father. If anything, Brad looks a lot paler than he left, and the gleam in my father's eyes makes my heart sink.

Brad heads straight back to the box of decorations without a glance my way and my father heads across instead and winks at Sammy Jo. "Hey, babe, Scott Macmillan, local vicar and father to this sweet little girl beside you."

"Dad, please." I groan with embarrassment, but Sammy just laughs. "I'm pleased to meet you, Mr Macmillan, or do I call you Reverend? I never know."

"Scott's fine. So, do you live near here, do you come to church and can I count on your help with all things Christmas?"

Sammy grins. "I live very close, Valley House to be exact and I'm married to the brother of the one who you appear to have scared within an inch of his life."

She laughs and I hold my breath because in one sentence she has summed up the situation perfectly and I wonder what my father will say.

He just laughs and whispers, "I may have had a stern word. Something along the lines of picking up vulnerable women and the repercussions of that. I think we're singing from the same hymn sheet now."

My gaze flicks to Brad, who is looking so defeated I feel incensed on his behalf and as I look at my dad with a rising fury, he just winks. "I told him I'd get him in shape. We're due a hike in the hills later on today."

"Dad, no!"

I share a despairing look with Sammy Jo, who just shrugs. "Sounds like an, um, bonding experience."

"I thought so. I mean, I need to get the measure of the men around here and I may as well start with him. He seemed eager enough."

"Only because you probably scared him half to death, honestly dad, why can't you just stay out of things?"

Turning on my heel, I head over to Brad, resisting the urge to stick two fingers up behind my back as I go. Typical of my father, an extreme workout designed to humiliate and exhaust any potential suitors that will probably end up with a lesson in self-defence where he gets to knock seven bells out of his 'trainee'.

Crouching down beside Brad, I say apologetically. "You don't have to go with my father, just tell him you've changed your mind."

Brad looks behind me nervously and I can feel my father's eyes boring into my back.

"It's fine, I could use a workout."

I block my father's view and say with concern, "Please don't let him win, Brad."

"What, the workout?"

I laugh. "No, just don't let him bully and intimidate you. He's got to learn I can make my own decisions and my own friends, whether he approves or not."

"That's just it…"

"What is?"

"At the moment, he doesn't approve of me and I want to prove him wrong. To be honest, I can't wait to change the look on his face when he sees I'm not that bad, really."

Sighing, I rock back on my heels and, taking a deep breath, say with a sigh. "You'll never win against him, Brad. You see, my father wasn't just a military vicar for all his service, he was part of a special ops team and they wrote the fitness handbook. He will drive you to exhaustion and I would hate to be the cause of that."

Brad's smile is frozen in place as he hisses, "I really wish you'd told me that earlier."

He groans, "I'm screwed, aren't I?"

"Yes, I think you probably are."

It's almost comical to see the torture in his eyes as he whispers, "I thought I had this one in the bag. He's older than me and I have youth on my side. He has every trick in the book on his and there is no way on earth I can beat him. I think you should just kill me now and put me out of my misery because how the hell am I going to survive this 'exercise' in mid-winter with an SAS psycho hot on my heels?"

He looks so anguished, I can't resist giggling and then blatantly, with no regard for the hostile eyes watching our every move, I lean a little closer and to my own surprise, press a light kiss on his cheek and whisper, "I have every faith in you Brad Hudson, you saved me once, then twice and I know you can do anything you set your mind to. Failing that, use your knowledge of this area and cheat. I would if it was up to me."

I don't know if he's more shocked that I kissed him or that I told him to cheat, but a flicker of something that looks a lot like interest flares in his eyes as he stares at me with a slightly vulnerable look. I'm not sure if the battle lines were drawn in this moment, or they were always there under a light dusting of snow because I am going to be friends with Brad Hudson if it kills me and if not, he will die in the challenge, anyway.

CHAPTER 10

Mum sighs. "Honestly, honey, you'll wear those floorboards out if you don't stop for one minute."

"But it's getting dark." I peer out into the disappearing light and for the thousandth time worry about Brad.

"They've been gone for hours; do you think Brad's ok?"

"I doubt it." Mum chuckles and as I throw her a worried look, she rolls her eyes.

"He'll survive. That's all that matters, really. I mean, your dad's not a…"

She falters and I say roughly, "A killer. Is that what you were going to say because we both know he has been in the past and can make anything look like a very unfortunate accident."

"Relax, Dolly." Mum laughs softly. "That was years ago. No, he's just spending time with one of your friends, checking him out just to make himself feel happier that you're keeping the right company. It's fine. They're probably tucked up at the weird pub across the valley. The Blue Balls, or something crazy like that."

Thinking about how cold it is out there, I'd say that was a definite and mum sighs again. "Why don't I make us a nice cuppa and we can enjoy some girlie time? I mean, it's been so hectic since we moved, I haven't had a chance to see what you make of this place."

"It's nice, sweet even."

Turning away from the window, it's probably a good thing to distract my attention from Brad's obvious fight for survival and I head over and help dry the dishes that mum is washing.

"I like it here, mum, the people seem nice and the town is so sweet and cosy. A little quieter than we're used to but nicer for that."

"And the locals seem pleasant, maybe some more than others."

She grins and I roll my eyes, wondering whether to answer her or not.

"So, Brad." Mum won't give up and I shake my head as I place the plate on the scrubbed kitchen table. "I like him despite his reputation."

I fix her with a determined look and she nods. "I know."

"You know what?"

"How much you like him. He likes you too."

"He thinks he does but then again, if you believe the rumours, he likes a lot of girls, so I doubt I'm special."

"Ah, yes, the rumours. Do they bother you?"

"A little." I sigh and think about Brad and the stories I've heard of his wandering eye. Trust me to fall for the local bad boy, although bad is hardly the word I would use to describe the extremely personable Brad Hudson.

"People change, you know." Mum's voice filters through my thinking and I nod. "I know."

"I mean, take your father. He wasn't always such an upstanding member of the community."

"I know mum."

"When I met him, he was a rogue. A loveable rogue who had all the chat and all the right moves."

"Yes, mum, I know." I have heard this story a million times already, but she won't give up and gets that misty expression whenever she talks about my father, even after all these years.

"Yes, he was a bad boy with a heart. When I met him at the local disco, he made a beeline for me. Swept me off my feet physically and turned on the charm. I was besotted, Dolly, well and truly hooked and fell hard. Maybe that's because he spun me too quickly and we both fell on the floor and were nearly crushed by the mob, but emotionally I fell harder. When I learned what he did to earn a living, I was shocked but fascinated. I'd never met a soldier before and certainly not a man like him growing up in the depths of Lewisham. He was exotic, babe, a rare gem in a field of mud, shining out like the purest temptation that I seized with both hands and never let anyone else get a look in. Well, the rest is history because I followed him around the world like a love sick puppy and I haven't stopped since."

"Do you ever get tired of travelling, mum, wish you could stop and take a breath and spend long enough in a place to make it your home?"

"My home is where your father is, Dolly, and it always has been. If my family is by my side, I'm home and I don't need anything else."

"But what about me? I haven't got that luxury, mum. You have dad and that's great, but how will I ever find anyone when we don't stay longer than five minutes and during that time dad scares the living daylights out of anyone who is remotely interested in me?"

Mum smiles, looking as if she's lost in love land again when I mention my father. "Things work out in the end,

Dolly. I'm a great believer in that. If you're meant to find someone, you will, regardless of what your dad or anyone else thinks of that."

She looks at me with a mild curiosity. "Do you think *that* someone could be Brad Hudson?"

"Who knows?"

I stare out into the ever-growing darkness. "Then again I probably never will because dad is probably digging a shallow grave as we speak."

Mum laughs out loud. "Nonsense, your father's a changed man, at least…"

"What?" I stare at her sharply and she rolls her eyes. "Maybe not where you're concerned. A father never compromises when his daughter's hearts on the line and maybe he's just doing you a favour because if Brad is really keen to get to know you, he won't let the small subject of your father get in the way of that."

"I think we both know it's not a small obstacle, mum. More like a big, immovable, insufferable obstacle that could fall on him at any time and crush him to dust. Why won't he just let me make my own decisions? He's always been so…"

"Protective, loving even. Don't knock it, babe. Love is a powerful weapon that most of us never learn how to use wisely. Love also blinds you to the harsh realities. Your father doesn't have that love dust in his eyes when he sees who comes calling, only the truth, and if Brad is wrong for you, he will know within ten minutes in his company. Trust him, babe, he's a skilled man in many ways and will soon have the measure of Brad Hudson."

There is absolutely no getting through to my parents because they are blind when it concerns me and my brother Beau. Just thinking about how lucky he is to have left home already makes me yearn for my own freedom. I need to spread my wings and discover who Dolly Macmillan can be and I will never get that chance all the time my parents control my life in this way.

It must be at least two hours later that my father bursts through the door looking as if he's taken a gentle stroll through the forest. He opens his arms as my mum rushes into them and as they fold around her, I feel a pang in my heart. This is what love looks like. Even after all these years, they are still happy together. I watch as he presses a deep kiss into her hair and I hear him whisper, "I missed you, sweetheart."

He raises his eyes to mine, still holding my mum, and winks. "He's alive."

"What happened?"

Mum pulls back and stares at him anxiously. "You didn't put him off, did you?"

"Off what? No, that man has learned a valuable lesson today."

An icy feeling claws my heart like a heavy frost on a cold winter's morning. "What did he learn?"

"The power of preparation, mental strength and working as a team. Guys like him are used to the easy life. Getting what they want with zero effort and then moving onto the next shiny object. He has no ambition, no killer instinct and just a desire to have it all. If you ask me, I've done him a favour, realigned his thinking and shown him that not everything in life is easy and sometimes the sweetest rewards are hard earned."

"What did you do, dad?" I am so worried for Brad and from the look mum throws me, she shares it.

"To build a man up, you need to break him. Brad may be feeling a little out of his comfort zone right now, but he'll thank me for it in the long run."

"Dad, please." I feel like shaking him. "Is Brad ok and

please tell me he's safe at home recovering from the near-death experience you undoubtedly put him through?"

"Relax honey, Brad's fine. It's all good."

He winks and says loudly, "Anyway, I could murder a bath and then a beer. Maybe not in that order."

He grins at my mother. "How about you fetch me a beer and then join me in the bath? That could work."

Mum is off and running to the fridge before he even adds the full stop to the sentence and I groan inside. Great, another night wishing the walls weren't paper thin and trying everything possible to drown out their enthusiasm for spending time together.

I really need to get a life and fast.

CHAPTER 11

My eyes are heavy and there's a fog in my brain that I really hope lifts soon because I don't think I slept a wink all night. Mainly worrying about Brad but also trying to block out the obvious party going on in the next room made for a very disturbed night.

Wearily I shower and try to ignore the slightly antiquated system as I shiver under a trickle of luke-warm water while freezing in the sharp frosty air that seems to follow me like a lovesick fool. Which is just my luck because after last night, I doubt anyone else will. Word will get out about the maniac vicar guarding his daughter like a minotaur and my life will be over in Dream Valley before it began.

With a heavy heart, I dress for the day and wonder what delights are in store as we contemplate the first service my father will take since we arrived.

Sunday is always a busy day for any vicar and so I mentally prepare myself for another one. The locals will be curious, hopefully making the short journey to crowd the church and judge the new vicar and his family. Mum will be in her element and take over like she always does and I will just exist on the side-lines and do what I'm told, like *I* always have.

I head into the warm kitchen, grateful that one room in this house is above freezing at least and mum smiles. "Did you sleep well, babe?"

The fact I have the black hole of Calcutta underneath my eyes right now should be the answer she needs and I nod stiffly, "Ok I guess, given the noise."

She doesn't even look ashamed and just throws my father a flirtatious look and grins. "Sorry, babe, blame your father."

I try not to think about what goes on when they're alone but they make it impossible to ignore and as I see my father bare chested in the middle of winter, looking as if he's sunning himself on a beach, I shake my head. I wonder what the parishioners would think if they saw their vicar now. Decorated like an Egyptian tomb with ink and menace. The images of broken skulls and captured birds scripted in ink all over his body, intertwined with flowers and weird Latin verses that he always told me was his motto for survival. A man's man and a woman's dream. That's always been my father which is why his chosen profession is a little surprising when you are faced with the alpha male that is Scott Macmillan.

Mum drops a plate of bacon and eggs with all the accompaniments in front of him and he smiles up at her with a mixture of love and lust making me roll my eyes because she is just as bad. Dressed in a silk kimono and probably not a lot else, she looks as if she's done ten rounds in the boxing ring and sleep never featured in her night at all.

Her gaze rests on him a little longer than usual and they share a secret smile that shuts the whole world out and I envy them their passion. I always have because nothing gets between them and their insatiable love for one another. *I want that.* I want a man to look at me as if I hung the moon and polished the stars but it's doubtful I'll ever find it all the time I'm living with them.

Sighing heavily, I sit opposite my father and reach for the teapot to pour myself a much-needed hot drink and mum says suddenly, "Oh babe, this came earlier, it was pushed through the door."

"What is it?"

She hands me an envelope with elegant script lettering on the front.

The Vicarage.

"I don't know but it looks posh."

My dad's eyes narrow. "Open it."

My fingers shake a little, probably from the fact they're freezing, and I draw out a cream invitation card and read.

You are invited to join us for Carols by Candlelight. Sunday at 7pm at Valley House.
Mince pies and mulled wine and the spirit of Christmas await you. Just bring your best singing voice and a heart full of joy and laughter.

Dad snorts. "Priceless."

Mum shakes her head. "I feel as if I've stepped back in time. It sounds good though."

Turning the card over, I see nothing else and smile. "I think it's sweet. Shall we go?"

"Obviously" Mum laughs. "It would be rude not to and I can't wait to get a look inside that place. Camilla spoke about her home and it sounds right up my street. We'll talk about it at lunch when they come for Sunday roast."

"For god's sake, Tina."

Dad thumps the table with frustration, and I prepare myself for fireworks.

"You haven't..."

"Only the Hudson's, babe, it will be fine."

Looking around the small kitchen, I catch my father's eye and giggle at the torture in his as he raises them and shouts, "For now! I'm guessing the first people through that door will be asked to stay behind so we can 'get to know one another.' Honestly, if you haven't invited half of Dream Valley by the end of the first prayer, I'm not the freaking local vicar who has to deal with this madness."

"Relax babe, it's doubtful anyone will come, anyway."

Mum laughs and I join her because if we get ten people, we're lucky most services. It's a constant source of conversation trying to think up ways to attract the people of whatever town we're in to come and actually go to church and we still haven't cracked it, despite mum trying to make church a cool place to be, minus the freezing temperatures.

Dad sighs with a resignation he only offers my mother and she rubs his shoulders and purrs, "I'll make it up to you, honey, don't worry about a thing."

Dad just shakes his head and carries on eating and mum winks and slides a plate of food in my direction with a smile. "Eat up, Dolly. I'll need all your help today preparing the vegetables and sorting out the crockery. This is going to be such fun."

* * *

AS ALWAYS, we huddle in the church half an hour before the service in the hope that someone actually shows up for once. Not the usual faces, the stalwart parishioners who turn out, rain or shine, to do their duty, the same ones who listen to every word and agree in its entirety. The usual squad who keeps the church going are bound to be here.

It's the rest we want. The new faces who have lost touch with worship. Those people who think religion is in the past and only turn up for special occasions like midnight mass and the Christingle service. Christenings, weddings and funerals are the only reasons they come and we want to attract them outside of those celebrations. It's mum's New Year's goal every single year and to my knowledge, she's never achieved it.

I'm not sure if Dream Valley is the right place to make all her dreams come true because from what I've seen, there aren't that many here in the first place. Maybe that will change in the future when Brad's brother's development gets underway, but for now, I'm sure of a very quiet Christmas and I'm not that sad about that, anyway.

Dad is changing into his 'uniform' as he calls it and mum is slipping her 'business card' into the hymn books. She is ever hopeful the God Squad are interested in YouTube, but I've always found it to be the opposite of that.

As I wait, I check the candles are lit and spray a room freshener down the aisle and around the front door. The last thing mum likes is a musty church and we get through cans of room spray every year. This one is 'yuletide energy' and I could use a burst of that myself because after the move and the subsequent anxiety attack every time my dad mentions Brad Hudson, I could use a re-charge myself.

"All set girls?"

My father's loud voice rings through the church and mum nods. "All done, honey, but there's no sign of Mrs Judd yet."

"She's not coming."

"Why not?" I share an anxious look with mum because

without her we are minus an organist and will have to rely on dad's karaoke version of hymns.

"Her sister fell ill, and she's gone to Durham to be with her."

"That's too bad, poor thing and at Christmas as well."

Dad nods. "It's fine, I've set up the karaoke machine; no one will know the difference."

"Are you sure about that, honey, because Camilla told me Mrs Judd only knows a handful of tunes and if something else comes on, they'll know in a heartbeat."

"It doesn't matter. We need to broaden our hymn horizons, anyway. I was thinking about White Christmas, Silent Night and Oh Little Town of Bethlehem."

I struggle to contain the giggle that the look on my mum's face causes, and she shakes her head. "The Elvis versions, I'm guessing."

Dad laughs. "Indulge me, babe."

Mum grins. "Only if I can have, 'I saw mommy kissing Santa Claus' from, A Holly Dolly Christmas."

"Only if you find me a Santa suit pronto and I'll hastily oblige."

Rolling my eyes, I turn to the door as the first of the congregation arrives and I smile at the small elderly couple who are dressed in their Sunday best.

"Welcome, welcome, come on in."

Mum rushes towards them like one of Santa's reindeers taking flight and they look a little worried, probably due to the fact she is wearing some kind of white feather-like jacket and leather trousers.

"I'm Tina Macmillan, the vicar's long-suffering wife and his better half. Come in and know that you are very welcome."

Dad rushes forward and introduces himself, and I bite my lip when I see the horror on their faces. My parents are definitely not the stereotypical vicar and his wife, and I wonder what Dream Valley will think of that.

A few more locals drop in and by the time the service is due to start, at least three pews have people occupying them, and the resignation in my father's eyes makes me feel sorry for him. He tries so hard, a little too hard sometimes and never has the joy of a full house on a normal Sunday, unless you count his own afterwards when mum invites most of them back for a lovely roast dinner and a gossip.

Then my heart flutters when I see Brad heading inside, closely followed by Camilla and what appears to be the entire Hudson family. Thanking God for the fact they will fill a few more pews, I look anxiously at Brad, who is looking extremely uncomfortable as he throws worried looks at my father.

Camilla sees me and shouts loudly, "Dolly, over here, let me introduce my family."

I'm not the only one who hears and my heart sinks when both mum and dad head that way too, causing Brad to position himself behind his three brothers without making eye contact with any of us as he appears to find the floor very interesting.

I join my parents and Camilla says with pleasure lacing her voice, "Allow me to introduce my family. This is Marcus and his beautiful wife Sammy Jo. They're newlyweds you know, so sweet."

I look with interest at Marcus, who looks a little irritated to be here at all, nod as his wife smiles sweetly, "We've met already."

I don't miss the interested look Marcus throws my way, and I'm guessing Brad had a lot to say about my family last night and my heart sinks. The fact his brother is holding on tightly to his wife's hand makes him seem less scary somehow because it's obvious he cares for her a lot due to the look in his eye when he smiles down at her.

"This is Jake and Florrie who you've already met and Dom, my second eldest. Oh, and you've met Brad, of course."

She sighs, "Show your face, Brad, don't go skulking around there at the back for goodness' sake."

I don't miss the slightly evil look my dad gives him, or the slight shaking of my mother's head as she throws him a sympathetic look, and I wonder what really happened last night.

Luckily, they all start drifting away to take their places with my parents as welcome escorts.

Grabbing hold of Brad's arm, I pull him back and say in a whisper, "Are you ok?"

He looks at my dad and sighs. "I've been better."

"I'm sorry, Brad."

I feel so miserable because it's obvious my father's completely put him off and yet when he looks at me, I see a softness in his eyes that takes me by surprise a little.

"It's fine, Dolly. I suppose I'd be the same."

Dragging him into a pew at the back of the church, I say with a worried frown, "What happened?"

"I'll tell you later, but I've never felt so exhausted in my life, both mentally and physically."

I see my dad laughing at something Marcus is saying, and it irritates me because why is he so nice to one brother and so appalling to the one beside me?

To my surprise, a hand grips mine and laces our fingers together and Brad whispers, "I won't let him beat me."

I just stare down at our fingers and feel my heart thumping with expectation. Turning to face me, Brad smiles and leans slightly closer, whispering, "Meet me later, Dolly. I need to know something before I put up the biggest fight of my life."

"What?"

"If you feel the same."

"Dolly, babe, over here, dad needs your help."

Guiltily, I look up and snatch my hand from Brad's, but I already know it's too late just from the smirk on my mum's face.

Scrambling to my feet, I whisper apologetically, "I'll see you later, I promise."

As I walk away behind my mother, I'm a mess inside. I do want to get to know Brad, more than I should for my sanity, but I'm already preparing for him to break my heart when he moves on to the next in line.

CHAPTER 12

My job appears to be karaoke machine operator and for once I'm glad there are only a handful of the locals to witness this whole debacle.

My face burns as I hear dad finish up.

"Moreover, we have all had human fathers who disciplined us, and we respected them for it. How much more should we submit to the Father of spirits and live! They disciplined us for a little while as they thought best; but God disciplines us for our good, in order that we may share in his holiness. No discipline seems pleasant at the time, but painful. Later on, however, it produces a harvest of righteousness and peace for those who have been trained by it."—Hebrews 12:9–11.

I know why he chose this particular sermon and haven't missed the hard look he directs in Brad's direction for the entire service. I also don't miss the amusement on the faces of Brad's family as they take pleasure in the misery he must be feeling. It's so obvious my father has it in for Brad Hudson, and I know it's because of me. He doesn't want to encourage a man with Brad's reputation to come anywhere near his protected daughter. The fact he was the biggest scoundrel around himself, if you believe my mother's stories, makes him a hypocrite in my eyes and all it does is make me determined to get to know Brad even more because like Brad, I will not let him win.

My dad turns and nods and my heart sinks as the opening bars of Silent Night play out and as the congregation stands, I prepare myself for what we are about to receive.

I'm not sure if it's the shock on the faces of the congregation, or the laughter in their eyes that mortifies me the most but as dad proceeds to sing a la Elvis Presley and mum backs him up with her finest impersonation of Dolly Parton, I want the ground to open up and swallow me whole.

In fact, they can be heard above everyone, given the fact they are wearing headsets with mics attached and it's like a duet of the most embarrassing kind.

My face burns and I can't look anyone in the eye as they completely murder the 'hymn' and as I raise my eyes to God and beg for forgiveness, I can only hope this torture will be over before I resort to cracking open the communion wine.

My pain is not even over yet because as soon as the last note is cut, my father stands and warmly introduces my mother, who is doing the reading today, which is not really so bad. The only trouble is, she insists on reciting Dolly Parton's, 'Hello God' and as my dad looks at her with so much love, the rest of us are looking at her with a completely different expression on our faces.

As a double act they are one of a kind and I have never really got over the way they carry on regardless of the looks they're given and people's opinions. It's as if they live in their own little bubble of happiness and I envy them for that. Does it really matter what people think, anyway? Possibly not, but just sometimes I wish they would tone it down a little and be normal for a change.

We plod on and after two more hymns, each one more excruciating than the last, we finally reach an end and yet the light shining in the eyes of the congregation tells me they were entertained at least.

I really wish I could slip away with Squirrel somewhere for the rest of the afternoon but have the added misery of lunch with the Hudsons to worry about. I'm guessing Brad is dreading this as much as I am and while my parents are otherwise occupied chatting to the dear elderly couple who look quite happy about things, I slide up beside Brad and whisper, "Come on, we can slip outside through the side door and avoid my parents."

He nods, looking so relieved I worry again what happened last night and as we step into the cold frosty air, for once I don't even register the chill because my anxiety is that bad.

Heading the short distance to the house, to let Squirrel out, I don't know where to start and Brad takes the opportunity to laugh softly. "Your parents put on quite the show back there, it was…"

"Embarrassing, weird, indulgent…"

He grins. "I was going to say different. I enjoyed it though and I normally hate church."

"Brad Hudson, hush your mouth and repent your sins." I say it in my best Dolly Parton accent and he laughs. "You sound so sweet, like your namesake, in fact…"

He stops and pulls me around to face him and I see a tenderness in his eyes that takes me back a little as he takes my hand and smiles, "You are so pretty, Dolly, I don't think you realise that."

"Did my father mess with your mind in more than one way last night? You're deluded."

I laugh, feeling very pleased with my life right now and he turns serious all of a sudden and leans closer. "If I only ever get one shot at this, Dolly, I want it to be now because, despite the protection you've got, I'm the fool who can't see past the fact I like you—a lot. It may cause me physical harm, end my life even, but it would all be worth it if you felt just a fraction of what I'm feeling."

"Brad I…" I don't know what to say because I feel–a lot where he's concerned, but I'm still wary of tossing my heart out to be wrecked by him. My father thinks I'm impressionable, a fool even, but I'm all too aware of Brad's reputation and the fact he could say this to all the girls. I'm a little more guarded over my heart and want to believe he's interested in me but then again, he's interested in a lot of girls, so I say with a sigh, "I would like to get to know you but only as friends. It has to be that way because I'm a little protective of my heart and I have a feeling…"

I break away and he reaches out and turns my face to his and whispers, "Tell me."

Just staring into those sparkling blue eyes makes me drown. Takes me under into a place I could lose myself forever and never make it back. So much desire, interest and curiosity fill them it's impossible not to be affected and I finish up with a slight hitch in my voice, "A feeling that you could break me."

Turning away, I say brightly, "We should let Squirrel out and then you can tell me what happened last night."

I hate that I've broken the spell and ruined a special moment, but I have no choice. We've just met and I'm not ready to sacrifice my own principles for a pretty boy anytime soon. If we are to have any kind of relationship, it's as friends because then at least we would have one far longer than anything else.

Once we let Squirrel out into the garden, we head into the vicarage kitchen and I switch the kettle on and reach for a couple of mugs.

"So, what happened? I'm dying to know?"

"Funny you should say that." He leans against the wall, looking like a tortured soul, and sighs.

"It started out ok, a gentle jog through the fields that was quite pleasant. It helped chase the ice away from my veins and for the most part, your dad just gave me fitness tips. Then he upped the pace a little and proceeded to rattle off a list of names of, um, local ladies I know and asked me about them. It was as if he had researched my entire back catalogue and I had to account for every date and every reason why it never worked out."

My heart beats a steady beat of 'I did warn you' as Brad confirms what the rumours have told me already. He has a *back catalogue*. That alone should warn me off because who the hell refers to their past dates as a back catalogue?

"Anyway, then it got really weird. He started pushing me in more ways than just physically, which I was really starting to feel the effects of. Suddenly, the questions changed, and I started to feel really uncomfortable."

"Like what?"

I hand him a mug of tea and he says gratefully, "Thanks, angel."

Just that one sentence alone wraps me in a yearning for more of the same and I mentally chastise myself for being so gullible and I watch as he takes a sip and then sighs. "Things like, where would you least like to be shot, what part of your body would you prefer not to lose and what do you want to be *if* you grow up?"

Resisting the urge to giggle at the pure torture in his eyes, I sip my drink looking annoyed for him but he does paint a very amusing picture as I imagine him running for his life – literally, with my furious father hot on his heels shooting psychological bullets to spur him on.

"It was when he remarked that he buried people for a

living and that nobody would ever question a freshly dug grave that really got me sprinting for home and it was as if I was given a shot of adrenalin as I reached that high most athletes strive for in training. Suddenly, my body had a life of its own as it upped the ante and I could have won an Olympic gold because I didn't feel a thing, other than an incredible overpowering need to get away from him fast."

I can't help it and burst out laughing at the tortured expression on his face and for some reason, it pushes out the edge developing between us as I guard my vulnerable heart. Brad reacts the same and we can't stop laughing, which drowns out the fact we're no longer alone and we hear, "There you are, we were wondering what had happened to you both."

Looking up in surprise, I see the interested faces of Brad's family and my mother and the slightly aggressive glint in my father's eyes as he stares at Brad with a look that could cut him down on the spot and I sigh inside. Here we go again.

CHAPTER 13

As expected, mum has bitten off way more than she could chew and the sheer number of people crowded into the small vicarage makes for a great deal of manoeuvring.

The men retire to the living room for a pre-dinner drink, leaving the women to help my mum with the roast dinner. There are no prizes for equality in this house because mum couldn't care less and just likes to dispose of the men as quickly as possible, so we can gossip about how useless they are even though she never gives them a chance to help out, anyway.

"Typical guys." She rolls her eyes. "They get to drink the medicinal brandy while the women do all the work."

Camilla nods. "It was always that way in our house. Anthony was such an alpha male and never lifted a finger to help around the house."

Florrie is laying the table with Sammy Jo and laughs. "Jake's not so bad. He quite likes cooking and can make a mean spaghetti Bolognese."

"Then make him show Marcus please, that man would prefer to eat out every night than actually cook."

Sammy rolls her eyes and mum nods. "Yes, I recognise another man fresh out of the cave. What are we going to do about them?"

She turns her attention to the vegetables and as she chats to Camilla, I help the others with the table. I say table, but it really consists of the farmhouse table with a trestle table from the church hall butted up at one end. We've also raided the hall for some fold up chairs and moved the rocking chairs into the snug. There's not much room to move in here and yet somehow we have managed to accommodate everyone and the table looks quite pretty with mum's finest china laid out and a little vase of festive foliage quickly gathered from the garden, set alongside burning candles that create a warm and magical glow.

Sammy lowers her voice. "I don't know what your dad did to Brad yesterday, but you should have seen him when he finally fell through the door. I had one finger on my phone to dial the paramedics."

My heart sinks as Florrie nods. "He was gasping for air and looked destroyed. Maybe he pushed himself too far."

Sammy laughs. "He looked absolutely terrified, and it took a while for him to recover. Maybe fitness isn't Brad's thing."

They look at me with a curious gaze and I sigh. "I'm so sorry but my father's a little overprotective, shall we say, and Brad has paid the price for that."

"Are you..." Florrie prepares to ask the question I think is on all their minds and I shake my head vigorously, "Just friends, which is why this is all so unnecessary."

Sammy nods, as if she understands what I'm going through. "My dad would be the same, although probably not quite as successful as yours. I mean, Brad must have a death wish to go up against him, surely."

Once again, my heart sinks as they insinuate that it's probably not worth the near-death experience pursuing me would bring and Sammy says kindly, "If you want something badly enough, you will do absolutely anything to make it happen. It will be interesting to see if Brad is as determined as I think he is."

"We're just friends, nothing else."

My words sound hollow even to my own ears and I don't miss the look they share. They obviously don't believe a word I say, and I sigh. "How can it ever be anything else? I've heard the rumours, Brad likes the thrill of the chase, it's obvious. Once he's caught them, he's off and running on to the next and when that supply wears thin, he'll be off travelling the world looking for fresh continents to conquer. I'm not a fool, I can see it all."

"I'm not so sure." Sammy smiles as if she is the guardian of a delicious secret and Florrie nods. "I agree. You see, Brad never talks about his dates - ever. In fact, we only find out who they are via Facebook and the village gossip. Occasionally we see them together, but it's never twice. You're different, Dolly. It's all he can talk about. The guys have been teasing him mercilessly, saying he's a changed man since you came to town, which is why they were so eager to come today."

"That and because Camilla's guilt tripped them into it." Florrie rolls her eyes. "They'll do anything for their mother, you've gotta love that about them."

Hearing them describe the close family bond they have with their mother sends a burst of heat to my cooling heart. I share that same value because I love my own so hard it hurts sometimes. Surely a man who loves his family isn't all bad and I wish like crazy Brad didn't come with a history that dates back to puberty it seems because it's like a massive barrier between us that I'm doubtful will ever come down.

Sighing, I say brightly, "Anyway, it will probably never be anything but friendship because Brad is intent on travelling and I expect we'll be moving on as soon as they realise we're a little too alternative for Dream Valley and send us to the Outer Hebrides or something."

"What about you, Dolly? Brad told us you were between jobs at the moment. Do you have any plans?"

Mum must be listening as always and shouts across, "I forgot to say, love..."

"Say what?" I look at her in surprise.

"Dad ran into Harriet Marshall from Valley Gifts yesterday, and she was putting one of those job notices in the window. Apparently, she's so busy, what with Christmas and all, and needs some temporary staff. It won't be for long, just a couple of weeks, but your dad said he'd mention it to you. It might be just what you need, to get away from us for a bit and earn some money."

Florrie looks excited. "Wow, I love that little shop. It's so pretty at the moment with the gorgeous window display and all those fairy lights."

Camilla nods. "Harriet's got exquisite taste and does a gorgeous gift-wrapping service. I pay her to do all mine and it's worth every penny. You should go and ask for the job, darling. I could give you a character reference if you like. In fact, I'll text her now. She's such a good friend. I'm sure the jobs yours if you want it."

I feel quite excited about this and nod enthusiastically. "I would love that, but it may have gone already."

"Leave it with me, I'll type out a text now."

Camilla reaches for her phone and mum starts dishing up and says, "Go and call them in, babe and tell your father to fill their glasses in there. I'm not sure I've got room on the table for bottles as well as everything else."

Quickly, I head the short distance to the living room and hear the loud laughter coming from inside, along with my dad's voice, no doubt rattling off the filthy jokes that he wheels out every time.

Sometimes I wonder why my father chose this as a profession because he's a real man's man and incorrigible, but somehow through all that testosterone he fell in love with God. Mum thinks it's because he's done some terrible things in his life and wants to make up for it now, and she's probably right. I know it wasn't easy doing the job he did, and he rarely talks about that part of his life. He still has friends from the unit, as he calls it, who often come and visit and occasionally I listen to their conversation of a time I could never imagine living through. My father has lived a hard life already and I worry about my brother Beau doing his best to live up to him. I suppose I'm not surprised that dad has such a low opinion of people who don't work hard and complain all the time.

Once again, my heart sinks because Brad doesn't really stand a chance with my father. He's everything my dad hates in a man. He doesn't work, has no obligations, no solid goals and a wandering eye. We are doomed from the start and yet there's still that foolish part of me that wishes for more.

As I push open the door, the first eyes that meet mine are Brads' and just for a moment, we stare at one another as if we're the only ones in the room. A connection of the most devastating kind, because I do want to know him more, on a closer level than friends. I already know I do because there is something about Brad Hudson that is different to anyone else I've ever met and for some reason, I think he feels that too.

CHAPTER 14

Things go steadily from bad to worse through lunch.

Somehow, we all manage to crowd around the table and enjoy a very squashed meal. Mum, as always, outdoes herself and the melt in the mouth roast beef and fluffy roast potatoes are as delicious as always. The vegetables are plentiful and a nice thick gravy accompanies the huge Yorkshire puddings that are mum's speciality.

The wine flows, and the conversation is delightful and should be the recipe for a very pleasant afternoon.

However, my father just won't let this Brad fixation rest and the conversation soon turns to more personal matters.

Leaning back, my father looks around the table with interest.

"So, tell me, Marcus, what do you do for a living?"

Marcus looks up and I regard him with interest because he seems to detach himself from normal life most of the time unless his wife whispers something in his ear and he gently rubs her shoulder and smiles into her eyes. Sammy Jo, in direct contrast, is warm, easy to chat to and full of good conversation and I like her – a lot.

His low, slightly husky voice holds everyone's attention as he says gruffly, "I'm a property developer. Mainly for other people, but I have my own exciting project due to start in the New Year."

"Oh yes," Mum interrupts. "Dream Valley Heights, I saw the signs."

"Yes, it should regenerate the area and bring much needed homes to the locals and their ever-growing families. I hope to update the school, the surgery and give Dream Valley a boost to keep it alive."

I can tell my father is impressed, which can be hard to achieve as he looks at Marcus in admiration before turning to Dom. "Are you involved in the property business?"

For some reason, they all laugh and Camilla raises her eyes, "Dominic would rather preserve the land and keep the environment as nature intended. He's more interested in a different type of business."

I look at Dominic Hudson and see a man much like his brother Marcus. More serious than the rest and exuding a raw power that is impossible to ignore.

Dominic carries on. "I run the building business. My father set up a chain of building supplies shops that I'm to inherit and it keeps me pretty busy."

"It sounds exhausting." Mum shakes her head and dad says to Jake. "Florrie told us you developed that game all the kids are asking Santa for this year. You are very talented."

Jake is the one most like Brad and it's impossible not to like him as he says cheerily, "I get paid to do what I love. I couldn't be happier right now. I have it all, a job that interests me and the woman of my dreams." He raises Florrie's hand to his lips, and she blushes, making us all laugh.

Then my heart sinks as he turns his attention to the

reason he asked the questions in the first place.

"What about you, Brad? What do you do to earn a living?"

His eyes hold him in a death stare as Brad looks around nervously. His brothers look angry on his behalf and Camilla interrupts, "Well…"

"It's ok, mum." Brad sighs. "To be honest, I'm between jobs at the moment."

My father leans back with a big look of 'I told you so' in his eyes as he looks at me as if to prove his point.

Brad carries on. "It's no secret I want to travel. I thought I'd take a gap year and see the world first."

"Is that right?" My father looks thoughtful. "That's interesting because I may have some contacts I could send your way."

"That sounds amazing." Camilla smiles, full of hopeful politeness. "Brad could use some suggestions, couldn't you Brad."

"Yes, um, thanks."

"You see…" My father is warming to his subject and my heart sinks. "I know of many charitable organisations who would love a willing helper. Someone to help build an orphanage or distribute aid. I have a few contacts with the Red Cross and they always need volunteers. The trouble is, I doubt that's what you had in mind when you say you want to go travelling."

"It sounds um, interesting but…"

"Oh no, darling." Camilla laughs. "Brad was thinking of taking off in his camper van and seeing where the open road took him. He has such a spirit of adventure, don't you darling. Just think of all the amazing places he will see along the way. Oh, to be young again."

"Yes, to be young again." My father ignores the death stare my mother is throwing him right now as he says roughly, "How old are you, Brad, twenty-one, twenty-two perhaps?"

"Twenty-two, sir." Brad looks so miserable I feel like interrupting but know better and just smile at him reassuringly.

"Twenty-two, you say. I had killed more people than my years when I was your age, Brad. Trained with the SAS and liberated many hostages. I had seen grown men weep as they faced their day of reckoning, and I saw mothers sell their babies just to feed the rest of their family. I have seen suffering and pain and all in the name of religion. I saw communities devastated by war and greed and I had a very big hand in that, all by the time I was twenty-two. I learned a horrible lesson – the hard way and I am not proud of my part in that but I did it because I was trained to defend our way of life, so men like you and your brothers could go about their business in a peaceful nation. However, when it comes to you, I doubt you can relate to that. A year off, you say, from what exactly? Studying, and living off your parent's hard-earned money. You see, Brad, it appears that the only thing you've earned in life so far, is your reputation and if you want any sort of relationship with my daughter, friend or otherwise, you will have to do better than that and prove me wrong about you."

I open my mouth to speak because the silence in the room is so tense, I think any number of people could snap under the weight of it but my mother gets there first and laughs loudly, "Oh, Scott, when will you ever give it up?"

She turns to Camilla and rolls her eyes. "He does this to all of Dolly's friends. He's only messing around, don't worry about it." She turns to Brad. "Hey, babe, I hope you like apple crumble. It's my dish of the day."

I think everyone here knows that was no joke but are too polite to say anything and as the conversation rumbles on around me, I stare at my father with a thousand thoughts on how I'll make him pay for this. He just leans back and stares at Brad with an amused grin and Brad is looking anywhere but him, and who could blame him.

No, my father has a huge problem and it will be up to me to put a stop to this once and for all.

* * *

AFTER LUNCH, mum tells dad to treat the boys to a drop of brandy in the living room, leaving us to tidy away the remnants of a very delicious meal. As soon as the door closes, Sammy whispers, "I'm so sorry, Dolly."

Florrie nods. "Poor Brad and poor you."

Ever the eaves dropper, mum says with a sigh. "I'm sorry about Scott. He's always been like this. No guys ever got a look in with Dolly. Nobody will ever be good enough for her and Camilla, you must hate us right now."

Camilla just shakes her head. "It's fine. Anthony was the same, no filter, you see. Said whatever he wanted at all times, leaving me to pick up the social pieces. It was exhausting and I suppose he would have been exactly the same. The question is, what are we going to do about it?"

Mum grabs the Baileys from the dresser and pours us all a huge glass each. "We need to do something. Poor Dolly will end up a nun at this rate and I won't get the grandkids I crave. Mind you, I'm pretty sure Beau is doing his best to keep his end up. Why are men so hypocritical all the time?"

It appears that everyone agrees with her and we look around the room with defeated expressions.

Camilla says with a sigh, "You know, where there's a will, there's a way. Why don't we give them a helping hand where we can?"

"I am still here, you know." I shrug, "I can look after myself and to be honest, we're just friends, anyway."

"Of course you are." Mum grins and the rest dissolve into

laughter. "We are, honestly."

"Oh, honey." Mum shakes her head. "To have a friend who looks at me the way Brad looks at you. And you're no better."

"How?" Now I'm deeply disturbed in case my face is betraying my mind and sending out all the wrong signals.

"It's obvious you like him too but are fighting it because of his um, past – sorry, Camilla, no offence."

"None taken."

She shakes her head. "We all know what he's like, but underneath it all is a man yearning for love. To find someone to commit to and whoever tames the beast will find a very loyal partner in Brad. There's a reason he only dates girls once, and that's because he's never met anyone he likes enough to try – until now."

I'm so embarrassed I don't know where to look and Sammy Jo says with a voice edged in sympathy, "Maybe we can help. Give you both some breathing space under the radar to hang out. You may be right, Dolly, and end up as just friends, but how will you ever know if you don't have the chance to find that out?"

"True." Florrie nods in agreement and Camilla says thoughtfully. "Tonight is carols under the Christmas tree, our annual offering to the village. There will be a lot going on and I could instruct Dolly to help Brad serve the mulled wine and the rest of us can keep Scott's attention on other things."

"Good luck with that, babe." Mum laughs and tops up our glasses. "He has eyes in the back of his head and an inbuilt radar where it concerns Dolly, but we could try at least."

Taking a huge slug of mum's favourite tipple, I feel the burn as it slides down my throat and wonder if all this subterfuge will be worth it because the thought of calling Brad Hudson my boyfriend at the end of this, is like catching sight of Santa as he delivers the presents on Christmas Eve – impossible.

CHAPTER 15

Mum is barely talking to dad, which means a night with no sleep for me – again. I know the drill and she will give him the cold shoulder for the rest of the day before an alcoholic haze surrounds her at the carols evening and they spend the rest of the night making up.

Dad obviously knows the drill because he doesn't appear overly concerned and just helps tidy the cottage before announcing he has a few calls to make.

This isn't unusual for a vicar on Sunday, as he keeps his appointments with parishioners who need his advice and to say a prayer for them or two.

Luckily, it gives me some time alone as mum decides to soak in a nice hot bubble bath and pamper herself after a hard day at the office, leaving me to take Squirrel out for a frosty afternoon's walk.

Due to the copious amount of Baileys I've drunk this afternoon, I leave the car behind, my parents one that is, because mine is still waiting for the engine doctor. Making sure to wrap up warm, I head out through the rickety gate and turn right instead of left into the lane outside.

It's such a lovely cold crisp afternoon as the sun tries to restore some heat to the valley, while the frost does everything it can to counteract that. Squirrel is pulling on the lead and I look out for the arrows pointing to a footpath nearby.

I've always loved exploring new places because you never know what you might find. A little piece of paradise perhaps, an undiscovered gem could be around just about every corner in an unexplored place.

Dream Valley is so quiet it gives me a lot of time to think and my dad's speech touched a nerve because how am I so different to Brad?

I'm in between jobs and unsure of the future, with no clear direction in sight. His little speech made me think because I am just the same, floundering with no purpose.

I'm so wrapped up in my thoughts, I don't see another dog coming and only the loud barks and angry growls alert me to the fact someone is walking towards us.

Frantically, I sort through my pockets for a dog biscuit that always guarantees to bring Squirrel to heel.

By the time I've got her safe on the lead, the stranger has reached me and I see a couple of women heading my way with big smiles on their faces amid a rosy glow to their cheeks.

"Sorry." One of them shouts as she puts her dog on the lead and the other one says with interest, "You're the new vicars' daughter, aren't you?"

"Yes." I'm surprised because I don't recall seeing them before, and she nods. "I thought so. I saw you in town with Brad Hudson and someone told me who you were."

"Poor you." The other woman laughs. "I'm not surprised though."

She rolls her eyes as my heart sinks.

My misery must show on my face because the first woman says kindly, "Listen, you will hear nothing more than gossip about the fact he's a ladies' man and likes to play the field and enjoy himself and why not?"

"You've changed your tune." The other woman laughs out loud. "Didn't you threaten to order a voodoo doll off the internet when he took your niece to pineland forest in his camper van?"

Can this get any worse?

Then it does.

"Only because there were two of them in the van with him. Disgusting if you ask me. Anyway, sorry, what's your name?"

"Dolly." My voice sounds as miserable as I feel and she smiles with sympathy. "Everyone can change, you know, and the fact it's the local dogging site shouldn't make us jump to conclusions."

"But you said…"

"Anyway, it's bloody freezing out here and we should let the poor girl carry on with her walk."

They make to leave and maybe it's the misery on my face that stops her, but the woman says gently, "Even the greatest rogue among us can change with the right incentive. Judge him on his actions with you and not other people. It may be different."

She smiles and heads off, leaving me feeling worse than before. Two women! For God's sake!

* * *

Valley House has come alive and as we park the car, my father exhales slowly. "Wow, how the other half live."

We take a moment to admire the view because this house

could sell a lot of Christmas cards. Flaming torches stand proudly, guarding an entrance that looks centuries old with none of the decay. An immaculate composite driveway leads us to a house that is imposing yet welcoming at the same time. Lights glow from every window due to the candles burning brightly on stone window ledges, and the enticing aroma of mulled wine greets us as we step inside the partially open door.

Wide eyed, we look around at a hallway straight from a movie set. A huge Christmas tree stands to the side, dripping with luxury and twinkling warm winter lights. Beautifully wrapped parcels spill out from underneath and the soft melody of old-fashioned Christmas carols is right up my father's street and his eyes light up with pleasure at the soft familiar tunes.

Camilla heads our way, looking like the lady of the manor; a designer's dream in red silk and black fur. She has a string of beautiful pearls around her neck and her make up is immaculate along with her hair style and she looks like the queen as she welcomes us.

"Welcome to Valley House. Come in from the cold and mingle in the drawing room. I will introduce you to everyone."

She links arms with my mother and says to my father, "They are dying to meet you, not literally, though. I'm sure you could use a night off."

Her loud laughter peals across the room and then she stops and says with a mischievous glint in her eye. "I don't suppose you could help Sammy and Florrie with the mulled wine, Dolly, you'd be such an angel if you could."

Spying Sammy Jo, hand in hand with her husband, chatting to Florrie who has Jake's arm wrapped around her shoulder, I giggle at the theatrical wink Camilla throws my way before dragging my father in the opposite direction.

Finding my way to the kitchen is easy due to my visit yesterday and the first person I see filling glasses with steaming mulled wine is Brad.

As he looks up, I love seeing the broad smile breaking across his face as he sees me coming, and I can't help throw one right back at him.

"Hi." I feel strangely shy and he nods. "Hi, angel."

As I head towards him, I feel the need to explain myself and dropping onto the bar stool, shrug out of my coat and say with concern, "Are you ok? I'm sorry about earlier."

"It's fine. To be honest, he was right, anyway."

"I thought the same."

He raises his eyes and I grin. "He could have been talking about me, too. It didn't make me feel good about myself if I'm honest."

"Same." He hands me a glass of wine and joins me on the bar stool next to mine and sighs.

"I think I need to edit my life."

"Me too."

We clink glasses and he says, "To a new life – for both of us. Whatever that will be."

"I'll drink to that." I take a sip and then turn my thoughts to the evening ahead.

"So, the carols. What happens here?"

To be honest, I could stay here all night in this warm cosy kitchen drinking hot wine and Brad groans. "Half the village descend on us and clear us out of mulled wine and mince pies, before attempting to sing with the Dream Valley choral society, who have been invited along with the kids from the local school to sing around the Christmas tree. Then when our ear drums have taken enough abuse, Santa arrives and showers the children with golden coins of the chocolate variety and we bid them all farewell for another year, after they have donated generously to the homeless and stagger back the way they came."

"Sounds like fun. I'm impressed that you raise money for the homeless, though. How much do you usually make?"
"£200, give or take a few pounds, although most of it is topped up by mum because she would feel bad donating any lesser amount."

"You know, I think I love your mum."

Brad's eyes soften. "We all do, everyone except my father it seems." He looks so angry I feel bad for him and he sighs heavily. "Dad never treated mum with the love she deserved. She was an angel living with a devil. He made her life hell, and it's up to us to make the rest of it heaven. You know, Dolly, your father was right to pull me up on my choices."

"No Brad, he wasn't." I shake my head. "He had no right to humiliate you in front of your family and make you feel bad about yourself. That is never right."

"Maybe not, but it got me thinking."

Taking another sip from my drink, I need the courage it will give me for this heart to heart he seems intent on having.

"You see, like I said before, I don't want to be like my father. He cheated terribly on my mum and she always turned a blind eye or forgave him when it came into the open. He was a cruel man and not just with her."

I hold my breath as he reveals a little of his past to me. "Once, I must have been eight or nine years old, he caught me smoking in the garden shed. He didn't say a word and just stood there and looked at me for a very long time before telling me to wait until he came back. I was shaking in my boots and imagined a good hard thrashing, but instead he returned with a box of two hundred cigarettes. You know, the ones they sell in Duty Free. He told me I had to smoke every one of them before I could leave the shed. Then he turned and locked me in."

"That's terrible, child abuse even."

"I know that now, but back then I thought I had no choice. I suppose I got through twenty before I was sick. There was so much smoke in the shed, the gardener called the fire brigade and when they arrived, they burst in with their hoses pointing right at me. Not only was I sick and humiliated, but I was choking and probably scarred for life. Mum was enraged and the shouting match could be heard in Riverton, but he defended his actions by telling her it was to teach me a valuable lesson."

"Did it?" I reach for his hand and squeeze it gently, and he smiles. "I never smoked again, if that what you mean, so I suppose it did. Maybe what I'm saying is, and this is not an excuse, but the reason well…"

"Go on."

"The reason I 'date' so many women is I'm trying to replicate that lesson, so when I marry the person I fall in love with, I will never be tempted to stray. It terrifies me that I'll be like my father and I'm trying my best to do that damage now, when it affects nobody but me. That's the reason I never see them twice, so they hate me and move on. To get this out of my system and save my heart for the right woman."

Tears fill my eyes because despite the nature of this story, it's probably the most beautiful thing I've heard and then Brad leans closer and whispers, "I think I've found that woman in you, Dolly. Don't ask me why, but when I'm with you, I don't see anyone else."

It would be so easy to fall head over heels in love with Brad Hudson at this moment. So easy to throw caution out into the snow and dive straight into something that could be incredible. If only we had that luxury, but the moment our lips almost touch, we hear voices outside as Camilla shouts,

"They're here! Everyone to the Christmas tree and bring your finest singing voice."

Brad grins. "I really hope there's a few Elvis and Dolly Christmas carols. I could sure use the entertainment."

Grinning, I love how he makes me feel. Like the impossible is only a decision away.

CHAPTER 16

If I could take a photograph and title it 'Christmas' it's this one. A small crowd of people surround the Christmas tree, holding glasses of mulled wine and balancing homemade mince pies that are handed around on silver platters by the Hudsons. The lights are twinkling in the darkened hallway and the scent of cinnamon cloves and spices scent the air as a feast for the senses. Flickering candlelight creates a romantic atmosphere and all around me is perfect festive bliss.

The door is open to a crowd of carollers, holding lanterns burning with flickering candles that dance along to the tunes on the wisp of frosty air. Dressed warmly in hats and scarves, their gloves gripping their song sheets, I love the sight of the cherubic faces of the innocent as they fidget and stamp their feet on the light dusting of snow on the ground.

There is not enough room for everyone in the hallway, so we make do with the warmth from the flaming torches either side of the door and all sing along to haunting Christmas carols including, Silent Night, Hallelujah, and Oh Little Town of Bethlehem to name but a few. Even mum and dad's voices don't sound above the crowd as everyone puts their hearts and souls into creating a little piece of Christmas magic. Somehow, Brad's hand creeps into mine as we stand shoulder to shoulder, singing with the rest of them but only really conscious of each other.

Even the curious gazes of the visitors doesn't dampen my spirits. The nudges, the smirks and the rolled eyes of 'here we go again.' They think me deluded, a fool and yet another conquest, but they know nothing at all. First, we are friends. That's where it ends with a little dusting of magic thrown into the mix. Maybe it could be more, hopefully even, but right at this moment, my heart is intact because Christmas and Brad are my two most favourite things in the world right now.

The final carol is sung, and we hear the bells approaching and my heart fills with happiness when I see the excitement on the faces of the small children. Santa rolls to a stop in a sledge festooned with fairy lights, carrying a sack bulging with chocolate coins. The laughter, the gentle teasing and the joy on everyone's faces is the most welcome sight, and it's hard to imagine anything ruining this warm glow surrounding me right now. Should I trust Brad? Probably not, but everyone deserves a chance in life—even a lovable rogue.

* * *

GROANING, I open one eye and sigh. I'm not sure what time we finally got to bed last night, but it was several hours later before the noise subsided in the next room and I finally got a moment's peace. Mum and dad were high on adrenalin, Christmas spirit and lust when we crashed back in the early hours.

Luckily, dad was so distracted at Valley House, I got to

spend most of my time with Brad and as I spent time with him and his family, a piece of me fell in love with the dream.

However, in the cold light of day, I must face facts and have a job to go to, courtesy of Camilla, who received a text from Harriet Marshall. The job is mine if I want it and I should report for duty at 9am to learn the ropes and begin a very busy day in Valley Gifts.

"Here you go love, hair of the dog."

On cue, Squirrel barks and we both laugh as mum slides me a coffee with a tiny hint of brandy in it.

"I'm fine mum, I didn't drink much."

"Then hand it back and I'll pour you a tea instead. I could use a double, what a night."

"Where's dad?"

"In the church, probably praying for forgiveness after that stunt he pulled yesterday." She rolls her eyes. "Poor Brad. What must he think of us?"

"It's fine mum, Brad doesn't hold a grudge."

"Then he's a better man than your father gives him credit for. Anyway, do you fancy a full fry up today to set you up for the day ahead? I'll drop you a packed lunch off later, or better still, we could grab a girly lunch in the Cosy Kettle. That looked so inviting the other day."

"Just cereal and toast for me thanks and yes, lunch would be nice."

"Great, I'll pick you up at two."

She busies herself with grabbing what I need, and it reminds me I should really be thinking of moving on. Relying on my parents for just about everything makes me no better than Brad and so I say slightly nervously, "Um, mum, I've been thinking."

"Steady on babe, it's too early to be thinking anything."

She grins as I roll my eyes. "Well, after dad's Brad lecture yesterday, it got me thinking."

"No Dolly."

"What, no thinking?"

"No, anything. I know what you're going to say, and that little lecture wasn't aimed at you. You will stay with us until you are sorted and not before. Can you imagine your father's rage if you actually declared independence from us? He would be incensed and probably stake out your new home. No, it's different for you."

"Of course it's not. I can't live with you forever, you know. No, I need a plan, to work out what I'm going to do with my life, and I was kind of hoping you would support me in that."

She sighs and sits down opposite and slides a plate of toast my way.

"We'll put our heads together and see what we come up with, but I'm not going to lie. I've been dreading this day."

"What day?"

"The one when you don't need me anymore."

I'm concerned to see her eyes fill with tears and she blinks them hastily away.

"I'm only thinking of it." I feel so guilty, and she sniffs. "Even that fills me with horror. I hate the fact I won't see that you're safe. I will always be wondering if you're eating enough, warm enough, and happy. What if someone takes advantage of you, treats you badly and makes you cry? You might not tell me about it, and I would never know. You could be breaking up inside, and I wouldn't be there to make it all better. How will you live? Money is hard to get and easy to spend. What if you go without, worse than that, don't have enough for the luxuries in life? I need to know that you're ok, Dolly, because you're the part of me I'm most proud of."

"I'm sorry, mum." I genuinely am because I never considered my mother's feelings at all.

She sniffs. "It was different when you went to university

and lived away. I pretended you were at school still, a kind of boarding school. Having fun like they do on the films, like you were at Hogwarts, or something along those lines. I always knew you were coming home and would still need your bed with the pink frilly comforter on top. I arranged your things knowing you still needed me but preparing myself for the day when you would move on and start a new life that I only get to visit sometimes."

She sniffs, and it's breaking my heart, and I'm not sure what to do. I need to leave at some point in my life, but it appears that my mum isn't prepared for that happening.

She sighs and sniffs, blowing her nose into the tissue she always keeps in her dressing gown pocket.

"Take no notice of me, babe. I'm a silly mummy with no common sense and a whole lot of emotion that boils over sometimes. You do what's right for you and know that I'll always support you every step of the way. I'm your mum, of course. It's what I'm here for."

I smile and it feels a little awkward eating as she slowly deteriorates before my eyes. Telling me one thing and battling the tears that tell me another. Why do I feel so guilty? I only said I needed to look at a career path. What will she be like when I do leave home? I may have to restrain her just to let me leave.

Sighing heavily, I smile and say breezily, "Anyway, I'll have to leave you today. I have a job, at least for the next couple of weeks. Can you drop me into town?"

"Of course, I'll just throw on a pair of leggings. I won't be long."

Seeming a little brighter, she heads off and I pour myself another mug of tea from the ever-present teapot.

I'm not sure what will happen in my future, but whatever it is, my mum will just have to find a way of dealing with it.

CHAPTER 17

*V*alley gifts is the prettiest shop I think I've ever seen, and Harriet Marshall is lovely.

She welcomes me in, and I stare at a woman who exudes warmth and personality. She must be in her forties and has dark brown hair tied in a ponytail and her green eyes twinkle behind a pair of tortoiseshell glasses. She is also extremely glamorous and wears her leopard print dress with panache and her wrists jangle as she waves her arms with an exuberance that's infectious and says happily, "I'm so happy you're here. We are going to have so much fun in the run up to Christmas."

The first hour is spent teaching me the cash register, the credit card machine and how to wrap the gifts that require the gift-wrapping service. She even has one of those chilled cabinets with handmade chocolates inside and often tells me to help myself to a treat. I notice that she treats herself often and I'm not sure if they are there for sale, or consumption, because the stock starts dwindling by morning coffee.

We must have had at least twenty customers already before she says with a sigh, "I don't suppose you'll head next door and fetch us a couple of coffee. I'm exhausted already and it's not even lunchtime and I need a shot of caffeine to get me through."

"Sure, what can I get you?"

"A latte and whatever you're having. It's on account so no need to pay. I settle up at the end of the week."

"But I should..."

"No need. It's in the job description. Complimentary coffees and more chocolate than you can eat."

She grins and I can't help but smile as I head to the Cosy Kettle because working with Harriet is a dream come true.

However, as I make the short journey, I hear, "You won't be laughing this time next week."

Turning, I see a dour faced girl around my own age, glowering at me from a table on the veranda outside the coffee shop.

"Excuse me." I look around me in case she's talking to someone else, and she says roughly, "You heard me. A few more days and you'll be dumped along with half of Dream Valley and you're a fool if you think otherwise."

"I take it you're referring to Brad."

My voice is tightly controlled fury because this girl definitely doesn't have my best interests at heart, and I guess she's got a page in his back catalogue.

"Of course I'm referring to him. Just so you know, you're not so special. Brad has the hots for any female with a pulse around here, so get used to rejection. I see it in your future."

"Why are you doing this?" I feel nothing but pity for the girl who looks so bitter it's almost tangible.

"Because I've been where you are now. Full of happiness and hope for the future. Feeling special and as if I matter. Only to wake up the next morning to stone cold reality when he doesn't call or acknowledge me in any way. I'll admit you're lasting longer than most. What's it been, two days already? A virtual marriage where it concerns him, but you'll see. He'll move on and you'll become a member of a very dirty club. The Brad Hudson rejects of Dream Valley. I'll keep your seat warm."

Despite her animosity, I see the genuine hurt in her eyes, and I feel sorry for her more than anything. She must have really liked him and it's only now when I see the repercussions of his actions; it drags me right back down again.

"I'm sorry." I genuinely am and I sit opposite and say gently, "I'm Dolly. I suppose if we're to belong the same club I should at least know your name."

"Evelyn."

"Pretty name." I smile and she looks at me strangely. "Why are you being nice to me? I've been a bitch to you."

"Because despite everything, I think you mean well and I take it as a warning. Who could be upset about that?"

"I suppose." A little of her animosity falls away and I see a pretty girl staring back at me with a little less bitterness in her expression.

"If it's any consolation, he likes you more than most. He wouldn't have held your hand last night and blanked the world out."

"You were there?"

I'm surprised because I don't remember seeing her and she laughs. "It appears he wasn't the only one."

She sighs. "I'm sorry, Dolly. I don't mean to come across as a bitch. I suppose I'm just jealous because despite his sins, Brad *is* great company. Maybe he sees you differently. I hope so, anyway."

"But we're just friends, really."

"That holds hands and can't look at anyone else."

She does have a point and I know how foolish I sound, so I shake my head. "I've heard the rumours. It seems that's all anyone wants to tell me, but Brad is impossible not to like.

We are just friends. It could be more, I suppose, but I'm listening to the warnings hiding behind a giant red flag. Maybe this time Brad won't get the chance to walk away from me because we aren't involved."

Evelyn smiles. "I wish I'd played it cool. You know, I feel like such an idiot. A foolish woman who let her heart run away with her common sense. Don't take up your membership in this club, Dolly. Just don't sample the goods unless you're prepared to deal with the withdrawal. Addiction is a destructive force and most of us around here are addicted to the pleasure that is Brad Hudson."

Feeling bad for her and who knows how many others, I still feel quite sick about the ever-growing number of them. I smile. "I should go. I've only been sent out for coffee and it's my first day on the job."

"Then good luck, and I don't mean with Brad." She laughs. "I meant the job because that's definitely more reliable than him."

As I walk away, I feel torn in two directions. I can't ignore his past, his reputation and the fact so many women have been damaged by him. Will I end up as another discarded soul, lying on the side lines watching him move onto the next person? Then again, he's so different from that behind closed doors. He's an enigma, a problem and a test of my resolve, but he's also a man I can't seem to shake from my heart.

* * *

The Cosy Kettle is as warm and friendly as I remember and Miranda, the owner, is working hard behind the counter. "Can I help you, dear?"

"Harriet sent me for coffee. I'll have the same if I may."

"Sure, it won't take long."

As she makes the drinks, I appreciate the bustling coffee

shop set in the small parade of shops that makes up Dream Valley high street. There aren't many and yet they all seem busy, and I wonder about such a small place. They appear to have loyal customers, which tells me a lot about the community and as I think about it, I'm brought back to the conversation when Miranda says, "All noted on account."

I smile my thanks and she says with a smile, "So, I saw you're spending time with Brad."

My heart sinks. Great, here we go again.

Preparing myself for the incoming warning, I'm surprised when she laughs softly. "You're a lucky girl if you can crack that armour he wears, metaphorically, of course."

"What do you mean?" This is new, and she sighs and leans in and whispers, "Brad is a kind, decent guy, who never really catches a break around here. There's a lot the people of Dream Valley don't know about Brad Hudson, only the bad parts."

Now I'm interested and she nods. "Don't listen to them and trust your own judgement because if the rumours are true and he is keener on you than most, maybe you will be the making of him."

She smiles as if she's guarding a secret that not many others know and turns away, leaving me with a little more hope than five minutes ago and a desire to know what secrets he's keeping close because I'm not sure even his family have the measure of him and now I'm keen to know more.

CHAPTER 18

Mum rushes in like an electric storm, full of energy and just as destructive.

"I love this place." Harriet smiles as she sorts through the various shelves, tossing random objects onto the counter and claiming that everything's adorable, or exactly what she's looking for and I resign myself to mum spending a small fortune on stuff she will tuck away somewhere and forget about it.

She's always been the same. Everything is done to extremes. If she wants to bake, she bakes all day and fills the freezer. If she decides to buy a plant for the garden, she buys enough to fill it. Shopping online is her preferred drug of choice, and the delivery van turns up most days with the latest bargain she couldn't live without.

It's always a constant red flag to my father, who is always shouting when the latest credit card bill comes in and he is presented with the damage. Most of it goes back, but a lot of it stays and I think he only works to pay her credit card bill.

Harriet isn't complaining, though, and as mum tells her

she's taking me to lunch, Harriet promises to wrap the gifts beautifully in our absence.

Luckily, Harriet was fine about us having lunch and I made sure to cover for her while she slipped out the back for her sandwich and pasta salad.

"So, what's it like working in Valley Gifts? I must say I could spend many pleasant hours in there."

We are sitting at a table in the corner, one of only a few available due to the lunchtime rush.

"I'm really enjoying it, mum. Harriet is so lovely, and she's really busy, as you would expect a couple of weeks before Christmas."

Mum says happily, "I'm pleased for you. You need something to occupy your time."

We quickly order a couple of lattes and a ham and cheese toastie each, and I look around me. Once again, the Cosy Kettle is brimming with customers, and I wonder where they all come from. People that seem to all know one another call out greetings as they pass, and the smiles are bountiful. Miranda, the owner, is a friendly woman who seems to know everybody by name and the young girl she has working for her is rushed off her feet.

I wonder if that's why she's so surly because she seemed quite abrupt when she took our order and it appears my mum thought the same as she leans in and whispers, "That girl could use some staff training, either that or a boyfriend."

"Shh mum, she'll hear you." I giggle because my mum says it how it is, and sometimes it can cause us a lot of trouble.

"So, what are your plans this afternoon?" I look at her with interest, but for some reason, she looks a little guilty and I wonder what mad scheme she has up her sleeve.

"Oh, just delivering some toys and stuff for Camilla to Riverton. She asked if I would, and I thought it would be a good chance to do some Christmas shopping."

"What now? It will be busy. Why didn't you go this morning before the rush?"

"Things to do, babe, always things to do."

She smiles as Laura drops our food on the table with a scowl and mum shakes her head. "She could use a little enlightenment in her life. Maybe I'll give her one of your dad's cards and ask if she'll drop by the vicarage sometime."

"Don't you dare, the poor girl." Shaking my head, I start cutting into my sandwich, wishing I could just lift it to my mouth with my fingers instead, when mum laughs softly and says brightly, "Brad, over here."

My hand freezes mid-air as I watch Laura's expression change in a heartbeat and it completely transforms her face.

Then my heart starts thumping as I sense Brad behind me and, for some reason, a shiver of excitement passes through me as I contemplate seeing him again.

I really should get a grip around him because this friendship thing should be just that. Not this yearning I seem to develop every time his name is even mentioned.

"Hey, that looks good enough to eat."

He flops down into a spare seat and says brightly, "I could sure use one of those."

As he looks up, as if by magic, Laura appears with a flirtatious smile and mum rolls her eyes as he says lazily, "Laura, sweetheart, I haven't seen you in a while. How are your parents? I heard your dad was finished with his treatment."

"Good thanks, Brad and yes, he finished a couple of weeks ago and things are looking good."

"I'm pleased, you must be all so relieved."

"We are." There's a longing in her voice, a slight shake to it, that tells me she's affected by him almost as much as I am, and I wonder if she has a section in his back catalogue. What is it about this man that has the women of Dream Valley panting at his feet and tripping over themselves to do whatever he wants with them?

Mum catches my eye and smirks as he orders the same as us and, as Laura reluctantly leaves, she laughs softly. "So, that girl did learn to smile."

"What do you mean, Laura's a sweetheart?"

Brad looks confused and mum laughs out loud. "Oh, to be in your world, Brad Hudson. You see a different picture than the rest of us."

I shrug. "It must be nice to be popular."

"Oh, we are just friends. She's a strange girl, a little abrasive at times, but has a good heart. Her father's just had cancer, and it's been a worrying time for all of them. Luckily, I heard he's clear and they can start living in the normal world again."

Now I feel bad because it's obvious there's a reason for her frown and mum says sympathetically, "Oh, that's terrible, the poor lamb."

We all look across at Laura, who has reverted to scowling at her customers and mum sighs. "You just never know the turmoil some people go through on a daily basis. We just judge by appearances all the time, never really knowing the secrets they are dealing with. I should remember that when I form opinions."

"Me too." I feel so bad, and Brad lifts the mood by saying cheerily, "So, what's up? This is a nice sneaky lunch. How are things going at Valley Gifts?"

He turns that blinding smile on me and I feel the heat surrounding me like a force field as I smile. "Good thanks. Harriet is lovely and I'm enjoying meeting the customers. They seem nice enough and her stock is a pleasure to sell."

"That's good."

Mum's phone rings and she answers it, leaving Brad free to lean in and whisper, "I enjoyed our evening."

"Me too."

"We should hang out together tonight. What do you think? I could show you the local pub, expand your horizons."

Every reason why I should politely decline is battling to be heard and luckily, I am spared from answering, when Laura gently places his ham and cheese toastie in front of him with a secret smile. "Can I get you anything else, Brad?" She is so openly flirting with him, it would be amusing if a tiny dart of jealousy wasn't piercing my heart right at this moment, but he just says, "No thanks, Laura. I've got everything I want right here."

He flashes me a smile and I hate that I flash Laura a triumphant smile, as she scowls and stomps off and I wonder if this is going to be my life here. Point scoring with the local single women every time Brad pays me more attention than them. I don't want to be that woman, so I try to switch off my emotions and attack my food more than a little faster than is good for me.

Mum sighs heavily and slaps her phone on the table.

"Bother. I'm in a conundrum now."

"A what?" Brad laughs, and she groans. "That was Ingrid, one of the parishioners who is interested in discussing yoga classes with me. I have to meet up with her this afternoon to iron out the details and can't head to Riverton now."

Brad smiles. "Yoga. What's that all about?"

"Mum's a teacher and is thinking about setting up classes here."

"Yes, I am, but Ingrid already has it covered, so I'm meeting to discuss any joint opportunities we can work on together. You know, I have so many ideas I'm absolutely brimming with them."

Brad nods. "Sound interesting."

"You should check us out, then again, probably best not

to. I don't want my ladies distracted by the local legend Brad Hudson flexing his muscles in the room."

She rolls her eyes as we both share a grin, and she sighs. "You'll have to tell your mum I couldn't deliver her gifts today. I could do it tomorrow though."

"What gifts?"

"Stuff for the local hospital. She's bought a few toys and wrapped them up for the children and has some food parcels for the food bank. I was thinking of going in and doing some shopping, so I offered to take them."

Brad interrupts, "I'll take them. I'm heading there, anyway."

"You are?" Mum looks relieved. "That would be great. Thanks."

He turns to me. "Do you fancy a ride, Dolly?"

He winks, causing mum to laugh out loud and me to nearly spit out my latte and in between choking, I stutter, "I'm working."

"Leave it with me. I'll have a word with Harriet. She owes me a favour." He grins and I feel the blood draining from my face because Brad and Harriet, surely not.

Mum nods. "You should go, Dolly. Enjoy an afternoon shopping and soak up the Christmas atmosphere."

"I'm not sure I can. I've only just started at Valley Gifts, and I can't leave Harriet in the lurch already."

That and the thought of my father tracking me down to Riverton high street and staging reconnaissance on us. I wouldn't put it past him, and I sigh inside. It doesn't bother me, but it's not fair on Brad. His life will be made a misery every time he steps out with me, and so, out of compassion for him, I should limit our meetings to the bare minimum.

Mum looks thoughtful and is probably thinking the same as me and we revert to eating in a companionable silence as we ponder the fact that my life sucks.

Once we finish, mum says cheerily, "I'll settle up. Why don't you head back, Dolly? Brad can help me unload the car into his."

Grateful to escape, I nod and can't jump up quickly enough. "Thanks, mum. Can you pick me up at 5.30?"

"Sure babe, no problem."

As I head off, I'm relieved to get back to a place where I can function without thoughts of Brad distracting me from sanity because all the time I'm around him, I'm fighting to keep my heart from betraying me and sending me into madness.

CHAPTER 19

*H*arriet puts the phone down as I head back inside, and I take a deep breath of pure pleasure because Harriet's shop smells of all things Christmas. The soaps and diffusers mingle with orange cinnamon garlands, and the scented candles mix together in a heady rush of pleasure. She doesn't seem as busy now and appears to still be wrapping my mother's purchases. and she smiles and cocks her head towards the chiller cabinet.

"Fancy a chocolate, Dolly."

"I'm fine thanks." I have decided to resist temptation in training for resisting Brad. I'm going to say 'no' to everything to train myself not to expect much and it feels good to take a little control of my urges for once.

"Can I help?"

Harriet shakes her head. "I'll be fine, but I do have something you could help me with."

"Ok."

"I have a few donations I need to drop off to the hospital." The alarm bells deafen me as she continues.

"That was Brad on the phone, such a lovely boy, asking if

I needed anything dropping off. He mentioned he was going there for his mother and offered to take you with him to represent the shop."

I'm not sure if it's in my imagination, but she looks as if she's making this up as she goes along, and I sigh inside. Why does everyone bend over backwards to accommodate Brad Hudson and his demands? It's as if he has cast a spell over the women of Dream Valley, me included, and we can't deny him anything.

Even Harriet won't look me in the eye and just rushes around, pulling out boxes of brightly wrapped gifts.

"I've been saving these all year. Samples from suppliers mainly. End of lines and things I can't sell. Every year I donate them to charity and this year our chosen one is the hospital. They have many children there over Christmas and local businesses have organised donations to help out."

I'm not sure if I believe her but it's such a noble cause I take her word on it and as the door opens and the cold blast from the street enters the warm shop, I shiver a little.

Brad enters and says cheerily, "Afternoon, ladies. The charity bus awaits any passengers or parcels to join me on my mission?"

Harriet smiles and nods to the pile on the counter. "These are ready to go. What about you, Dolly? Do you fancy going on my behalf?"

I actually give up. It seems that what Brad wants, Brad gets, and I would look an idiot if I said, 'actually I'll pass this time.' I have been backed into a corner, not so skilfully I might add, and I raise my eyes. "Ok, it will be interesting."

I'm not sure if my eyes are tricking me, but I see Harriet share a look with Brad that tells me this is a conspiracy I was never going to get out of and sighing, I grab an armful of the parcels.

Brad grabs the rest and smiles. "Thanks Harriet, I'll bring her back before you close."

She laughs. "It's fine. Maybe show Dolly my competition in Riverton. I would welcome any ideas she can pick up."

"But…" I feel so bad because she is paying me to take the afternoon off, and she grins. "Honestly, Dolly, you'll be doing me a favour. Call it staff training."

That doesn't make me feel any better and I vow to offer to work and make up the hours, but this is out of my hands, so I resign myself to being skilfully played and follow Brad outside.

"Come on, pretty lady. Let me introduce you to Riverton." It's impossible not to relax around him and I feel quite excited for the afternoon ahead.

His van is parked across the street, and I sigh. My father would blow a fuse if he thought I was riding around with Brad in his camper van and I wouldn't put it past him to head to Riverton to intercept us.

As I take my seat beside him, I try to forget about my father because I'm an adult and can surely do what I want, and I really should stand up to him.

As we start the journey, I laugh softly. "You're a bad man, Brad. I'm guessing you had no intention of going to Riverton today."

"Actually, I did."

"Christmas shopping?"

"Not really."

"What then?"

"You'll see but know this, Dolly. What you see today must remain our secret because quite honestly, I have a reputation to protect, and word can't get out about this."

He slides me a smile and I roll my eyes. "I know all about your reputation, Brad and if it was such a secret, you wouldn't have offered to take me with you."

I laugh but he looks so serious it makes me stop as he says softly, "Maybe it matters to me what you think of me. Normally I don't care. I'm used to people thinking the worst, but well, I don't want you to agree with them."

He looks so genuine, I think back on my conversation with Miranda, where she told me to give him a chance and not to listen to gossip. Maybe this is the day I discover the real Brad Hudson and I'm hoping it's someone I like.

I think we drive for twenty minutes before a loud rendition of Jail House rocks comes from the back of the van and I stare at Brad in horror. "Is my mother back there?"

The distinct sound of my father's ring tone on her phone is haunting me, and he laughs.

"No, but she must have left her phone in one of the bags."

"Oh my god, I must get to it." I stare at him in horror. "If she doesn't pick up, he'll be tracking her inside of five seconds and we don't want to meet him anytime soon."

Now Brad looks worried, and I scramble into the back and start searching through the bags resting against some kind of kitchen area. I try to ignore the made-up bed that sits at the back of the van, trying not to think of Brad's back catalogue earning their page in it by way of that bed.

The phone stops ringing, luckily and by the time I locate it a thousand excuses have flooded my mind as to where she is right now and as I scramble back into my seat, I look at Brad with despair. "What are we going to do?"

"Turn it off." He shrugs and I shake my head vigorously. "We *never* turn our phones off. He would know something's up immediately."

Suddenly, it rings again, and I say with a groan, "It looks like it's your mum this time."

"What, calling yours?"

"Yes, she probably wants to know if she's delivered the goods yet."

"You make it sound like we're drug dealers or something." Brad snorts and I roll my eyes as I answer it. "Um, hi…"

"Dolly, it's mum, I've borrowed Camilla's phone."

"Mum, you left your phone in one of the parcels. This is a disaster."

"Not really, it was part of a well-executed plan, so listen to me."

"You planned this?"

Brad looks at me and grins and I wonder if I've been set up by three very conniving people, but for what?

"Listen, Dolly, if dad texts me, call Camilla's phone and I'll tell you what to reply. If he calls, just text him back that you're driving. You know how he hates that."

"But won't he know it's me?"

"No babe. I swapped phones with you at the Cosy Kettle and dropped yours off at the shop. I'm waiting it out at Camilla's, enjoying a nice gossip while she fills me with coffee and cake. Enjoy your afternoon and I'll meet you at Valley Gifts at five and dad will be none the wiser."

"But I feel bad. What if he asks me a question and I let slip I've been to Riverton? I'm not sure you've thought this one through, mum."

"Details, details. Now just go and enjoy yourselves safe in the knowledge that your father is locked away in the bishop's office in a meeting about church rules or something equally boring. Enjoy."

She cuts the call and Brad laughs. "So, angel, we have the afternoon free from worry for a change. No one to watch us and a few hours to enjoy ourselves."

Now I'm worried because it hasn't escaped my attention that we are travelling in a van with a great big bed behind us and Brad has a reputation for entertaining in it.

"Is Riverton far?"

I sound as if anxiety is my middle name as I struggle to

breathe and Brad nods. "Another twenty minutes and we'll be there. What music do you like? I'll see if I've got it on Spotify."

"Oh, anything you've got will be fine. I've been brought up with a very eclectic taste in music."

Brad cranks up the volume and we are soon listening to Christmas tracks on repeat as we speed through the frosty landscape in search of civilisation.

CHAPTER 20

I love Dream Valley, but I crave Riverton. Finally, a virtual metropolis and my eyes are wide as we crawl through the traffic towards the hospital. The pavements are crowded with people clutching their warm coats, wearing brightly coloured hats to keep off the chill of Winter. Cars screech past and dogs bark and I see the happiness on the faces of the children, in direct contrast to the pained looks of anxiety on their parents as they clutch bulging shopping bags, while caught up in the Christmas rush.

I've always loved these weeks before Christmas. Festive events to attend, Christmas fairs and wreath making classes. Shopping for the ingredients needed to make the Christmas treats and delicacies and stocking up on mulled wine and mince pies, among other things.

Decorating the tree and writing the cards, all make Christmas special and catching up with friends inside brightly lit restaurants and bars, makes me feel warm inside because at Christmas it appears that everyone is happy.

"You know, Dolly, not everyone is happy at Christmas."

I do a double take because did Brad just read my mind or something? That is some skill he's got there if he did.

"Why do you say that?" I'm curious and he looks so sad it surprises me.

"This hospital will entertain many sick children on Christmas day, not to mention the adults. Not everyone in there will have a family to spend time with and that includes the staff."

"Is that why you chose this as the charity this year? It's a nice thought."

"Partly. Anyway, it wasn't my decision. It's the local parish council who decide. We just go along with their decision and do our best to help."

He parks in a space in the car park, and I look behind me at all the bags we have to carry.

"Do you think we should call a porter?"

I raise my eyes at the sheer scale of this operation, and he shrugs.

"I'm sure we'll manage."

As we load up, I shiver a little in the icy air and long to get inside. I feel a lot of admiration for Camilla and all the people who have donated time, money and effort to bringing some Christmas cheer and I love that Brad is helping too.

We stagger under the weight of the bags into the reception, and I watch as Brad charms the lady on the desk, despite the fact she's old enough to be his mother. He just can't help himself and yet somehow, it's that cheeky chap part of him I love. It's almost impossible not to like him, which I suppose is why he found it so easy to earn his reputation.

She directs us to the children's ward, and I look around with interest. Despite where we are, they have tried to make it as jolly as possible. With tinsel and Christmas trees and the

CHRISTMAS IN DREAM VALLEY

odd string of fairy lights to make the sterile space more festive.

We finally reach the reception area and my heart sinks when a pretty nurse looks up and smiles in delight. "Brad, long time no see."

"Hi Denise." Brad looks pleased to see her and I wonder what page number she is in his back catalogue.

She looks at me with interest and smiles. "Hi, I'm Denise."

"Dolly, pleased to meet you."

I don't miss the interest in her eyes as she looks between us and the fact Brad smiles in my direction and says sweetly, "Isn't Dolly pretty, Denise, like a little Christmas fairy."

Denise laughs but probably because of the panicked look on my face. Why would he say that?

He is smiling at me and so is she and it feels a little uncomfortable, so I say quickly, "Where shall we put these?"

"Oh lovely, more donations. Come with me. I'll direct you to the room we've set aside for wrapping."

She takes a couple of the bags from my laden arms, for which I am eternally grateful and as we pass down the corridors, my heart twists in agony at some of the small bodies hooked up to machines, looking lost in their hospital beds. It appears this unit is home to the more serious cases, and I see parents with their heads bent as they hold hands over their child's still body and feel their heartache with every step I take.

We turn right and I see a group of children playing in what appears to be a playroom and their laughter should fill me with hope but all I feel is emotion when I see the tubes in their throats or their shaven heads. They are all so sick and it should be against nature's law because why them? They haven't even begun to live their lives yet and don't deserve this torture and uncertainty they must live with.

Brad is chatting with Denise, and I wonder how they

know one another. She doesn't seem hostile in any way and so maybe they went to school together or something. I shouldn't always jump to conclusions, but I can't help it. He's a man with a reputation, of course, and I have nothing else to go on.

We enter a small room that is already stacked high with boxes of children's toys and Brad whistles. "This is a job and a half. Do you have to wrap every one of them?"

"Yes." Denise sighs. "They have to be sorted in age group and then wrapped with the right wrapping paper that tells us if they're male or female and what age group. Then they go into big bins that are wheeled out on Christmas morning.

"Who does the wrapping?" I can't imagine the nurses having time for that, and Denise smiles. "Volunteers mainly, some staff who are before a shift, or just finished. We get it done somehow."

"I would love to help." I surprise myself by volunteering, and Brad nods. "Me too. Let me know when you're ready to wrap and we'll be right here. You've got my number, haven't you?"

She looks at me as I shuffle on my feet and then nods. "Yes, I've got your number, Brad, haven't we all."

She rolls her eyes and Brad just laughs, but I fail to see what's so funny about throwing your phone number around like confetti without any thought, like he apparently does.

Denise sighs and looks at her watch. "I'm sorry guys, the doctor's about to start his afternoon rounds. I'll be in touch and thank you so much for the donations. They will go to very good homes."

We follow her back along the corridor and I hate hearing crying coming from a small room that we pass. I can't help looking inside and see a man comforting a woman as they stare at a small boy who looks to be asleep. As we pass, Brad says in a strangely gruff voice, "Will he be ok?"

Denise shakes her head and turns away and instinctively I slip my hand into Brad's because I'm an emotional wreck and I don't even know anyone here.

Brad looks as upset as I am, and we follow Denise in silence towards the exit.

As we head outside, I feel like the luckiest person alive right now because I have my health and the only problem in my life is an overprotective father.

"It makes you think, doesn't it?"

Brad's voice sounds rough around the edges, and I squeeze his hand. "We are so lucky. I hope we're never in that position those poor parents are."

I hear the words I just spoke and say quickly, "I don't mean, um, us exactly, as parents, at least to the same child..."

"I know what you meant." Brad chuckles and squeezes my hand back. "I'd love children one day, at least four."

"You'll be lucky to find someone to agree to that."

I laugh as he shrugs. "I can be very persuasive."

"I heard." He just laughs out loud and as we hit the street outside, I look around at normal life going on outside these walls.

"What next?"

"I want to show you something and then I'll treat you to a coffee in the high street and soak up the Christmas atmosphere."

"Where is this place?"

"Not far."

Brad has gone all mysterious and I follow him with curiosity, noting his hand hasn't let go of mine for a second.

As we walk, I can't help but ask, "So, Denise. How do you know one another?"

"We went to college together."

"Did you..."

Brad stops and the look in his eyes tells me my answer

before he even speaks. "I'm sorry, Dolly, you must think I'm a monster."

"I'm not sure what to think, Brad. You are so sweet and kind and yet there's this promiscuous side to you that I can't understand. I know why, but when does it stop? When you run out of prospects?"

He sighs heavily. "I've stopped."

"Really?" Like any addict, I'm not sure if Brad even knows the meaning of the word 'stop' and he sounds so apologetic when he says, "Dolly, I'm not that bad."

"Really?"

That I don't believe, and he shakes his head with a worried frown. "I know it seems that way; there have been enough examples already, but it's not as bad as you think."

"Tell me then."

"Most of the time, I just enjoy their company. Take them for a drink, a meal, or go to the cinema. There may be some kissing involved, but…"

"Sometimes there's more."

Picturing my dad's, I told you so grin, makes me sigh inside.

"Anyway, like I said, not anymore, because do you remember when I said I got to twenty cigarettes and couldn't stand anymore?"

"Only twenty, really?"

Brad looks away and says quickly, "Anyway, I just don't want that life anymore. I've moved on and want something better."

"That's good to hear. So, what are your plans for this better life?"

He stops beside a door in the wall that has definitely seen better days. The paint is peeling and there are cobwebs wrapped around the pillars outside, and Brad looks a little worried.

"I want you to see this first, which will show you why I've decided on my future plan."

He looks quite vulnerable as he turns the handle, and I'm almost fearful to follow him inside.

CHAPTER 21

I'm not sure what this place is, but it smells kind of strange and I feel the trepidation build as I follow Brad down a dusty hallway. It's obviously not a warm and cosy tearoom or anything even remotely resembling a gift shop, and I wonder where we could be heading.

Brad seems to know exactly where we're going as he says over his shoulder, "Despite appearances, I feel more at home here than anywhere else."

Now I'm worried that this could be a furtive second home for Brad, and this is where he auditions for roles in joining his back catalogue.

I hear another rendition of Jail House Rock infiltrating the silence of the hallway and groan. "What now?"

Stopping, I glance at mum's phone and see a text from my father.

Babe, I'm dying a slow death here. Tell me you're waiting for me at home with the whipped cream on standby because I need something to keep my interest motivated.

Brad says, "What does it say?"

"I'd rather not tell you."

I feel a little worried about my parent's sanity right now.

Brad looks over my shoulder and laughs out loud. "Wow, I have a new level of respect for your father."

"It's probably innocent. He always did love my mother's apple pie and says it keeps him sane in a mad world."

"Sure, Dolly, it's the apple pie — obviously."

He grins. "The question is, though, what are you going to type back?"

"How about…"

I start typing and as I finish up, Brad smirks. "Maybe not the response he was hoping for, but I dare you."

As I press **send,** my message makes its way along the unexplained web traffic road and I stare at my reply with a sense of satisfaction.

I'll keep it hot for you.

Brad grins and whispers, "You, or should I say, your mum, what is she keeping hot?"

"The apple pie, of course."

I shrug as he smirks, "I doubt he'll read it that way."

Another text comes through, and Brad laughs out loud.

Wear that red number I like and be ready. Santa's heading home with a sack full of treats.

Brad grabs the phone before I can stop him and, holding it above my head, types something out and presses **send**.

"What have you done?" I stare at him with a mixture of horror and laughter and as he drops the phone into my hand, I stare at it, feeling the heat race through my body like a line of dynamite that's fuse has been lit.

I've never been a patient woman and may just rip off the packaging in a hurry to enjoy what's inside.

Brad, what will he think? What will my mum say when she finds out that we've been sexting on her behalf?

"You'd better warn her then and give her time to head home and start cooking – I mean, those apple pies don't cook themselves, you know."

Fixing him with a fierce look, I dial Camilla's number and mum answers.

"Are you ok, and having a nice time?"

"Listen, mum, dads sent you a text and I've replied on your behalf. I may have got my wires crossed, please tell me I haven't. I'll send them to you."

"Sure, can't wait."

I forward the texts to mum and almost immediately I get a laughing emoji back and those three little bars that tell me she's typing.

Soon the message comes through, and I groan.

Next time he texts, send this and remember I'm here for you, babe.

Hey Santa, remember Christmas comes only once a year, so make it a good one.

"I can't send that." I stare at Brad with horror and actually feel a little lightheaded.

"Why not?"

"Because they are my parents!"

I stare at him with a mixture of revulsion and disgust and he shrugs. "So what, if they were my parents, I'd love it. In fact, any affection my dad showed my mother was never seen in public. At least your parents love one another and still have fun. Lots of people don't make it that far and if anything, it makes me want that for my future."

"What whipped cream and a racy red number?"

"If you insist, Dolly, I'm game if you are."

He winks as I blush as red as Santa's suit and quickly push

CHRISTMAS IN DREAM VALLEY

away the disturbing image of my father hauling his sack of treats in my mother's general direction.

As I struggle to push away the mental image of my father hot footing it home as we speak, I follow Brad into a room that makes me blink in surprise.

It appears to be a huge kitchen, canteen even, with fold up trestle tables lined up like soldiers and plastic chairs placed at short distances against them.

At one end of the room is a large counter where the smell of food emanates like a siren to my hunger.

Dotted around are several men and women who look as if they've seen better days and yet as they look up, I hear many shouts of, "Hey, Brad." and "Look what the cat dragged in." and "Wow, who's your friend?"

Brad replies with a cheery laugh and a greeting to everyone in turn by their name and I look in surprise when a woman behind the counter shouts, "Just in the nick of time and you've brought reinforcements. I could love you forever, darlin'."

Brad turns and says as an aside, "That's Sadie, she runs this place."

"What is it?"

I kind of know already just by the sight of the diners, and Brad says with a sigh. "The homeless. People down on their luck who come here for food, a change of clothes and sometimes a bed for the night."

I look around in astonishment and catch the eye of a young man who looks fresh out of his teens. He nods and looks away and Brad whispers, "That's Joey. He's new here. His parents kicked him out when he got in trouble with the law, and he had nowhere else to go. I saw him begging for change outside the local coffee shop and told him about this place."

Brad shouts, "Hey Joey, any news?"

He looks up and shakes his head. "I've registered with the local council, but it could take months."

Sadie shouts, "Did you follow up my lead with that friend of mine?"

Joey nods. "He was out when I called, and I couldn't leave a number."

"It's fine, leave it with me, I'll send him a message."

Brad turns and says in a low voice, "Sadie has some connections with a farmer in Kent. He's always on the lookout for people to help out on his farm and it comes with a caravan and food. She's sent lots of people his way, but not everyone wants the job."

"Why not? I thought they'd be happy to have somewhere warm and dry to stay and it's a start at least."

"Not everyone wants to start again, Dolly. Some people see this life differently and love the freedom and lack of responsibility it gives them. They are happy to drift along, taking the odd meal here and there to help out, before moving onto the next town and the next shop doorway. Some get lucky and start again, but not everyone's prepared for what that involves."

He points to a man sitting hunched over what looks like a bowl of soup, and he whispers, "That's Lol. He's been on the streets for years, despite having had many opportunities to start over. He used to be married and even has children, but they left, and he hasn't seen them since. He hit the bottle and isn't interested in kicking the habit, despite the number of times we've tried to help him."

"We?"

Brad nods, looking proud. "I come here a lot and help out. Most days actually, and some nights. Sadie does a good job but can't do everything and so I do what I can. Get support from local businesses, lobby the council, raise the shelter's profile and try to make a difference."

I'm so shocked, touched and a little in awe of Brad at this moment because who knew he was an angel in a devil's clothing?

He places his finger on my lips and winks. "Just don't tell on me. I have a reputation to protect."

He turns and says over his shoulder, "Come on, we'll give Sadie a hand for an hour and then I'll treat you to a hot chocolate in the local coffee shop. We'll feel as if we've earned it then."

For some strange reason, the tears almost blind me as I think about the bad press Brad deals with every day back at Dream Valley. My own father's judgement of him makes me more upset than anything and if only he could see what I see, he would change his mind like a rocket heading off the pad at Kennedy Space Center.

Time passes quickly in the shelter and as Brad serves the food at the counter, I busy myself by loading the dishwasher and clearing the plates from the tables. Christmas tunes play out from hidden speakers, and the atmosphere is joyous rather than depressing. It's warm bright and pleasant in here and as Brad jokes with the men and women who line up for food, I think I fall a little harder for him because he has shown me a different side to the lovable rogue that I feel extremely privileged to witness first hand.

CHAPTER 22

The Toasty Tipple is Brad's favourite coffee shop in Riverton, and I know that because he told me at least ten times on the way over here.

We left the shelter after promising to come back soon and as we walked hand in hand along the bustling streets of Riverton; I felt a little differently about my cheeky companion. Contrary to popular belief, there is a different level to Brad Hudson that very few get to see, and I've decided this is the side of him I love the most.

As we push inside the coffee shop, the deeply satisfying aroma of coffee, chocolate, and laughter assaults my senses and the fact it's freezing like the North Pole outside makes this now my most favourite place in the world too.

Brad guides me to a seat by the window that has only just said goodbye to the previous occupants, and I settle down in the chair gratefully and flex my frozen toes inside my boots.

Brad joins the line of patient customers who patiently wait for a beverage prepared by the 'best Barista in the world' according to the lettering on the backs of the staff and I snuggle down with contentment, feeling just slightly guilty

CHRISTMAS IN DREAM VALLEY

that I should be working and not enjoying illicit time with the man my father disapproves so strongly about.

As I wait, I look out at the street and enjoy people watching, a particular hobby of mine. Couples walk hand in hand, some laughing, some looking bored. Mothers push prams or try to manage unruly children who have more excitement in them than they can contain, given how close it is to Christmas. Brightly coloured shopping bags with festive slogans hold items needed for a very happy Christmas and I feel so content for once in my life because for some reason this feels like home.

Brad head back balancing a tray and I smile.

"You are constantly saving my life. You're an angel."

He winks as he drops the tray on the slightly sticky table that hasn't even been cleaned from the last customers.

"I'm not going to disagree with you, babe, because I want you to think only good thoughts about me to counteract the ones I'm constantly thinking of you."

Laughing softly, he looks amused as I feel the blush staining my cheeks as he reaffirms his interest in me.

Sliding the steaming hot chocolate towards me that is topped by a mountain of whipped cream, he laughs at the slightly desolate look on my face. "It's not only your father who has a liking for the whipped stuff. Wrap your lips around that and tell me how good it is."

Shaking my head, I groan. "You're a bad man, Brad Hudson, and I doubt I'm the first one to call you that."

"No, but you're the first person I've brought here. The first person I've let inside my life and the first person I've ever wanted to impress."

"I doubt that." Shaking my head, I lick a little of the cream off the top of the drink and Brad's expression makes me giggle as he looks at me with a tortured frown.

"What?"

"You, Dolly. I don't think you realise how gorgeous you are. There's a certain innocence about you mixing with a wicked woman that I am aching to explore."

"That's what worries me."

Leaning back, I fix him with a despairing look. "How can we be more than friends when there's a huge wall between us?"

"We knock it down and go there, anyway."

"You make it sound so easy."

"One thing I've learned is that you only get one life and what you do with it counts. It's why I'm different from my brothers. They want to make something of themselves, make a difference with money at the heart of it. Marcus gets to build his property empire and takes satisfaction in leaving behind something for future generations. Dom wants to be better than my father and expand his empire and Jake wants to be the number one gaming genius in the world, striving for a certain level of fame. I don't."

"What do you want?" I lean forward because this is the first time he's ever shown any interest in anything other than travel and he looks almost animated as he says, "I want to make a difference to people's lives and not for monetary reasons either."

"Go on."

I smile my encouragement and he leans forward, an excitement burning in his eyes that's contagious.

"When my father died, he left me all his savings in his will. It adds up to rather a lot of money and I only get it when I marry and stay married for two years."

I'm beginning to feel a little uncomfortable, wondering if that's the reason for his sudden interest in one woman. To get his hands on the money.

He carries on. "I don't want to succeed on the back of my father. The money is nice to have and one day I'm sure I'll be grateful for it, but it's set me free to do something I have wanted to do for some time."

"What?" His enthusiasm is infectious and now I know he's not interested in proposing anytime soon, at least marriage that is, I relax a little.

"I want to travel. That part is true, but not for the reasons your father thinks, or anyone else for that matter."

"Then what?"

"You've seen where I hang out. Those people never seem to enjoy life anymore. They get treated like dirt from the people who have much more than them. Walk past them huddled on the ground, labelling them as addicts or alcoholics. Fearful they will steal their purse or wallet, or physically assault them, perhaps. Nobody sees them for what they are and to a degree, I don't blame them. Nobody wants to see suffering, I certainly don't and if you turn a blind eye, you can pretend to yourself that it's not all around you."

He sighs and looks at the line of customers still waiting to be served. "Does it really take much to buy a second hot drink, or a second cake and drop it in the lap of the man struggling to survive in the shop doorway. Does it physically hurt to throw them a smile and ask how they are? Offer up a warm coat that you're thinking of throwing in the recycling bin, or perhaps asking if there's anything they need. Not many people like to confront poverty and suffering because it makes them stop and think and they don't want the trouble."

Every word that Brad speaks fills him with more enthusiasm and I think I fall a little in love with the gorgeous man opposite as he bares his soul.

"So, my big idea is to devote my life to helping others. I don't need to work for money. Your dad was right that I'm content to live off my parents and not lift a finger to join the rat race. Instead, I want to set up a travel agency and any profits will be spent taking under-privileged people, sick children and those who never catch a break, to enjoy something the rest of us take for granted. Maybe a night in a hotel, a spa break or a trip overseas. By selling holidays to those who can afford them, I intend on using the profits to give something back to those who can't and so in some roundabout way all those people who prefer to look the other way, will actually be doing their bit without even realising it."

He slumps back in his seat and looks so happy about his vision that I could cry. Who knew my knight in shining armour was so noble? He keeps his charitable side close under wraps and I'm sure everyone would forgive him every transgression and cut him some slack when they learn what a big heart the local playboy really has.

"You have a noble vision, Brad, but why a holiday? Wouldn't it be better to offer them somewhere to live, help them get a job, somewhere to call home?"

"Perhaps, but not everyone wants that. Not everyone is homeless who I want to help. Some have homes and struggle to pay the bills. The luxuries in life are sacrificed just to eat and buy second-hand clothes. Those with children face emotional ruin as their children mix with richer ones who have all the latest clothes and toys. They want the same, but it's an impossible dream. They are the people I want to help. Pay for them to enjoy a mini break somewhere to give them a taste of something their friends enjoy most years. Perhaps take them shopping to buy clothes or toys as a special kind of treat. I'm not saying I can save the world, but if I can make a difference to anyone's life, it will be worth it. I've never had to work for anything. Your father was right about that too, but I will work 24/7 to help someone else have just a small part of something I was handed by honour of my birth."

I reach for his hands and, as he grabs mine with a twinkle in his eye, I smile. "Then I admire you for your dream and I want to help. Let me help at the shelter and be a sounding board for your ideas. I think it's an admirable goal in life and it's changed how I think about you."

"Does this mean..." he grins and I shake my head. "It means that I'll be your friend. The jury's still out on anything more."

"You're a hard woman to impress, Dolly Macmillan."

"Then keep trying."

Sitting with Brad in the Toasty Tipple, surrounded by the Christmas rush, is probably where I've felt happiest since I came to Dream Valley. Here, anything is possible. Everything is a new adventure and I think I've found a place I could happily make my home.

CHAPTER 23

The entire journey home, we talk and bounce ideas back and forth about how to make Brad's dreams come true. By the time we reach Valley Gifts, we have the bones of a plan and I have agreed to help Brad look for suitable premises to rent in Riverton to set up his travel agents. As we exit the camper van, Brad pulls me back and says with a serious tone to his voice, "Please, can we keep what I showed you today between us? I'm not ready to let my family or any of the locals know what I've been up to. It would seriously ruin my image."

He winks and I stifle a snort of laughter but nod. "Of course, your secret's safe with me."

"Pinky promise."

He curls his finger and I wrap my own around it and shake. "Pinky promise."

We head into Valley Gifts and Harriet smiles. "Mission accomplished?"

"I think it was." Smiling at Brad, who for some reason is now loitering among the shelves, Harriet raises her eyes. "Anything I can get you, Brad?"

CHRISTMAS IN DREAM VALLEY

"Thanks, Harriet, just browsing. I need to get some gifts for my family, and I could use all the help I can get. Did I hear you say you gift-wrap too?"

"Anything for you, Brad."

This time I roll my eyes and she giggles and nods towards the chiller. "Chocolate, Dolly."

"I'm good thanks."

The door opens and mum rushes inside like a snowstorm, dressed in a flurry of white and accompanied by a chilly wind.

"Thank God you're back, babe, and remember not a word about today. We won't lie but we won't offer the truth about where we've been. Hopefully, it gave you a bit of breathing space."

"Thanks mum, I had a great afternoon."

She grins when she sees Brad holding a scented candle and looking like a lost sheep among a herd of cows.

"Hey, Brad." He looks up. "Your mum would love that candle. She told me she was running out of them only a couple of hours ago."

"Do you think?" He looks a little relieved, and she nods. "Harriet will even wrap it for you. One tick on the gift list is one credit card transaction away."

His decision is made, and he hands the candle over with a smile of relief. "I may just bring my list in tomorrow and see what you can help me with. All this shopping is exhausting me."

He winks as he grabs his credit card and as his gaze lingers on me, it makes me feel extremely warm inside.

Mum looks between us with a triumphant smile and I'm so grateful to her. At least she's allowing me to make up my own mind, unlike my father, who made his up the moment he discovered Brad's reputation.

* * *

We head home and I reflect on a very enjoyable day and mum says with interest.

"So, what happened? Did Brad make his move, and did you let down your guard and if so, leave your father to me?"

"We're just friends, nothing more."

"So, I wasted all that careful planning. You disappoint me, Dolly. You should have seized the moment and dived right in. I know I would."

"And deal with the repercussions of that. No, poor Brad doesn't deserve the trauma dating me would bring. Maybe one day, who knows, but for now I'm just keen on settling in Dream Valley and seeing where the experience takes me."

"Then you need to broaden your experiences. Honestly, Dolly, you really don't take after me."

Mum sounds frustrated, which makes me smile. She longs for me to 'have a life' as she calls it, but I'm a little more protective of my heart than most, largely due to the fact I keep on getting it wrong.

Some of my past boyfriends haven't lasted longer than one meeting with my father, proving to me that I'm just not worth fighting for and it's scarred me a little. Surely, I'm worth a little tenacity. Someone who fights my corner and doesn't care what challenge they face. Maybe that's my father's plan, and he does it on purpose. To see who can stand up to him and rise above the threats and bullying. I know that's not how things are supposed to work, but dad will never change, and it will take a very special person to break down his reinforced walls.

As we turn into the drive of the vicarage, I see my father has barely made it home before us and I'm surprised when the passenger door to the Toyota opens and mum says, "Who's that?"

"I don't know."

As we peer through the windscreen, I almost think I'm hallucinating and blink twice, because surely not… it can't be.

Mum obviously sees him too because she says incredulously, "Is that…?"

We both look as the two men turn and watch our arrival, and my heart starts thumping with disbelieving horror.

"Lucas."

Mum says it at the same time and as we stop, dad wrenches open the door and peers inside, looking very pleased with himself.

"Look who I found."

He looks at me with a gleam in his eye and I stare at the newcomer with a mixture of anger and happiness.

Two emotions that combat each other every time I'm in this man's company because Lucas Harrington is the exception to the rule, my ex-boyfriend and the only man my father can tolerate for longer than an hour.

"But why… how?"

Dad grins. "I heard from Todd the other day and he told me Lucas was nearby and at a loose end and asked if we could put him up. You know how I feel about helping out a mate and so here we are."

"But you never said." Mum looks as shocked as I am, and he shrugs.

"I thought it would be a nice surprise."

More like his trump card to dispose of Brad, and I know the probable reason for this act of kindness, and it definitely wasn't to help out a mate. More like to help himself.

My heart thumps as I exit the car and I see Lucas Harrington in all his muscled glory, standing before me looking as fit as ever. A friend of Beau's both in childhood and in their chosen profession, Lucas has been part of my life ever since our fathers served together in the special forces. Like Beau, Lucas took up the challenge and they serve together and are as close to brothers as you can get.

I always had a huge crush on Lucas. Probably due to the fact he is seriously gorgeous and totally unattainable. At least I thought he was until the Christmas they joined us at Crab Creek Nature Reserve, and we altered our relationship.

The fallout was huge and lasted for months. Beau and my father were completely against it, but Lucas won them over and after lots of fist fights and barbed comments, my family accepted the situation and watched like predators from the side-lines.

Then Lucas was posted on a secret mission and broke up with me for my own good. At least that's what he told me, but I knew it was probably because he was bored and ready to move on, anyway.

Now he's back and I don't know what to make of that and as he steps forward, his megawatt smile touches me deep inside like it always has done.

"Hi, Dolly, you're looking good."

"Lucas." I smile my welcome and outwardly appear cool and polite, but I'm a mess inside. How do I feel about Lucas walking into my life and worst of all, as a house guest?

Gingerly, I test my heart that was so cruelly battered when he left and find it's not so bad. Maybe time has healed the wound because that yearning I always had for him is the barest flicker of curiosity and I'm happy about that because I need this man in my life like a bad dose of the flu.

Mum interrupts the reunion with a loud, "Look at you, Lucas, honey. I swear you've got even more muscles than the last time I saw you. Don't you guys believe in coats and jumpers? It's bloody freezing out here."

She runs up and give him a hug and fusses over him like any mother would and I hate that I drool over the sight of those huge bear wrestling biceps that are now covered in tattoos as he wraps those arms around my mother and says sweetly, "You're looking good, Tina."

"Hands off." My father grins and pulls my mother away and says in a voice filled with satisfaction. "Come in, son, we'll get you settled in."

Son. That just about sums up my father's feelings for Lucas. He accepts him, likes him and approves of him. Three things that definitely don't relate to his feelings about Brad. Now Lucas is here, dad will be trying to throw us together just to spite Brad, knowing that Lucas is probably about to be posted elsewhere imminently but not until he has earned his stay and scared off the local Romeo.

Part of me wonders if dad's telling the whole truth. A little coincidental maybe, probably just another plan to disrupt my love life and if it is, and he's playing games with my heart, he's about to discover that sometimes life doesn't go according to plan and he's too late, anyway.

CHAPTER 24

After listening to Lucas's story and catching up with news regarding Beau, mum says, "Why don't you take Squirrel for a walk, Dolly? Show Lucas the area and leave me and your dad to prepare supper."

Hoping to God it's apple pie and cream, I say with a sinking feeling, "Ok, that sounds good."

Great, now I'm to entertain the man who broke my heart and pretend that nothing's wrong and I'm not sure if I can do this.

Making sure to wrap up warm, I throw a cursory look in Lucas's direction as he shrugs on a padded jacket and slips his feet into his military boots. I hate that he looks so good, better than ever and even the slight suntan he has makes me wonder what horrific place he's spent time in lately. In fact, just thinking of what he does to earn a living makes my soul weep for him and Beau because it can't be easy and so I should at least be friendly.

We head outside and Lucas falls into step beside me and as soon as we're out of sight, he says in a husky voice, "I'm sorry, Dolly."

"For what?" To be honest, the list is lengthening by the second because just by being here, old wounds are resurfacing and causing me pain.

"For breaking up with you."

"I'm a big girl, I handled it."

My voice is cool to match the outside temperature because I did handle it to a degree. I cried, raged and vowed the blackest revenge, but my heart was shattered when he walked away.

"If it's any consolation, I regretted it the minute I left you."

"Two years ago." Thinking about the fact that this is the time of year Lucas was preparing to break me, doesn't make this any easier, and I sigh. "Listen, we've both moved on and, to be honest, I don't think about it anymore. I'm trying to forgive and forget and get on with my life, so don't worry about it, things like this happen all the time."

"Is there someone else?"

"No." It annoys me that he thinks that's the only reason I'm not jumping into his arms and forgiving him instantly. Does he really think I'm that shallow?

"Are you sure it's just your dad…"

The ball of anger inside me is growing by the second as I imagine my father telling Lucas abut Brad and probably enlisting his help to rid me of my next biggest mistake. He probably engineered this whole visit as yet another trick up his sleeve to keep Brad away from me and I'm weary of it all. Weary of my father interfering in my life. Weary of my brother backing him up and weary of always trying to do the right thing.

"My dad has it wrong."

I sigh. "Listen Lucas, we've only just arrived in Dream Valley and I'm finding my feet. Yes, I've spent time with a local lad because he's been so kind and seems keen. Yes, I like him, but for now we're just friends, despite what my father thinks."

"That's good to hear."

"Why is that good to hear?" I feel so frustrated because where was Lucas when I was breaking apart the months after he left me? He never called, never wrote, and never cared. It was obvious because if he did, he would never have left and now just expects to head back into my life and say he's sorry and all will be forgiven. Well, it doesn't work like that and once again, I need to be strong around the hot guy because the next time I fall in love, it will be after having done a thorough risk assessment for my heart.

Squirrel chases a bird, and it makes me smile. She always has that ability, and Lucas chuckles beside me.

"I missed the little one too."

"She's fun to be around."

In fact, I think I love my dog more than anything else because she is always happy to see me and never lets me down.

We head around the field and out through the rusty gate towards the woods and despite the fact it's freezing out here, it's good to breathe in the sharp air. The landscape is barren and frozen in a state of shock as the animals curl up underground in their burrows or high in the trees in their nests, trying to wait out winter and long for the first signs of spring.

Having Lucas beside me is a strange plot twist I never saw coming and I'm interested to know his plans.

"So, how long are you staying?" Christmas isn't far away, and I wonder if he's here for that.

"I'm not sure. I think I've got leave until after Christmas and then who knows where I'll end up."

"And Beau, is he ok?" I am always so fearful for my brother. It's like a constant worry gnawing at me inside. I don't know how mum copes with the worry of it all and I feel the relief settle my heart when Lucas chuckles. "Still the same annoying brat, but he's good. I think he has leave in the New Year. He was way down the list to request Christmas, so I think he's spending it on a secret mission in the desert."

"Is it dangerous?" I hate what he does, what they both do, and Lucas sighs. "Most of them are. There's always a risk, but we're trained soldiers, Dolly. We work as a team and Beau is good at what he does."

Good at what he does. Killing men and removing targets. Rescuing hostages and disabling threats to our country and allies. Once again, I hate their life and thinking of the one Brad wants to create sits a lot better with me.

I wonder what Brad will think when he finds out Lucas has come to stay. Probably not a lot. I know I wouldn't, but will it just be another reason why he should give up the chase and admit defeat? As soon as one obstacle clears, another one rears up and I expect he will hold up his hands and surrender because there's only so much any one man can take, surely.

Lucas is quiet and so am I because this feels extremely awkward and after a while, he sighs heavily and stops me by pulling on my arm and swinging me around to face him. "Dolly, we really need to talk and stop stepping around the real reason I came."

"Which is?"

"You, of course."

My heart starts thumping wildly as I look at my own reflection in his aviator sunglasses, looking small and afraid under the enemy's gaze.

"I've done a lot of thinking over the past two years. I broke up with you because you don't deserve this life. Waiting for the phone call that tells you I never made it. Always wondering if I'm ok and keeping one eye on the horizon. I never wanted that for you; you deserve more from life.

It wasn't fair to chain you to this job and so I made the hardest decision of my life, to set you free. To find someone else and build a life for yourself. Not become a military wife with no roots. Following me from base to base in the hope of a few snatched days here and there. That wasn't the life I wanted for you; I love you too much for that."

"You said, wanted."

My voice shakes slightly as he opens his heart to me, leaving it open in the frosty air of mid-winter and I must respect him for that at least.

"I've changed my mind."

He gently strokes my face and just feeling him touch me again, brings back so many memories and I close my eyes against the tears that were never far away where it concerns him.

"So, what are you saying? You want me back, to try again and bring me into that life with you?" I try to get a grip on my emotions and ask the million-dollar question.

"Yes."

"Lucas I…"

I look away because I can't deal with this right now—if ever. When Lucas broke up with me, the broke part featured heavily in my life for many months after that. I returned to university and threw myself into my studies, sworn off men for life. Living with two soldiers was bad enough but dating one and dealing with the subsequent emotional battering that brought made me swear off them for life. I haven't met anyone since, until Brad, and that's why this is so hard to cope with. If Lucas had come and told me this a year ago, I would have fallen into his arms with a delighted sigh of relief, but things have changed. *I* have changed, and it doesn't help that he was always so good looking and ticked every box in my head when I designed my dream man.

"I can't deal with this." I look up into his mirrored shades, wishing I could see his eyes. He has always been good at keeping his feelings shrouded in mystery, whereas I have always been an open book.

He nods, but keeps me anchored on the spot, seemingly in no hurry to let me go, and says gruffly, "I've surprised you, and I'm sorry about that. Staged an emotional ambush and you need time to think. Let's just take things slowly and see what happens. Enjoy the next few days and you can show me this sweet little place you have found yourself in. Who knows, miracles may happen, and we will rekindle something that should have always been kept burning. Protected at all costs, and I'm the fool who doused the flames. I've done a lot of thinking and I can't change the fact that all roads in my life lead back to you Dolly Macmillan and I deserve to wait for as long as it takes you to forgive me."

Turning away, I shiver against the cold and say in a small voice. "We should keep moving, it's cold."

I know I'm acting as cool as the temperature outside, but who can blame me? This is all too much. Discovering Brad's secret and then finding Lucas on my doorstep is messing with my mind. Maybe I just need to step back and distance myself from both of them and let fate decide for me because one thing's certain, when it comes to my heart, I can't be trusted not to make a complete mess of things.

CHAPTER 25

We head home after a slightly frosty walk in more ways than one, and as soon as we reach the warmth of the fire, I feel my inner calm resurfacing.

Shrugging off my coat and many layers, I sit in the chair with Lucas opposite me and wonder when my life got so complicated.

Seeing him here, all muscle and testosterone, messes with my mind. He was always so gorgeous in every way and if this is a test of my resolve, it's an extremely good one.

My parents fuss around us and I glare at my father as he hands Lucas a beer and quips, "It's good to see you, son."

Son. For goodness's sake, can he make this any more obvious?

I listen to them catch up. Tales of Beau and the mad things he's been doing. Mum is like a dog with a bone and interrogates him as if he's fallen behind enemy lines. I feel sorry for her because she worries about Beau so much and I note the anxiety in her eyes as she questions his best friend.

Then there's the man himself. So cool, handsome and every woman's dream. A fighter, a soldier and not just

CHRISTMAS IN DREAM VALLEY

anyone either. A crack shot sniper and a man who could take on a small army and win single-handedly. Yes, Lucas Harrison is Kryptonite and I need to handle him with care because I must decide if I can deal with such explosive material in my everyday life.

I don't miss his furtive looks my way. The desire in his eyes for something we once had. A sense of normality in a crazy world. Someone to write to, dream about and come home to whenever he gets the chance. Can I be that person? I thought so once.

It all seems so natural, normal even, as Lucas slips back into his position in my family as if the last two years never happened. Mum adores him and was just as broken as I was when he called time on our relationship and despite the fact dad gave him an extremely hard time, along with Beau when we first got together, he soon grew to love him, probably more than me as it turned out.

Just seeing their happy faces as they enjoy spending time with him makes me doubt my own mind. Brad or Lucas. I have a decision to make. The new or the old. The safer bet against a tentative attraction. One who has learned his lesson and decided it's me he wants and the other wants me because he never has. The challenge, the one just held out of reach and the trouble is, my heart could easily go either way.

I make my excuses and head to my room and decide on an early night. The walls in this place are paper thin and my heart sank when I heard my mum say with encouragement, "Just give her time."

Even mum is on Lucas's side, and I really thought she was team Brad. Well, I'm team Dolly and I'm not going to be swayed either way and I may just decide to turn my back on both of them.

* * *

Waking up the next morning is a little surreal. It's pouring down with rain, which matches my mood perfectly. I'm almost fearful to go to breakfast because Lucas will be there. A constant reminder of every reason I should take him back.

However, as I venture tentatively inside the kitchen, it's only mum frying bacon and looking a little tired.

"Dolly, babe, there you are. The boys are out for their run so it's just us girls, which is good because I wanted to have a word in private."

She pours me a cup of tea from the teapot and one for herself and takes the bacon off the stove for a brief moment.

"Listen, we don't have long, but I just wanted to see how you are. That can't have been easy last night and well, I'm worried about you."

I feel my heart sag with relief as I see the concern in her eyes because for the first time since Lucas arrived, I feel as if I have a person who is on my side.

"I'm confused, mum." I say with a sigh and lean back in my chair. "It was a shock seeing him here and hot on the heels of a very nice day with Brad. What do you think I should do?"

I ask because I could really use a helping hand right now and she sighs, looking troubled.

"If you ask me, which you have, so I'll offer my opinion. I don't think you should make any decisions either way. They're both great lads in their own ways. Brad is the unknown. The loose cannon with not a great track record. But there's something deeper about him that's telling me to give him a chance."

I'm surprised because I didn't see that one coming. Brad certainly doesn't give off the deep vibes and mum must have listened to the gossip along with my dad.

"Then there's Lucas. The soldier we know and love and lives a life we're familiar with. The fact he's taken two years to realise something that should have hit him the moment he left, makes me wonder about the timing."

"Dad?"

She nods. "I did wonder, but he denies it, so we must give him the benefit of the doubt. Just don't do anything hasty and live with it for a while. Lucas doesn't have long and certainly doesn't have the right to a decision the minute he steps back into your life. Make him sweat or send him away. The decision is yours, but at least you have options. I suppose, that's good, isn't it?"

She grins and I can't help but giggle at the look in her eye and as she joins me, the door opens and two panting men burst into the room, raising the levels of masculinity to toxic levels. Mum catches my eye and for once I know just what she's thinking because, good God, these men would test a nun's resolve.

Flexing muscles and thin shirts clinging to bulging biceps is a very welcome start to the day and as my eyes connect with Lucas's, I see the passion in his as he looks at me with an obvious desire. It's almost too much and I feel my heart fluttering like a butterfly caught in a net because how can I choose? It's just not fair.

Mum shrieks as dad pulls her against him and bats him away with her hand, the tea towel flapping from the other one.

"Not until you shower. Hurry up though, the breakfast's nearly ready."

Lucas winks as he heads off to shower and change and any normal girl would be putty in his hands.

As mum catches my eye, she raises hers and despite it all, we grin like two cats who have had a full home delivery of cream.

CHAPTER 26

Luckily, I have a job to distract me from Hobson's choice at home and mum drops me into Dream Valley for a very welcome shift at Valley Gifts. Lucas is heading to Riverton to catch up with a friend who lives not that far away, and my dad has a full day ahead, meeting parishioners and arranging the Christmas service.

Harriet looks up when I push through the door and smiles.

"Morning Dolly, it's a shame it's raining, we'll probably be quieter today."

"I'm sorry."

She shakes her head. "Don't be, I have boxes of gift-wrapping to do, and you can help if you like."

"I would love to."

To be honest, I love nothing more than wrapping exciting parcels in beautifully decorated paper and tying satin ribbons, before decorating the top with little sprigs of fake foliage and glittering decorations. It's a real love of mine and as I set to work, I congratulate myself on finding this job at all.

Christmas carols play out from the speakers and soon Harriet and I are deep in conversation and sheets of wrapping paper. I discover she has never married out of choice and just prefers to enjoy the odd date with a like-minded individual. She lives above the shop and has a cat named Merrill. Her last holiday involved walking in Wales with a group of fellow enthusiasts where she met Derek, her holiday companion.

"He lives in Merthyr Tydfil, and we always enjoy our weeks away."

She has a dreamy look on her face as she tells me every detail about Derek, who sounds really sweet. "We're taking things slowly though, because it's important not to rush into these things and just enjoy a few weekends away and the odd week in the Lake District."

"How long have you been, um, seeing Derek?" I'm interested to know what a long-distance romance is like, and she smiles. "Five years."

"That's a long time."

"Not really when you've only met up a handful of times, but that may change in the new year."

"Why?"

I am fascinated to hear her story, and she sighs as she twists a red satin bow and slips a sprig of fake berries underneath it. "He's asked me to move in with him and I am seriously tempted."

"You are?" I hang onto her every word because this could be life changing for Harriet.

"What will you do?"

"I've been thinking about that a lot, and I've come to the conclusion that the only thing keeping me in Dream Valley is Valley Gifts. I could sell up, or rent, I'm not sure what, and take Merrill with me and move in with Derek. He has such a sweet bungalow in the valley and as he's retired, we could spend our days walking and exploring together. I've also concluded that life's too short, and I should just throw caution over the cliff at Rocky Cove and head that way to a new life. Does that sound impulsive to you, Dolly?"

I suppress a giggle and say solemnly, "I don't think so. You've given it five years already and this is surely the next step."

Harriet nods, her eyes shining with an excitement I wish I could bottle and take sips of before starting the day because my life is complicated more than I can deal with right now, so it's great to absorb myself in someone else's, distracting me from mine.

The door opens and a blast of icy wind blusters inside and I hear a familiar voice. "Darlings, what a rotten day."

Looking up, I see Camilla Hudson dressed like a fisherman. Covered head to toe in a bright yellow rain mac, with a matching hat on her head and wellington boots. I try to keep a straight face as she gasps, "I knew I should have stayed at home but I'm meeting a friend.'"

She rolls her eyes. "We're meeting at the Cosy Kettle for lunch and as I'm early, I thought I'd tick a few more gifts off my list beforehand."

"A friend." Harriet grins and Camilla nods, looking very pleased with herself. "Yes, I side swiped a rather fetching man who looks a little like George Clooney in his profile picture. Well, I could use a bit of George in my life, so I arranged to meet and greet. Do you think I look ok?"

Harriet catches my eye, and I don't know what to say as Camilla stares down at her attire and laughs. "Silly me, how can you tell? Wait there."

She starts to strip off layers of oilskin and I blink as she steps out of it in a blue dress that sits just above her knees, with a beautiful necklace shining in her ample cleavage. Her hair has been freshly coloured, making her look ten years younger and Florrie must have done her make up because she looks as if she's just stepped out of a magazine. As she pulls off her wellington boots, she stands in stockinged feet and reaches inside the huge bag she is carrying and pulls out a pair of fashionable stilettos and looks absolutely incredible.

"Wow, Camilla." That's all I can say as Harriet nods her approval. "I think you look beautiful. He's a lucky man. Um, how old is he?"

I'm surprised at the question, probably because of the way she said it, almost as if she was afraid to ask, and Camilla smirks. "My age unfortunately, Harriet, but he looks good enough."

Camilla turns to me and grins. "I have a reputation for dating men way below me in years. What can I say, cougar alert and proud of it?"

It makes me laugh. "Well, what's a number, anyway. If you can catch them, why not?"

"Exactly, darling." She throws me a keen look. "So, how did your day with Brad go yesterday? He actually stayed in last night, which was nice for a change. Usually, he's off on the open road with that camper van and only God knows who else."

Thinking about Brad heading off to the shelter makes me want to defend him, but he asked me to keep his secret and I'm not about to go against his wishes. So, I just smile politely. "We had fun."

"You'll always have fun with Brad." Harriet nods at Camilla's comment and I'm guessing I would. He's fun-loving, easy going with a heart of gold. He also has principles and a social conscience, which I love. In fact, the more time I spend with Brad, the more I like him, which is why it's so unfortunate that Lucas has come calling.

Camilla peruses the shelves and decides on a lovely scarf for Florrie and some bath oil for Sammy Jo. Then she chooses a smart leather handbag and some sunglasses for her housekeeper, Mrs Jenkins.

"Please, can I leave you to wrap them, and I'll collect them after my date?"

She smiles as she settles up with Harriet, who nods. "Of course, we'll start them straight away."

Camilla takes a deep breath and says with a sigh, "Wish me luck, ladies. Here's hoping he's handsome, cool and loaded. Good humoured and not averse to a wicked night away, preferably next Thursday."

She winks as she totters out on her heels and Harriet shakes her head as the door closes behind her.

"I love Camilla Hudson and when I grow up, I want to be just like her."

She grins because Harriet is probably the same age as Camilla, but nowhere near as youthful in her outlook of life.

"You know, Dolly…"

She points to the chiller. "Maybe we should grab a chocolate reward and then I'll take a trip next door to fetch our coffees. I may just time it so I can take a look at this George Clooney lookalike for myself."

"I wish I'd thought of that."

I laugh as she hands me a tray of chocolates and I select my favourite and pop it in my mouth, loving the delicious taste explosion it creates on my tongue.

"So, I won't be long, and I'll make sure to report back every detail."

She heads off, leaving me knee deep in wrapping paper, with a very happy smile on my face.

CHAPTER 27

Lunchtime comes and I have a visitor and my heart flutters when I see Brad heading through the door armed with a soul shattering smile.

"Hey pretty lady, can I tempt you to lunch, my treat?"

Harriet smiles and nods her approval. "You go, Dolly, you haven't stopped since you arrived. Take your time."

"Are you sure?" I feel bad because Harriet has also worked hard and only took thirty minutes in her flat for her usual pasta salad and pitta bread.

"It's fine, it's not busy, due to this damn rain that just won't go away."

She peers through the steamed-up window with a doleful expression, and I nod. "Ok, but we're only next door, so come and get me if it gets busy."

Brad interrupts, "Actually, we'll be in The Olive Tree."

I look at him in surprise, and he grins. "The Italian restaurant, a few doors along. I've taken the liberty and booked us a table. Their pasta is amazing."

Harriet nods. "It sure is. I eat there most nights now because I hate cooking for one."

Thinking that explains the copious amounts of pasta salad she consumes, makes me curious to discover the delights of The Olive Tree for myself.

Walking to the restaurant with Brad reminds me of who I'm hanging around with because it's as if a local celebrity is in town. It's only a few doors away and yet he is continually stopped and makes polite conversation, all the time holding my hand so sweetly. I don't miss the curious looks thrown my way because even I know this is an unusual sight. Brad Hudson doesn't do dating. He does a lot of the rest that goes with it but never takes a girl out more than once and I see a few curious looks at our tightly clasped hands and can't help but feel very smug about that.

Eyes follow me wherever I go, and I see whispered comments behind girl's hands as they try to disguise the envy in their eyes and it's like a powerful drug being on the arm of someone most would kill for, and I try not to let this madness distort my view on this.

As we finally step inside the warm and welcoming door of the sweet Italian restaurant, we are greeted by an attractive woman with long dark hair and flashing green eyes.

"Good afternoon, Maria, you are looking particularly lovely today." Brad grins and shaking her head, Maria laughs softly. "Honestly, Brad, you really should take a day off with the charm."

She looks at me with interest and smiles her welcome. "You must be Dolly. I've heard a lot about you, mainly because you have bewitched our local Romeo, which is big news around here."

Brad laughs as I roll my eyes. "We're just friends, that's all."

"Who hold hands?" Brad raises our clasped hands and smirks, and Maria laughs. "Keep telling yourself that. The rest of us don't believe a word. Anyway, I've reserved you a sweet table by the window so you can flaunt your 'friendship' to the desolated women of Dream Valley some more."

She grabs some menus with a grin, and we follow her to the table by the window and Brad holds out my chair like a gentleman, before taking his seat opposite me.

"Can I get you a drink while you decide?" Maria enquires, and I nod. "Just some still water please, I'm trying to be good."

"Same." Brad grins and Maria laughs. "You have got it bad then, Brad, because *good* isn't a word I'd associate with you, or any of your brothers to be honest."

She heads off and Brad pretends to look hurt. "And I thought everyone loved me."

"As the lady said, keep telling yourself that."

Grabbing the menu, I try to decide between spaghetti or pizza, which is just a couple of things I like on a menu that may have been stolen from my wish list of food and I sigh with delight. "I love Italian food; this is a good choice."

Brad nods. "Me too. My family eats here a lot. Not only does Maria run the best restaurant for miles, she also runs the *only* restaurant for miles."

He laughs and I find myself settling down into his easy-going company.

Brad looks at me with concern. "You seem a little distant today, is everything ok?"

I'm surprised at that because I thought I was doing a good job of keeping my emotions balanced but obviously not, and I sigh. "It's not good I'm afraid."

"What isn't?" He looks anxious.

"We have a visitor and I'm not sure I'm happy about it."

"Who?"

He looks so worried, I hate telling him and so just throw it out there, "My ex-boyfriend."

The look on his face is one that affects me deeper than I

imagined. He looks as if I've stabbed him in the heart because his face falls and he appears lost for words. The disappointment mixed with regret is obvious to see and I hate that I've put those feelings there.

"I'm sorry, Brad. My father invited him as a favour to his friend. They worked together and are more like brothers and when he asked if we could put Lucas up, he was never going to say no."

"But you went out with him, how long ago?"

"Two years."

I take a deep breath. "He broke up with me and I haven't seen him since."

"How do you feel about him now?"

"I don't know." I hate my indecision because I can see Brad quickly building a wall to hide behind and I feel bad for that, wishing I could tell him not to worry.

Instead, I reach across the table for his hand and smile a reassurance I'm not sure I can give him.

"It changes nothing. I still want to be your, well, friend and it won't change a thing between us."

He grasps my hand and rubs his thumb over mine and stares deep into my eyes.

"But I want to be more than just your friend. I thought you knew that."

Maria interrupts the million-dollar question with a cheery, "Are you ready to order?"

"Of course." Pulling back, I seize the menu and rattle off my order and wait for Brad to do the same and as soon as Maria walks away, he says quickly, "I don't want to pressure you into anything, Dolly. I would hate that myself. Just know I'm here for you. I want to see where this could go, and I've never wanted to do that before. Please don't be put off by my reputation. I'm not proud of it and I haven't helped the rumours I know, but I'm really not as bad as everyone makes out."

"I know."

I smile and feel bad that I've caused a little of the light to die in his eyes and he was being so sweet in bringing me here. The trouble is, Dream Valley is a very small place and I know it would reach his ears in no time at all and I wanted him to hear it from me first. Despite how bad I feel about it, I can't give him any reassurances of my own feelings. I can't even reassure myself, so what chance do I have of choosing between them? It's an impossible situation to be in and despite the fact some people would think I've had my Christmas gifts delivered early, I don't share that joy. I want a simple life, a man who loves me and no drama. Now I just need to work out what I'm going to do about it.

CHAPTER 28

Despite my bombshell, lunch was amazing. The food in The Olive Tree was seriously scrumptious and I could happily eat there every day. Now I can see why Harriet has a pasta fixation. I probably would too if I lived so close to this gastronomic delight, and I feel a little full and could really use a good walk to help burn some of it off.

Brad appears subdued and as we part company, says with a little desperation in his voice. "Are you free tonight?"

Thinking of Lucas and how bad it would look if I left him with my parents, I feel my frustration growing by the second.

"I'm sorry, Brad I'm not."

"Lucas."

"Partly but also because dad's planning the Christmas service, which usually involves rehearsing our part in that."

"What do you have to do?"

I groan and think I must have post-traumatic stress because years of embarrassing myself in his various services are coming back to haunt me.

"Oh, he just does a little play, you know, like the nativity but usually centred around his sermons 'to give them life' and create a more visual form of enjoyment, usually designed to embarrass me in the process."

"Can anyone join in?"

"Don't even think about it." I roll my eyes. "You would never recover."

He grins. "No, I'm serious. You see, I need to step up my game and prove to your father that I'm a worthy successor to Lucas, the visitor from my personal hell. I will fight for you, Dolly, and use my charm where he will no doubt use brawn."

He looks so upset my heart softens and I smile with a reassurance I'm not sure is required in this instance. "After dinner, usually around 7 o'clock. We'll be in the church. I'll tell him to save you a part."

"Thanks, Dolly."

"You're a strange man, Brad." I shake my head and grin. "I'm not sure if that's a really sweet thing to do, or you're missing some common sense. You may regret this very rash decision."

"If I'm spending time with you, whatever he makes me do will be worth it."

He steps a little closer and as he fixes me with his sparkling blue eyes, my heart skips a beat because let's not forget, Brad has a very powerful weapon of his own in the looks department and as he directs that piercing gaze onto me, it's difficult to think of anything else.

He leans closer and whispers, "I've never taken things slowly before and I want to kiss you so badly, but I want to be the good guy for once and do things the right way."

He shifts even closer, as I hold my breath and good guys can take a hike because surely every girl likes a bad boy and right here, in this moment, I want him to kiss me so badly, protocol and good intentions can take a break.

"But I want to be better this time. Do things properly unless…"

He looks into my eyes and grins, a little of devil returning, "You want otherwise."

It would be so easy to lean a little closer and see what all the fuss is about, and I almost think I will, until I hear a giggle and looking over Brad's shoulder, I see a couple of young girls watching us with interest. I pull away regretfully because I will not fuel the gossip in Dream Valley, especially where it concerns him.

"Hold that thought, I'll take you up on it in a less, um, public place."

I look behind him and he grins, seemingly not caring if the whole of Dream Valley is watching and just whispers, "I'll hold you to that."

Stepping away from Brad is like wrenching a limb off and that surprises me because when did he become so necessary to my existence? As he watches me head into the brightly lit shop, I replay the scene on repeat with a very different outcome. The one where he pulls me into his arms and declares his undying love for me and plants true love's kiss on my willing lips, before whisking me away to happily ever after.

Yes, that's what I want. Somebody to come in and sweep me off my feet because I don't want to choose between the devil and the deep blue sea, anyway.

* * *

Harriet smiles. "Good lunch?" I know she's interested in my relationship with Brad, along with most of Dream Valley probably, but I'm also a spectator in this waiting for things to unfold and I smile. "Great, thanks. I really loved The Olive Tree."

"Yes, Maria is so good at what she does. The place is always busy, which is no mean feat in a town this size. People come from miles around just to sample her delicacies and I will miss it terribly if I relocate to Wales."

"You said *if*, are you undecided?"

"Not really, but I know fate sometimes has its own agenda and something could happen to throw my plans off course."

She looks worried, so I smile reassuringly, "You'll be fine. Life has a habit of working out, I really believe in that."

Wishing my own life would work out right for once, I distract my own turbulent thoughts and say with interest, "Did Camilla come back and tell you about her date?"

"No, they're still there."

"It must be going well then."

Harriet nods. "When I went to grab the coffees, he had his back to me so I couldn't get a good look."

She wanders over to the window and strains to look outside. "I can't even see them from here."

"Well, it is next door, so that doesn't surprise me."

Laughing to myself, I wonder if Harriet has gone slightly mad, and she grins. "I'll let you in on a little secret. You see that shop across the street."

"What, the hairdressers?"

"Yes. Well, at the right angle, I can catch sight of the people inside the Cosy Kettle through the mirror they have in the window."

"Why have they got a mirror in the window?"

Rushing over, I look across the street and laugh softly when I see a huge mirror, centre stage, in the middle of the shop window, reflecting our enquiring faces back at us and half of the Cosy Kettle.

Harriet says with a hint of laughter in her voice. "I asked Jemima that once. She's the owner and a brilliant hairdresser. She said if people were looking in her shop window, they were probably thinking of a new hairstyle, or at least a tidy up. If they saw their own reflection staring back at them, they would hate it and head straight inside and book an appointment. A sort of reverse shop window psychology because nobody is happy with their own reflection when they stare into a mirror and she's banking on it pulling in more customers that way."

"Does it work?"

"It's hard to get an appointment, so yes, I suppose it does."

"She's a genius."

"She sure is. It wouldn't work for me, though. I need people to want what's in my window, which reminds me I really should change it and replace some of the items that I'm running low on, for ones I have an abundance of."

As she starts reshuffling the window, I head to the back of the shop to stow my coat and bag and almost as soon as I return, the shop door opens, bringing inside a burst of cold air and an extremely merry Camilla Hudson.

I look up and see a very happy woman swaying in the doorway, with slightly pink cheeks and a sparkle in her eyes. Harriet glances across at me and grins before saying, "I take it the date was successful."

"In every way. Honestly, ladies, I fell on my feet there. The man is a dream."

Harriet moves fast and leaves what she's doing, and we look at Camilla with an air of expectation.

"Well, his name is James, and he's a retired banker. Earned his money and then took early retirement two years ago. We have so much in common and like doing all the same things."

"Like what?" Harriet is hungry for all the details, and I am no exception.

Camilla smiles dreamily. "He loves sailing, orienteering, and basketball."

"I never knew you were into sports and physical activity, Camilla."

Harriet looks confused and Camilla shrugs. "In my mind I'm a little curious, but he doesn't need to know the details. Well, we've arranged to go sailing in the spring on his fifty-footer. it sounds huge, doesn't it?"

Her eyes are wide, and I nod. "I think that sounds quite large."

We all giggle as she says dreamily. "He asked me to go rock climbing with him in the Brecon Beacons, too. That sounds like fun, wouldn't you agree?"

Harriet looks concerned and I share it.

"Won't that be a little um, more physical than you're used to?"

"Oh, Harriet." Camilla laughs happily.

"How hard can it be? No, I'm up for most things and definitely with a George Clooney lookalike. I've invited him to come around tomorrow and check out my lodge house. Who knows, I may even persuade him to check me out in the process, a girl can dream, anyway."

"Is he good looking?" Harriet obviously needs to know everything and Camilla sighs.

"Better than George Clooney, way better. He has gorgeous salt and pepper hair with that designer stubble that's all the rage at the moment. Really sexy, you know. His smoky grey eyes were full of wicked intent and the fact he couldn't tear them away from mine was a serious tick in the box. He looks in good shape and wears really nice clothes, so the attraction was there almost instantaneously. Yes, I'm keen to see where this goes, but I need the boys to check him out first."

"How?" Images of them running a full background check and requesting references spring to mind and she giggles like a teenager. "I'll invite him to dinner, and they can suss him out. Ask some well-placed questions and decide if he's genuine or not. You never can tell and he could be a philanderer, a rapist or a murderer. A girl can't be too careful these days and before you know it, they've spiked your drink and taken you for everything you own. No, I need my family to do the background checks, so I've decided to throw a little dinner party tomorrow evening. He's up for that and I wondered if you would like to join us, Dolly. I know Brad would love me forever and I'm keen to see what you think."

"Me?" I feel so privileged to be included in this gathering, and Camilla smiles. "Yes, I have a good feeling about you and Brad, and I'm usually not wrong."

"Of course, I'll come. What time?" I jump at the chance because an evening away from Lucas and my parents could be just what I need, and I wonder why I'm so eager. When she mentioned me in the same sentence as her son, it felt right somehow. Brad and Dolly, Dolly, and Brad; we sort of go together and I'm starting to look for him by my side when he's not there and wonder what he's doing. When we are together, it feels so natural and even though he has a tarnished reputation, it doesn't bother me half as much as it should.

"Then it's settled. Tomorrow night at seven. James is arriving at 7.30 and we will all be briefed and ready to give him the grilling of a lifetime."

As Harriet places Camilla's wrapped purchases in a large paper carrier bag, I feel excited for tomorrow. I hope this evening doesn't put Brad off me for life because now he's agreed to be part of the service, the full horror of what he's agreed will come back to bite him hard and it will probably ruin Christmas for him, forever.

CHAPTER 29

Mum picks me up at 5 o'clock and says cheerily, "How was your day?"

"Good thanks. We were busy in the shop and Brad dropped by and treated me to lunch at The Olive Tree."

"Did he now?" Her tone is playful, and I shrug. "It was nice."

"I'm glad, honey. What are you thinking about the Lucas situation? Have you thought any more about it?"

"It's difficult, mum. If Lucas had come back a few months ago, I would have probably given it a second chance. Everyone deserves that at least, but now…"

"There's Brad."

"What do you think of him, mum?"

"Well, don't tell your father, but I like him, despite his reputation. You know, Dolls…" She sighs. "That second chance you were talking about applies to him, too. So, what if he's played the field a little. They all do, at least all the men I've ever known. It's what makes them see something worth keeping when they meet her, which is why I'm not surprised you're in this – situation."

"In what way?"

"Take Lucas, for instance. He's probably run rings around that field in the last two years. I'm guessing he hasn't been short of female company when he's on leave, or on a night off. Brad appears a good guy who likes female company, so they're no different. But I see the way they both look at you, Dolly. It's something else, more than attraction. It's a yearning for something we all want. A friend, a lover and someone to come home to at night. Sex is one thing, but friendship counts for a lot more and that's when it hits the baddest boy of them all. When they connect the dots and see the whole picture. Unfortunately for you, they have both connected the dots at the same time and come to the same conclusion and now you have the power my girl, so use it wisely."

She laughs out loud, and I must admit, she does make it all sound simple. But which one will I choose, if any? Maybe I should look for someone less attractive, less intoxicating and not liable to break my heart the moment they get bored.

We reach home in no time, and it shocks me that I'm already thinking of the dusty vicarage as home. In fact, I can't believe I've settled in so well to life in Dream Valley. It usually takes months and by the time I feel secure and happy, we're off to the next parish and the next dusty vicarage. But this is special. I can feel it and I wonder if that feeling has anything to do with Brad. If he wasn't here, would I feel the same?

Lucas is back from Riverton and my heart sinks when I see him laughing with my dad as they watch a Christmas movie. Normally that's mum's thing and dad just likes to poke fun at it and ruin the magic it creates.

Dad grins as we head inside and pats the seat beside him.

"Hey, babe, the fire's hot and the company is even hotter."

He winks, and she shakes her head and says dismissively, "In your opinion."

I venture into the room, and Lucas shifts up on the settee and smiles. "I've saved you a seat, Dolly."

Sinking down beside him, I worry about how quickly we have settled into being a unit again and feel a little nervous about that.

I also don't miss that my dad mumbles something like, "I'll help your mother with dinner," and pointedly closes the living room door on his way out, leaving me with Lucas, a roaring fire and a romantic film.

I'm just surprised they didn't light candles and have the champagne resting in an ice bucket beside us, and then I see a lone flicker from the windowsill of a candle dancing in the breeze from the ancient window and my heart sinks. There it is.

The seal of approval from a man who has obviously decided it's better the devil you know. Someone he can control, manipulate, and understand.

Great.

Lucas slings his arm along the back of the chair, and it feels as if I'm suffocating. It doesn't help that he's looking seriously hot and not just because of the fire.

Lucas has always been good looking. That was never in doubt and very difficult to resist, which got me into this mess in the first place. He is also probably the only man alive who could stand up to my father and brother and swing their loyalty towards him and once again, I think of Brad and his hopeful grin, trying his best to win my father over. Hiding his caring heart behind a wicked smile and a reputation that is deserved in part, but not to the extent he lives with.

"I've missed you today, darlin'."

Lucas's voice drips sincerity and I say politely, "Did you meet up with your friend?"

"Connor? Yes. His family lives an hour away from Riverton, so we agreed to meet up. He was part of our unit for a while, but it wasn't for him, so he joined the Paras."

"What about you? What are your plans?"

I'm sure Lucas won't stay in the special forces for long. Dad told me it's a hard life that can ruin a man's soul and I worry about Lucas and Beau.

"That depends on you."

"Me?"

He turns and the look in his eyes leaves me in no doubt about his intentions where I'm concerned and he leans forward and whispers huskily, "I want you back, Dolly. Back in my life, to be my girlfriend and build a life with you. These past two years have been hell for me because you weren't part of my life anymore. I didn't just miss you today, I've missed you ever since I walked away and now I'm begging you for a second chance to let me prove to you how much I love you."

It would be so easy.

The heat from the fire, the romantic music from the film, and a man like Lucas declaring his undying love for me. Just one nod of the head, one slight move and the past two years would fade away like a bad dream.

His lips hover dangerously close to mine, and I feel intoxicated by some kind of hormone that is kicking in hard. This is what I want. Everything. A man who wants me so much, he will do anything to make it happen. Someone promising me everything, a future, and I wouldn't be alone anymore.

The only trouble is, I don't see Lucas when I close my eyes, I see Brad AND Lucas. What am I going to do?

"I need time."

I well and truly wimp out and lift my eyes to his and say with a quiver in my voice. "It's too much to deal with. You

CHRISTMAS IN DREAM VALLEY

hurt me. I don't think you realise what it was like for me and just coming here, being in the same room as you, is difficult."

He reaches up and strokes my face, gazing into my eyes with a heart wrenching look. Puppy dog's eyes mixed with a wolf because this man enjoys taking hostages and I'm no different. He is bringing out the big guns, and I have to remind myself that he will do everything to get what he wants.

Pulling away, I sigh heavily. "I can't do this. I need to think."

The sadness in his eyes doesn't help and so I stand and say firmly, "I'll go and see if my mum wants any help. Enjoy your film."

I make a swift exit and take in large gulps of air to restore the balance because I could have so easily given into what *should* feel right but somehow feels as if it's the wrong decision, for now, anyway.

The hopeful looks that greet me turn to despairing ones as they see I'm alone and I say roughly, "Brad's coming over later to help with the Christmas service. I told him you'd save him a part."

Dad looks irritated and growls, "Is he now?"

Mum fires him a warning look and smiles. "That's good of him."

"Yes – it is." I stare at my dad with determination, and he shrugs. "I can't guarantee anything because I've already enlisted Lucas's help. Leave it with me though and I'll see what I can do."

Mum pulls a face behind his back and says loudly, "Of course he can take part, the more the merrier. Anyway, we should get this dinner on the table because we don't have long before the good times roll."

Dad heads back to the living room, no doubt to start planning the second wave of attack, and mum shakes her head. "I told him not to interfere, but you know how pig headed he can be. I'm sorry, Dolly, just remember to do what's right for you."

"I will, thanks mum."

I distract myself by helping her with supper and when I call the men in, I try to ignore the pull of Lucas's eyes because he could hypnotise me with them, he always could, and it wouldn't take much to get me to agree to anything at all and so I try hard not to engage and keep things light and on safer ground.

CHAPTER 30

Brad is prompt, which probably annoys my father and as we all huddle in the pews of the increasingly cold church, I wait for more embarrassment to be heaped upon me.

When Brad arrived, Lucas was fixed firmly by my side and just regarded him coolly when I introduced them.

I saw Brad wince a little as they shook hands and the cold way Lucas just nodded and then laughed at a comment my father tossed out there didn't make me feel any happier about the evening ahead.

To make matters worse, Lucas pulled me by his side and hemmed me in so I couldn't move and, once again, slung his arm along the back of the pew with a clear message of ownership. Brad, meanwhile, was told to sit on the other side of the aisle—alone, while my dad stood at the front and told us what we had to do.

It was a definite him and us and I felt so sorry for Brad as he tried to look interested, while glancing my way every minute he could.

"So, this is the general plot."

Dad outlines his story and my heart sinks with every word spoken.

"The service is about trust. Learning to trust and that not everyone in life is how they look on the outside. People you think are good, hide a rotten core." He looks hard at Brad, who sinks even further in his seat if that's possible.

"Now, the story centres around the nativity, of course, it is Christmas, after all. Mary and Joseph have reached the stable and not everybody is happy about that. The evil innkeeper wants to prevent the birth of Christ and, in doing so, would destroy Christmas forever, because without Jesus there would be no Christmas. He has contacted Herod and needs to keep them locked in the stable until the soldiers get there to kill the newborn king."

I'm not surprised dad's service includes killing and covert operations. They always do and catching my mum's eye roll, I giggle.

Dad carries on. "The good angel, in this case, Dolly, learns of the dastardly plan and enlists the help of the shepherd in the fields, in this case, Lucas."

Dad smiles at Lucas and winks and for some reason that causes Lucas's arm to drop onto my shoulder and he pulls me close and whispers, "The perfect pairing."

Then he kisses my cheek and I want to burn with mortification at this very public marking of his territory.

"So, the evil innkeeper, in this case, Brad, locks the stable door and throws away the key. Seeing where the key lands, the shepherd waits for him to leave and then races to find it with the help of the light from the angel's wand. Together they save Christmas because sometimes the person with nothing has so much more to give."

Once again, he looks at Brad with a sneer and says, "The shepherd opens the stable door and tells Mary and Joseph of the dastardly plan and helps them onto the donkey that is

CHRISTMAS IN DREAM VALLEY

grazing by the manger. The angel and the shepherd help them on their way and the innkeeper, seeing what is happening, races out and tries to stop them. He grabs a knife from the folds of his clothing and, as he raises his arm to strike, the angel waves her magic wand and turns him into an angry elf."

I think this time I do groan out loud, but he shrugs and carries on. "As Mary and Joseph proceed to the nearest stable, the real nativity gets underway and as the baby Jesus is born, Christmas is saved. Mary and Joseph turn into Mr and Mrs Christmas and the angry elf is banished to the North Pole to toil in Santa's workshop for the rest of his days. So, what do you think? I mean, obviously your mum and I will be Mary and Joseph and then Mr and Mrs Christmas and at the end we will hand out chocolate coins to the children and sing Elvis's version of Here Comes Santa Claus."

Mum opens her mouth to protest, and he says quickly, "Followed by Dolly Parton's duet with Kenny Rogers, A Christmas to Remember."

I want to hide somewhere far, far away because this one is worse than most. What on earth must Brad be thinking because this is insanity at its most destructive? Praying not many come to church this Christmas Eve, I can only pin my hopes on that and mum claps her hands and says, "I printed off the scripts last night and have some amazing costumes lined up."

She shouts across to Brad. "You will look so adorable as an elf, Brad. The transformation from evil lowlife to sweet little elf will delight the children. And Dolly, you should see the sweetest little white fairy dress I ordered from eBay. It arrived this morning and you will melt the hearts of the whole of Dream Valley."

I cast an anxious look in Brad's direction, and he just

smiles and nods and as brave faces go, his is a good one and once again, my heart softens towards the rather cocky man who is doing his best to win my parents over.

Lucas chuckles in my ear. "I see your father hasn't changed. This should be entertaining."

"For the rest of the world, maybe. Do you think I can call in sick?"

"It will be fine. I'm right beside you, darlin' and if you'll let me, that's where I want to stay."

It feels so frustrating because Lucas has glued himself to my side and won't give me a second with Brad. As dad monopolises his attention away from us, I see Brad struggling to listen to what he needs to do. I'm certain those instructions will be delivered with dad's usual military precision, and I feel bad for Brad who must be wondering why he's bothering, and it's made worse when Lucas pulls me by the hand behind a stone pillar and traps me in a cage of muscle and intention. "Have you decided yet?"

"Lucas, please," I look around wildly for an escape and he presses in further and groans. "I know I deserve to wait for all that I've put you through, but I'm going slightly mad here. It's tearing me apart knowing I'm the one responsible for driving you away and that man out there, he's not for you, nowhere near good enough."

"In your opinion." I inject a sharp tone into my voice, and he sighs as he rests his head against mine.

"I deserved that and just so you know, I will make it up to you. I won't back down either, because some things are worth fighting for and it's what I excel at. That man, Brad, is it? He won't last. I've seen men like him before. He'll get what he wants and then not want it anymore. I don't want you to be another conquest, another notch on the bedpost of the legend that is Brad Hudson because your father filled me in, and he's worried about you."

Pushing him away, I say icily, "Then allow me to make up my own mind for once in my life. Give me a little credit for that at least and don't pressure me, Lucas. It only pushes me away."

I head back to the others with the anger growing inside me, which is fuelled even more when Lucas follows me out and pretends to wipe his lips in front of a despairing Brad and smirks at him as if he's already won.

It's just too much and I spin on my heels and head back to the vicarage and try to create as much distance from the lot of them as I possibly can.

CHAPTER 31

*H*arriet can tell something's up because I'm wrapped in my own thoughts for most of the next morning and after a while, she nods towards the chiller cabinet and says kindly, "I think we're due a chocolate break. Sometimes the sweet stuff can help cure most problems in life – or offer some comfort at least."

"Thanks, Harriet." I smile at her gratefully as she hands me the tray and as I pick my favourite praline cream, she says kindly, "If it helps, I'm a good listener."

"Is it that obvious?"

"To anyone with eyes." She smiles and leans on the counter. "I'm guessing it's man trouble."

"Why do you say that?"

"At your age, my dear, it always is."

"What about double man trouble? Two impossible choices to make and not that long to do it in."

"Oh, to have your problems, Dolly."

Despite everything, I laugh softly. "I suppose." I sigh heavily. "The trouble is, one is a past love who broke my heart, left me devastated and who I would have given anything to turn up and pledge their undying love for me even a couple of months ago. The other is someone new, exciting, unknown and yet sweet and kind."

"Interesting decision, and not one I envy you for. Typical really, fate does deliver things in bulk sometimes and that throws up some difficult decisions."

She looks thoughtful. "Do you have any idea what direction your heart is leaning towards?"

"Not really. You see, one of the 'problems' is currently living with us, and I have no room to breathe. The other is trying his best to be the perfect prospect but is facing barriers placed there by my father, who has made it perfectly obvious where his loyalties lie. He loves problem number one like a son and is doing his best to push me in his direction and has listened to the rumours surrounding problem number two and has made up his mind he's not the one."

"I see your dilemma."

She offers me another chocolate and grins. "Two problems deserve two chocolates."

Setting the tray back in the chiller, she says with a wry smile. "You know, it's perfectly natural to like two things equally. Take these chocolates as an example. I have two favourites and if I only had to choose one, I would struggle. If there was only one chocolate I could have for the rest of my life, I would struggle to decide. You see, they are so different in taste, but having the same thing all the time can get boring after a while. We look around for something new to tempt us and change it up a little. Now, I know I'm talking about chocolate here but if you think about it, isn't that also most people's relationships? We gorge on the one we love the most, but sometimes temptation comes in the form of something new. We take a bite and decide that is the best thing in life and much better than the one we have grown accustomed to."

"I'm not sure this analogy is helping me much, Harriet."

"Why is that dear?"

She fixes me with a look that makes me stop and think for a moment.

"What if I like them both equally?"

"Then picture it another way. If those two chocolates were on a tray and someone came in to take one and you had first choice, which one would you choose? If these two men were walking away forever, which one would you run after?"

She smiles. "In that split decision, you would make the right decision based on what you want the most. Your subconscious would kick in and you would know. You see, Dolly, it's all simple when you break down the process. You see, a wise man once said, 'life is like a box of chocolates' and who could argue against that?"

"Forrest Gump, I presume." I grin as she nods. "Who else?"

Picturing Brad and Lucas walking in opposite directions, who would I chase, if any? Do I know enough to choose?

The door opens and we straighten up in anticipation of a customer and my heart sinks when Lucas steps inside, filling the small shop with his muscle and confidence. He flashes Harriet a resolve shattering smile, and she stares at him in disbelief. Then he turns to me and throws me a look that should have me swooning like a lovesick fool as he says, "I was hoping to treat you to lunch, baby. I heard the local place is an experience I won't want to miss."

I look at Harriet helplessly and she raises her eyes, and the imperceptible shake of her head drives my problem home. It is an impossible decision because they are both desirable men with noble intent, and it will take a Christmas miracle to decide which one I should choose.

Harriet sends me to lunch with a smile and as I head into the Cosy Kettle with Lucas, I don't miss the jaws drop of several of the diners watching with astonishment. Even the men look impressed and they're not looking at me because Lucas is like a poster boy for every woman's dreams. Men want to be him, and women just want him, and I was never any different – until now, it seems.

Miranda smiles and looks a little confused as we approach the counter and I know she has got used to seeing me with Brad by my side and Lucas says in his husky voice, "Hey, darlin', I've been told this is the best place on earth to bring my girl for a treat." He winks and I cringe at the 'my girl' reference because once again, he is stamping an ownership on me I'm not sure I'm happy with.

She nods and says with slight awe, "Of course, I'll send Laura over to take your order."

I think Laura is there almost as soon as Lucas pulls my chair out and the wonder in her eyes as she openly stares at him makes me roll my eyes and look away.

Once again, I think of Brad, the usual recipient of all the attention in Dream Valley, and my heart softens a little as I picture his cheeky smile and genuine interest in the people of this town. A little too much interest in some perhaps but hiding behind that cheeky chappie is a man with a heart of gold and good intentions.

"What about you, baby?"

"I'm sorry." I must have tuned out there for a moment because they are both looking at me and I see Laura's pen hovering over her order pad. "Oh, um, I'll take the soup of the day and a roll. Thanks, Laura."

She scribbles on her pad and says dully, "Drink?"

"Latte, please." She looks at Lucas and smiles. "Is there anything else I can get you, sir?"

For some reason, her voice has gone all Marilyn Monroe and I stare at her in surprise as Lucas winks and says with a grin, "Maybe later."

A pink tinge flushes across her cheeks and her eyes are the brightest I think I've ever seen them and as she turns away, the look she shoots me is full of envy and a jealously I'm getting used to by now.

As she reluctantly walks away, I roll my eyes. "You've still got it, I see."

Lucas shrugs. "There is only one girl for me and always has been."

"Not always, Lucas, you have a short memory."

He leans forward and just him being in my personal space confuses me, as my heart flutters when he takes my hands in his. "I was a fool, Dolly, but it was done with all the best intentions."

"What, breaking my heart and walking away from me was for the best?"

My voice sounds hard and jaded because I haven't forgotten the storm he wrecked in my heart when he left, and it took so many sleepless nights and skipped meals before I could even stop thinking of him for a few hours. But time is a great healer, and I soon accepted that he wasn't coming back.

"It was hard for me too." He looks a little vulnerable, which isn't like him, and he sighs. "The reason I left was because of my job. So many guys have families that wave them off at the door, not knowing if they will ever see them again. Those same guys are wracked with guilt and their minds messed up because they miss their families and don't get to watch their kids grow up. When you're on a mission that takes over your life, it's exciting but scary at the same time. Every single one of us lives with the knowledge we may not make it back and that's not a burden I wanted to share with you."

"So, you left me because you wanted to protect me."

My eyes fill with tears, and he squeezes my hand. "Of

CHRISTMAS IN DREAM VALLEY

course. I would do anything to protect you Dolly, even walk away because that is not the life I wanted for you."

"Then what's changed?"

"I have." He raises my hand to his lips and kisses it sweetly. "Not having you in my life is much worse as it happens. It gives me a reason to come home and when you do the job I do, that's what gets you through. The other guys used to talk about their wives, girlfriends, and even people they were interested in. It keeps us sane and the only one I could think of and talk about, was you."

"Oh, Lucas." My eyes fill with tears as I sense his loneliness. He looks unusually vulnerable as he speaks to me from the heart for the very first time. Suddenly, I see a very different side of him, and it changes my perspective a little. "So, what now?"

He smiles. "That's up to you. If you can accept my apology and agree to let me make it up to you, I would arrange a house for us at the base and start a life together. You know, there are many jobs you could do, and the community is good. They will look out for you, and you wouldn't be alone when I'm on a mission."

He looks so animated it's easy to get caught up in the excitement of it all, and I can picture a good life with Lucas. I always could, but do I want it? Do I want him? It's almost impossible to *not* want him in my life, but do I want *that* life?

He smiles sweetly as Laura fetches our drinks and as she reluctantly leaves, he says softly, "Think about it, Dolly. I know it's a lot to spring on you, especially now you're settling down in this place. I'm offering you a new life with me, and I will never let you down again. I want to come home to you *every single time* and I want to make a life with *you*–nobody else. To see our children playing in the garden and annoying the hell out of you. To fill our lives with laughter and share good times along with the bad. I want to be your everything because you are already mine."

I almost can't see him through the tears that blind me because Lucas has always put up a good fight, and this is no exception.

"Ok, Lucas."

The hope in his eyes makes me regret my choice of words, and I sigh. "I'll think about it. Just give me some time."

He shifts in his seat. "The thing is…"

"What?"

"It's just, well, I only have this week and then I leave for the base in Scotland. They're holding a house for us and need my decision because there's a waiting list."

"Scotland!"

He looks worried. "It's ok, you don't have to move there for a few weeks. It's just that I'm needed back, and I have to know if you're coming with me."

Laura's back and sets a bowl of steaming soup in front of me and smiles at Lucas as she gently sets down his toasted sandwich and fries. "Anything else, sir."

"No, thanks, sweetheart." He winks and as she heads off with a sigh, I wonder if I should do the same.

CHAPTER 32

Luckily, we are so busy this afternoon I don't have time to dwell on the decision I must make in the very near future and as Harriet turns the key in the lock and hangs up the closed sign, she sighs heavily. "A nice deep bath followed by a Christmas movie is on my agenda tonight. What about you?"

Wishing I had that luxury, I sigh in much the same way as her, but for a different reason other than exhaustion. "Straight to the church for a rehearsal and then off to Valley House for dinner with the Hudsons."

"Oh, that's right, Camilla's new gentleman friend. You must tell me everything tomorrow."

"Of course." Grabbing my coat, I say thankfully, "I really appreciate this job, Harriet. You're a lifesaver."

"It's nice to have company."

I bid her goodbye and when I head outside, mum is waiting and as I slide into the warm interior of the Toyota, she smiles.

"Hey, babe, good day?"

"Interesting."

"Life can be. What did I miss?"

"Lucas."

She looks at me sharply, "What did he do?"

"Nothing really, just showed up for lunch and laid his heart on the table along with the food. What am I going to do, mum?"

She says nothing until we are halfway up the road and then sighs. "If you're asking me, then you have your answer already."

"In what way?"

"Listen, honey. Don't get me wrong, I love Lucas like my own son. We both do and nothing would give me greater pleasure than seeing you happy and settled with him. He's our kind, Dolly. We know him. Your father admires him and he's your brother's best friend. But that's us, honey, not you. I know how hard you fell when he upped and left. I wiped your tears and planned a long-suffering death for him if I ever saw him again, but it's not us that matter, it's you. I'm guessing you're hanging back because of Brad."

"Probably."

She sighs. "Two men, very different in some ways, but similar in others. You've known one for years and one for days. That tells me more than anything."

"Tells you what?"

"That maybe you've changed and are looking for something different now. Maybe you are using Brad as an excuse not to get back with Lucas because your heart is no longer in it. If you want my advice, good, and if you don't, I'm giving it, anyway. Tell them both to wait. There's no urgency, don't commit to either of them and tell Lucas you need more time and see how things develop with Brad. You have all the time in the world, my darling, and you don't have to make a decision now."

"But I do."

"Why?"

"Because Lucas is heading to Scotland and wants me to go with him. He's even put our names down on a house on the base."

"There'll be other houses." She sighs. "Listen, Dolly, don't make the single most important decision in a young girl's life based on a tenancy agreement. Tell Lucas you need time and if he thinks that much of you, he will wait."

"Thanks mum." As always, she gives me clarity on things and takes away a little of the pressure and she's right. Of course, I shouldn't rush into things with either of them and now I feel a lot better telling Lucas my decision. Which is that I haven't made any decision at all.

Mum says lightly, "Are you going to that dinner tonight?"

"Yes, Brad's taking me after rehearsal. He texted me earlier and asked."

"He's a sweet boy."

"Hardly, mum." I giggle and she laughs with me.

"In some ways."

"Yes, he is." Thinking of 'sweet' Brad and his cheeky smile makes my own appear and I raise my fist at the timing of all this because why did Lucas have to come crashing back into my life now? It's just not fair and thinking of him, I say, "What are your plans tonight?"

"We're eating and then I've persuaded your dad to take Lucas to that pub in town, The Blue Balls. Rather apt on this occasion, don't you think?"

I cringe but can't help laughing along with her because mum is a very hard woman not to be wicked around. She's always made me laugh, and this is no exception, but I'm glad Lucas will be going somewhere and not dwelling on my 'date' with the Hudsons.

We park outside the vicarage and make the short walk to the church, and when I see Brad's van parked outside, I feel excited to see him. I do miss his company because he makes me laugh and I'm enjoying getting to know him.

As soon as we get inside, Lucas is waiting by the door and grabs my hand before the door even closes. "Dolly, I've been waiting for you. Your father says we should practise our lines."

Dad heads our way and nods. "Yes, your first scene is together, and I thought you should get into character. Brad will be practising with us because in the first scene we beg for a room for the night. Nail this beginning and tomorrow we can get to the good stuff."

Looking past him, I see Brad looking so uncomfortable on his own, I feel bad for him, but he just raises his eyes and grins, making me smile. I love him for the effort he's putting into this because I'm not sure I would be as patient if I was the one watching him with a past girlfriend. It reminds me we have no history at all, unlike the man who is crowding my personal space right now, so the only thing I can see is him.

We all get on with the job in hand and as Lucas sits beside me in a pew, we start reading our lines, which distracts our attention for a while.

It's all so bad and really cringe, which makes us laugh a little as we struggle to take this seriously. Unlike my father, who is shouting direction to mum and Brad like a Hollywood producer and Lucas laughs softly. "Your dad will never change. I still can't believe he's ended up here."

"What, Dream Valley or his job?"

"Both I suppose. It's a world away from the armed forces. I understand why he did it though."

He sounds pensive and impulsively, I reach for his hand. "Things will work out for you, Lucas. If not with me, then with someone else who will be so lucky to have you. Who knows, you may also get the call from God, and this could be your life in the future."

He looks absolutely horrified, which makes me giggle and he sighs. "That sounds a lot like goodbye to me."

"Not goodbye, Lucas, never that, but it's a 'we'll see' I suppose. Just give me time and space because I can't make a decision right now."

"Because of him." He jerks his head in Brad's direction and I slowly shake my head. "No, because of me."

Trying to put into words what's in my heart, I say regretfully, "I just can't make that decision right now and it's not because of Brad. You've come back into my life and exploded a cluster bomb of emotions, and I'm still dealing with the fallout of that. You see, I'm at a crossroads myself and I'm not sure what I want. I just need to settle here for a while and find out what that is. Not a choice between you or Brad. I'm choosing me."

Leaning forward, he rests his head on mine and stares into my eyes and whispers, "Then you have my word I will give you all the time you need. Let's just enjoy this time we have and when I leave, it's on the understanding you know where I am – to a degree, of course, and if you want to take me up on my offer, I'll come and get you."

His lips hover so close to mine I am tempted to taste my past and see if it's still as good as it always was, but a crashing sound makes us jump and as I look up, I see Brad on his knees, frantically trying to gather up the flowers that were so beautifully arranged in the stand by the altar.

"Sorry." He looks anything but and Lucas growls irritably, "He did that on purpose."

"Probably." Despite myself, I laugh out loud and as Lucas shakes his head, my father says loudly, "On that note, I need a drink. Hey Lucas, put my daughter down and grab your coat. Honey, you've pulled."

"What about your tea?" Mum sounds annoyed.

"Come with us and we'll eat at the pub."

She doesn't need asking twice and with a whoop of delight, she says over her shoulder, "I'll grab Squirrel and a coat and meet you by the car. Have fun at the dinner party, guys. Take pictures if you can, so I can cast my judgemental eyes over the guest of honour."

As everyone disperses, I feel relieved and as Brad heads my way and says cheerily, "Are you ready, angel?" I am more than happy to follow him outside.

CHAPTER 33

We head to Valley House and at first, it's a little awkward because now there's a very big elephant in the room who goes by the name of Lucas.

After a while, Brad says tentatively, "I'm sorry, Dolly."

"What for, the flowers?" I laugh as he groans. "Don't remind me. I've always been accident prone."

"Are you sure it was an accident?"

"Of course not. I kicked that pedestal in a rage when I saw where that man's lips were heading."

"My knight in shining armour, as always."

I keep it light, but it only reveals his intentions towards me and heaps on even more pressure and once again, as if he can read my mind, he says sweetly, "I just want you to know that I'm interested in us but if you choose him, I'll understand."

"Really." I feel a little disappointed at that, and he sighs. "I hate that he's here and living in your house. I hate that you have a history and have shared your lives. I hate that you were his girlfriend, and he has a greater hold on your heart, and I also hate that my reputation has come back to bite me because if I could change anything, it's that."

"You shouldn't change a thing, Brad."

"Why not? It would certainly help me with your father."

"Because it's what makes you, well, you. You have your reasons for your obsession with women and it comes from a lot of pain in your heart. You disguise it well, but I see it for what it is. You're just trying to come to terms with something you had no control over when you were younger, and this is your way of trying to deal with that."

"By being like him? I'm a fool if I think being like him makes it all better."

"No, but your intentions are good. You are trying to be *better* than him and I'm just surprised you want to keep that part of your life a secret. That's what I don't understand because if people knew the real Brad and how amazing he is, you would have a much easier time of it."

"Maybe I don't want that. Perhaps I want a hard time because then people's expectations will be low."

"You don't mean that."

"Maybe not, but my family is a dynamic one. You've met my brothers; know my father's history, and they are all powerful in their own way. Driven by ambition and a desire to make their mark in some way. I'm the same, but money doesn't interest me. I'm not interested in building a fortune, just to help. They would think I'm weak, a fool and think I've lost my mind because the Hudson men don't give money away, we multiply it and that's what's scaring me."

"Your brothers?"

"Yes. If they knew of my plans, they would take over. They wouldn't be able to help themselves. Marcus would see it as a money-making opportunity and set it up as a non-profit organisation to save on taxes. Dominic would use it to gain himself good publicity and tell me everything I'm doing wrong, and Jake would probably design a computer game around it and use my business to advertise it."

"Are you sure of that? It all sounds so cold."

"Welcome to my world, Dolly. The Hudsons are cold for a reason. Generations of them have followed the family motto to make money at all costs and keep it all for themselves. The fact my inheritance is so huge reflects that. My father's savings are vast and earn me enough in interest alone to live a comfortable life. Jake wants the investment portfolio because it's much the same. He can reap the dividends and not worry about money, all the time indulging in his love of design, not worrying if it pays the bills or not. Luckily for him, this latest game has just swollen his bottom line and not the one he sits on. No, I want to do this on my own, without any help and prove to them all that one Hudson at least, has the best interests of people less fortunate than us at heart."

"You're a good man, Brad."

"In some ways maybe, but not all."

He winks, and I find myself grinning like an idiot as he pulls into the driveway of Valley House.

"Will you accept my help?"

"In what way?" He pulls the car into a space and looks confused. "Can I help set up your business? It will give me something to do and make me feel good about myself."

"But you have a job with Harriet. You won't have much time, surely."

"I have all the time in the world for this. Harriet will close after Christmas and probably head to Wales in January. I'm between jobs and deciding on my future, so it will give me the welcome distraction that I need."

"And Lucas?" Brad is no fool and has probably heard the latest whispers concerning him, and I shrug. "Lucas will head back to work and has agreed to give me space to see what I want."

"What do you want?"

"I'm not sure. Though right now, I want to check out George Clooney and see if he's as nice as Camilla thinks he is."

Sighing, Brad pretends to disapprove, and I giggle as he says fiercely, "I'm with you there, and if there's any doubt in my mind, I'll send Lucas, actually, both Lucas and your father his way and watch from the window as they send him packing once and for all."

"My brave soldier."

He winks as I laugh out loud. "Here for you, Dolly, you can rely on me."

We head inside and it feels a lot like coming home. Valley House can make a person feel that way just by the delicious scent of Christmas that lingers in the air. The flickering candles that dance with joy as they welcome you inside. Sparkling fairy lights that adorn the beautifully decorated tree and the feeling of joy that surrounds the warm and cosy atmosphere as you step inside a home that wraps you in happiness.

"Darling, so lovely you could make it."

Camilla wafts towards us, a vision in white with a colourful silk scarf tied around her neck in a fashionable way. Her perfume reaches me before she does and she takes my hand and pulls me in for a hug, kissing me softly on my cheek.

"Come and warm yourself by the fire and grab a glass of champagne. To be honest, I've had three already because I'm so nervous. What if he's really dull, and one of those creepers you hear of?"

"A creeper, what are you talking about?" Brad laughs out

loud and Camilla shrugs. "You know, a man who won't go away. Hits on vulnerable women and misleads them to ruin."

"Don't worry, mum..." Brad slings his arm around her shoulders and pulls her tightly against him. "If anyone can spot a creeper, it's Dom." He laughs. "It takes one to know one."

"I heard that." A loud angry voice makes its way out of the living room towards us and we all giggle as we head inside the room.

The smiling faces that greet us lift my spirits as Florrie and Sammy Jo call out, "Dolly, there's a glass of champagne with your name on it over here."

I see the men of the family standing by the fire, deep in conversation, but they look up and smile as I head into the room.

Camilla follows me as Brad joins his brothers and whispers, "You look so good together, darling. I'm really praying for a Christmas miracle for you both this year."

Sammy Jo catches my eye and pulls a face and I laugh as she says loudly, "Don't wish Brad on her. For goodness's sake, Camilla, she will need to be a saint."

Florrie giggles, "Then it's a good job she's one step closer, living in the vicarage. He needs some heavenly inspiration to guide him, that's for sure."

Camilla pretends to be annoyed for him. "He's an angel. Why can't anyone else see that?"

"I can." I shrug. "What can I say? I see the good in everyone and I see a lot of it in Brad."

"Told you."

"What?" I stare at Camilla in confusion as she grins triumphantly. "I told you Dolly was made for Brad. She's been sent to save him from himself. I've seen it all before in one of those Hallmark movies. The one where the angel is sent down to earth to save a wicked soul. Someone who needs guiding onto the right path in life and then they fall in love, and she gives up being an angel to become his wife. It always brings a tear to my eye, and this is no exception. Well, if you want my blessing, you have it one hundred times over. Welcome to the family, darling. I'll set up a Pinterest board for you in the morning."

"A what?" It's impossible not to laugh at Camilla and her strange ways, and Sammy Jo grins. "Camilla has a Pinterest Board for everyone in her life. She'll have your house designed, your holidays mapped out and your wedding, baby shower and children's birthdays parties, all done by bedtime tomorrow."

Camilla shrugs. "It will give me something to do, dear, to distract me from my disastrous love life when George, or should I say, James, turns out to be a philanderer."

A loud ring on the doorbell causes her to jump and she shrieks. "Oh, my, he's here. How do I look?"

"Lovely, Camilla." We all heap praise on her, and she takes a deep breath.

"Wish me luck, girls, this could be every Christmas I ever wanted all rolled into very hot and tasty packaging."

As she heads off on her four-inch heels, Sammy Jo sighs. "I really hope he's the one. She could use someone in her life to distract her from ours."

Florrie grins. "I second that. You know, she called me in this morning to discuss flowers for my wedding."

I stare at her in surprise. "I didn't know…"

She holds up her hand. "Neither did I."

Sammy laughs. "I got the same invitation to discuss nursery schools. She said it would be a good thing to get our names on the register because they fill up quickly around here and the best ones get snapped up."

"But…" I stare at her stomach, and she says with horror, "No, Dolly, I'm not pregnant. Which is why you can see why we are all pinning our hopes on James/George Clooney being the one wish we all hope for this Christmas."

We hear footsteps approaching and lots of laughter and as they head closer, every single eye in the place looks in the same direction, praying for a Christmas miracle to walk through that door.

CHAPTER 34

*J*ames is a very pleasant surprise and I hear the sighs of relief echo around the room as everyone exhales the breath they were holding.

Gripping tightly onto his hand is a beaming Camilla who says proudly, "Here he is, the guest of honour."

I look with interest at the stranger and am pleased to see he doesn't look anything like a creeper. In fact, he appears quite comfortable being the centre of attention and says in a loud cheery voice, "I'm James, and Camilla wasn't lying when she said she has a beautiful family."

Brad steps forward and holds out his hand. "I'm Brad, also known as the favourite."

James grins as he shakes it hard.

"Then I'll stick with you, Brad, and you can tell me how one makes it to the top of Camilla's affections."

"Oh, James." Camilla giggles and Florrie nudges me as Jake introduces himself and one by one, we all take our turn.

As I shake his hand, he says keenly, "So, which brother is courting you, young lady?"

His brown eyes twinkle as he looks over my shoulder and

before I can answer, an arm slides around my waist and Brad says proudly, "That would be me. The thing is, James, courting is the operative word because I'm still trying my hardest to get Dolly to fall hopelessly in love with me."

"Once again, Brad, we'll swap notes because I appear to be in the same situation as you."

He raises Camilla's hand to his lips, and she giggles and says breathlessly, "Oh, James."

Resisting the urge to giggle again, I'm relieved when Brad whisks me away and whispers, "Sorry, Dolly, I hope you don't mind the introduction, it's just that I don't want him getting any ideas and switching his attention to you. I've got enough competition around here and can't risk it."

"Seriously, Brad. Do you really believe, 'Oh, James' would be interested in me? He seems quite smitten with your mother."

We both look across the room to see the couple with their heads bent close, laughing at something James is whispering in her ear, and I smile inside. Camilla looks so happy, and I'm pleased for her, because from what Brad tells me about his father, she could use some male attention and deserves to be the centre of someone's world for once.

Sammy heads our way, hand in hand with her husband Marcus, who never says much but seems pleasant enough and as they reach us, Sammy giggles and whispers, "I must say, Camilla has turned up trumps this time."

"This time?"

Marcus groans. "I'd rather not reminisce about the last few months. I'm just about to eat."

I laugh at the pained expression on his face as Jake says cheerily, "Nonsense, she's had a wild time and deservedly so."

Sammy Jo nods. "Well, remember the three firefighters she brought to our wedding? That was fun and made for some interesting photos."

"If you mean the one where she was pictured in a fireman's lift, laying across them all while they held her up, I think I'm still having counselling for that."

"The fact the rest of the family were behind her at the time and she was centre stage and dominated the picture was rather funny, you have to admit. I mean, your face was a picture, Marcus."

"Photographs usually are." Marcus rolls his eyes as his brother laughs out loud, and Sammy grins. "Then there was Mr Potato Head, as Jake called him."

"Why on earth would he call him that?"

"He looked like that toy the kids all got at Christmas. Bald head, thick moustache and glasses. It looked like a very bad disguise, almost as he if he didn't want to be recognised."

"You got that right." Marcus shakes his head. "It turned out he hadn't paid his taxes and the Inland Revenue has him on their 'most wanted' list."

"A master criminal, wow, interesting." I am riveted and Jake nods. "It turned out he owed over a hundred thousand pounds and was trying to seduce wealthy women so he could persuade them to help him out. I think mum was wealthy widow number five."

"How did you know?" I can't believe what I'm hearing, and Sammy says proudly, "Marcus asked his friend, Bob, the local policeman, to run a background check on him because he said he had shifty eyes and wasn't sure about his furtive ways. Bob stopped him when he left one night and ran a check on the number plate and took down his particulars. The subsequent arrest and conviction made it to the national news. Camilla dined out on that one for – well, I think she still is, so act surprised when she brings it up at dinner. She'll make out she was Agatha Christie or that Jessica Fletcher by the end of it and Marcus won't get the credit he deserves."

She stands on her tip toes and kisses his cheek sweetly. "He's always my hero though."

The fact he looks at her so proudly makes my heart skip a beat because it's obvious he adores his pretty wife, and the feeling is reflected back at him one hundred times over.

It makes me yearn for what they have. To be part of a team and settled. I could have that with Lucas if I just said the word, but our life wouldn't be like this. He would be away for most of it, leaving me alone on an army base somewhere, worrying if I'd ever see him again.

"The worst one was that friend of Dom's who showed up to take her ice skating."

"Now you are kidding me." The three of them grin and Brad laughs. "No, we're not. Dom answered the door, and that was the last mum ever saw of him. Apparently, he always had a Mrs Robinson obsession even at school and one of the teachers was dismissed because she was caught in a state of undress with him in the stationery cupboard."

"Classic." Marcus drawls, and for some reason we all look over at James and breathe a collective sigh of relief.

"It's a Christmas miracle. I need one of those." Brad whispers in my ear and I nod. "Same."

"What do you wish for, honey and I'll make it come true? I am one of Santa's elves and can have a word with the big man on your behalf."

He grins and I say apologetically, "I'm so sorry about that. You must wish you'd never agreed to do it."

"No, it's fine. I can put up with being ridiculed in public and made to look a fool as long as I'm doing something with you. Bring it on, I'll be the star of the show, just you watch and learn."

He winks and I'm not sure if this is the moment I fall a little bit in love with Brad Hudson, or if that love has been deepening every minute I spend in his company because right now, standing here surrounded by a loving family in a beautiful setting, I would never want to be anywhere else but beside the man who is just about ticking every box I've ever had in life.

* * *

Dinner is interesting, and Camilla's in her element. She sits at the head of the beautifully set table amid the festive centre arrangement with its burning candles. At least ten of them, which give off some serious heat and melt the butter pats, much to the delight of her sons, who make a big show of pouring the buttery liquid onto their bread roll rather than spreading it.

She looks amazing with James sitting beside her, who couldn't give her more attention if he tried. He seems so keen, and I must admit they do make a striking couple and not because he does resemble James Bond a little in his black dinner suit, with dress shirt and black bow tie. He looks distinguished and successful and keeps his eyes firmly fixed on his vivacious companion, whose delight is obvious.

"Florrie whispers, "Oh, James, is certainly living up to his name, he is definitely 00 heaven."

"I hope it works out for them."

I really do and Florrie says rather wistfully, "I hope so too. From what Jake told me, she was starved of attention from his father. He treated her like the hired help and reserved any affection for his many mistresses."

"Surely not. Poor Camilla." I look across in horror to see James laughing at something she said and feel my heart physically ache for the gorgeous Camilla.

Florrie sighs. "Fingers crossed, this is the one. She deserves some happiness."

Jake pulls her against him and Florrie giggles as he

nuzzles her neck and Brad rolls his eyes. "Do you two never stop? Please, I'm eating."

"Jealous?"

Jake grins in his lazy way as Brad groans. "Of course I am. I'm still in the desperate stage, hoping that Dolly chooses me over her extremely handsome, very fit, weapon of mass destruction, with a shared past and memories, ex-boyfriend."

Florrie looks interested. "I've heard he's amazing, a real poster boy."

Sammy Jo leans across the table and nods. "I heard he's like Ice Man in Top Gun. Laura from the Cosy Kettle is still getting over the shock of meeting him and is thinking of enlisting in the army in the hope they're all like him."

Brad nods. "He's fierce competition alright and I suppose it's Karma having a laugh because if anyone deserves to work hard for something, it's me."

He grins ruefully and I feel bad for him because Brad works very hard and nobody even knows, so I lean in and kiss him lightly on the cheek and whisper, "You have nothing to worry about. Just be you, that's good enough for anyone."

Brad smiles and I see the emotion glittering in his eyes as he whispers, "Thanks, babe."

I don't miss the delight on the faces of Sammy Jo and Florrie and the interested looks the brothers share.

Casting a look across the table at their other brother, Dom, I wonder about him. Of all of them, I have spent the least amount of time with him and as he listens to something James is saying, with Camilla looking on proudly, I wonder about his life.

Brad sees the direction I'm looking in and whispers, "Dom is all about the business at the moment. He says he's sworn off women until he makes it to the top of his game. He wants to be better than our father in every way and isn't interested in any distractions right now. Grumpy old sod."

He laughs out loud, and I suppose the description does fit him a little because he rarely smiles and looks as if the world annoys him on a loop.

So serious, a lot like Marcus and absolutely nothing like Brad and Jake. And for the first time, I can picture their father, who must have been a lot like him. Watching Camilla dazzle at the end of the table, I feel sorry for her because she needs a man who will let her shine, not dim her light, and I really hope James *is* that man.

CHAPTER 35

The food is scrumptious and I feel myself relaxing in good company wrapped in a haze of contentment, fuelled by the deep red wine that Camilla apparently has an abundance of. Spending time with Brad and his family is no hardship, and I find myself relaxing and enjoying an evening that came just at the right time.

With half an ear on Camilla's conversation, I almost spit out my wine when she says loudly, "Oh, yes, I'm a very active naturist."

Brad's low chuckle beside me makes me giggle as Marcus rolls his eyes. Before they can interrupt, James says with a great deal of interest, "Then you would enjoy a club I go to. We meet once a month and would love you to join us."

Sammy Jo stares in horror as Florrie almost chokes on her wine and Camilla nods enthusiastically. "Oh yes, that sounds right up my street, doesn't it, Dom?"

"If you say so." Dom shows a rare devilish smile as he catches his brother's eyes and Camilla beams around with excitement.

"We were always heading to Dreamy Sand beach at Rocky

Cove and enjoy being at one with nature. Goodness, the fun we used to have, I kind of miss those days."

James nods in agreement. "There's nothing like feeling the sun on your skin, warming every part of you and feeling free."

"Oh, James, we are a match made in heaven because I absolutely love a spot of sun worship. Maybe we could do it together some time, so much fun."

"Definitely, you know there's a place in Spain I always go to. Maybe we could sail there next year on my yacht and spend a few liberating days at the campsite. It would be so good to share it with a like-minded person to enjoy the freedom nature blesses us with."

Brad says with interest, "So, mum discussed her love of sailing with you then."

Camilla shakes her head imperceptibly because the only sailing she's ever done, according to Brad, was when they took the pedalos out as children.

"Oh yes, Camilla told me what an avid sailor she is. I still can't believe I found her. I think she's my soulmate."

He turns and gazes into her eyes and, to her credit, Camilla just nods as if she believes every word herself.

"So, this naturist camp club, tell me about that, James."

Jake can't help himself and James says happily, "It's not far from my home and I often go there to unwind. You know, badminton, tennis, a little bit of ping pong to get the competitive juices flowing."

"So, you're into ball games then." Brad can't resist adding and just about everyone, except the new loved up couple, are thinking very different thoughts right now.

Camilla nods. "I love a good whack on a ball. It takes out my aggression."

James's face lights up. "Then you'll find a willing partner in me."

"Super, darling, I'll give you a good thrashing."

Florrie actually can't speak right now and is pressing her lips to her glass in a bid to disguise her laughter and Brad says loudly, "So, mum. Tell James about how much you like um, nature. What was it again?"

James leans forward. "Naturism?"

"That's the one."

Camilla giggles. "Honestly, Brad, of all of us you should know more about that than anyone."

"She's got that right." Dom raises his eyes. "Brad's a constant visitor to Pineland Forest at night. They call him dogging Brad Hudson in Dream Valley."

I feel decidedly uneasy as Brad grasps my hand under the table and says loudly, "Don't believe a word of it, Dolly. It's a myth that everyone uses to explain my absence most nights."

My heart flutters with relief because I believe him, despite the rumours. After all, I'm the only one who knows his secret, anyway, so if Brad wants to use his reputation to deflect attention from his real nocturnal activities, I really should back him up on that.

"Yes, that's our Brad, such a lover of animals, he always has been." She turns and smiles at her adoring companion. "So, James…"

Camilla's voice rings out. "This holiday sounds super fun. What will it involve?"

"Yes, do tell, James, we may be tempted to join you, won't we, babe?"

Jake stares fondly at Florrie, who says quickly, "My sailing days are over, Jake. The last time I took to the high seas, I ended up with you. Once bitten, twice shy, as they say. I'm sticking to dry land from now on."

"Shame, it would have liberated our minds."

"Agreed, Jake. The sea is quite liberating. I love nothing

more than feeling the wind in my hair and blowing the cobwebs away. Do you have a date in mind, James?"

James looks so excited I almost feel sorry for him, knowing the boys are setting him up for a gigantic fall. Then again, knowing Camilla, she wouldn't be averse to trying something new and just go with the flow. I almost hope she does just to see their looks change from smug enjoyment to panic at the thought of their mum sailing off to Sodom and Gomora with a naked James Bond impersonator.

"Well, obviously, we need it to warm up a little, so maybe June is a good time. The children are still at school, and we can take off and enjoy our freedom without the crowds."

"Sounds amazing. I'll book it in my diary. So, what does one bring on these well-being holidays?"

"Just a smile and your toothbrush. Maybe a nice dress to wear around some of the small towns we dock in. Not a lot else though."

"Good luck with that." Dom snorts. "Mum's idea of travelling light is to forego her handbag. I hope you've got a decent amount of storage on your boat, James. You may struggle to leave the marina under the weight of all mum's clothes."

"Oh, James." Camilla laughs. "Don't listen to him, he's just winding you up."

James laughs out loud. "You had me going for a moment there, son."

"Anyway…" Camilla jumps up.

"Girls, will you help me bring in the main course? I heard it's your favourite, James, and have taken the liberty of preparing it specially. Meatballs, anyone?"

I don't think I've ever exited a table so quickly in my life and as we head out of the room, Sammy whispers, "Do you think we should tell her?"

"God no." Florrie grins. "This is the most fun I've had in

ages. Can you imagine her face when James strips off as he mans the wheel and lets the wind blow his inhibitions back to shore? Oh, to be a seagull on that particular mast at sea."

"Please use a different description, Florrie. I was quite hungry until now." Sammy's expression makes us giggle and as Camilla joins us, she smiles with satisfaction. "Well, this is all going rather well. What do you think, girls? James is a delight, isn't he? I may need to brush up on my sailing skills between now and June, though. I say brush up, I mean take a crash course and pretend I don't get seasick on the Isle of Wight ferry. Oh well, it will be so much fun to try something new."

As she walks off and busies herself with the meatballs, Florrie grins. "I give it one week before Dom tells her exactly what her new experience will involve. I doubt we will be seeing James in the new year. Shame really, he seems quite sweet in an alternative way."

Feeling a little sorry for Camilla, I nod in agreement, but Sammy just shrugs. "You never know, it could be a match made in heaven and she could discover her inner free spirit. Knowing Camilla, I wouldn't put anything past her."

We all look toward the women who is an inspiration to us all and in a way I hope she does go with it. I envy her the chance at least because I'm not sure if I could ever be so bold.

CHAPTER 36

Brad takes me home after a very enjoyable evening and as soon as we pull away from Valley House, he groans. "I'm sorry about my family. They should be sectioned for their own good and my mother never let out."

"I think they're great, special even. You are very lucky."

"I could be luckier." He grins. "If I get my Christmas wish, I will count myself the luckiest one of all of them."

"Your travel agency?"

I smile, hoping he makes it all happen and shows them just what he's made of, and he sighs. "No, Dolly, not the travel agency, although I am going to do my best to make that happen."

"What then?" Wondering if he has something else up his sleeve, which wouldn't surprise me, I'm taken aback a little when he says softly, "It's you, Dolly, you're my Christmas wish but it will take a Christmas miracle to drive away the current adversary who is probably cleaning his rifle in readiness to blow away the competition, permanently."

I'm a little stunned because I know that Brad is interested

CHRISTMAS IN DREAM VALLEY

in me. I feel the same, but it brings back my dilemma and with it the hopeless choice I must make.

"Listen, Brad, I…"

"It's fine. You don't have to say anything. I just want you to know I'll do whatever it takes to prove I'm worthy of a chance at least. I may not be the noble fighter, defending our freedom and making women's hearts flutter wherever I go, but I'm in unfamiliar waters with you, Dolly, darling. I've never wanted to try with anyone before, which is strange territory for me. It's not just because you haven't succumbed to my charms either, it's because from the moment you looked into my camper van window on that frosty road, looking like an angel with your innocent blue eyes peering out from under that white fluffy hat, I think I was reborn."

"Stop it, Brad, you're an idiot."

I roll my eyes and he chuckles softly, "Guilty as charged. I'm the idiot elf who thinks he stands a chance with the sweet, innocent angel. The idiot who tries a little too hard to impress her father, who wants me dead – obviously and the idiot who thinks he stands a chance against every woman's fantasy, otherwise known as your ex-love and my eternal adversary. But I'll play the idiot for as long as it takes to prove to you that my heart is yours for the taking. Which now makes me the idiot who bares his soul ready to have it trampled on by those big fluffy snow boots you seem to adore."

He looks so tortured it makes me laugh and he rolls his eyes. "At least I make you laugh, it's a start."

"Just be yourself, Brad. I kind of like who you are and wouldn't change a thing, except maybe…"

"What and it's done already?"

"I wish you would let everyone else know just how amazing you are."

He shakes his head. "Only when it's all done. The big

reveal, as they say, and so for now, I'm happy to let everyone think the worst of me just to keep them off my back. Talking of which, I'm heading to Riverton tomorrow evening to help out. Sadie wants to visit her family because apparently, they've been in touch and want to meet up."

"What's her story?"

He sighs. "She was an unruly teenager and dabbled in drinking that progressed into drugs. She fell in with the wrong crowd and ended up on the streets when her parents threw her out."

"That's terrible, poor Sadie."

"It happens." He shrugs. "Anyway, she lived on the streets and her life fell apart. It was only when she stumbled across the shelter that she found somewhere she fitted in. She's been running the place for the last year and it's helped give her a purpose. She lives there now and has a permanent place to call home and a noble mission to help others. There's a rumour she's keen on Matty, one of the social workers, and they've been getting closer."

"That's a lovely story."

"Not really."

He laughs. "Not exactly Cinderella, is it?"

"It has a happy ending, though. Fingers crossed, anyway."

"We can all hope for that. So, do you fancy helping out tomorrow evening? I could pick you up after work and we could grab a bite to eat first."

There's an anxious look in his eye and I feel bad about that, so I nod. "Of course, I'll help out. I'd love to."

"Will action man mind?"

"Probably, but leave it with me. I need to sort this situation out for everyone's sakes."

"What will you say?"

"I wish I knew. The trouble is, I care for Lucas a lot. I was in love with him. In fact, he was my first love. I can't just turn my back on that, which is why I'm struggling."

"I see." Brad's face falls and I feel bad for that too, but I can't make promises I can't keep because who knows what my heart really wants? I certainly don't and so I need to make a decision and live with it and move on with my life.

* * *

As soon as I step foot inside the little cottage, I sigh. Unlike Valley House, the rooms are small and rather dark and there's a draft blowing through the crittal windows. It's in direct contrast to the warmth and cosiness of Brad's home and yet this is where my family are. I love them more than anything, and I will do everything in my power to make them proud.

Venturing into the living room, I take comfort in the fire roaring in the grate and smile when I see mum curled up on the sofa with her legs on my dad and Squirrel on her lap. Stroking the little dog's soft fur, I say softly, "I missed you, squizzle."

Her tail wags adorably and I wish my life was as simple as hers.

Dad says gruffly, "You're late and have work in the morning. Lucas is in bed already."

"He is." Wondering if they've had a few too many beers at the pub, I'm surprised he's in bed because Lucas is normally the last man standing and mum shakes her head, looking upset.

"He's had some bad news, darling. I'm so sorry."

I sit with a slump on the settee and say fearfully, "What's happened?"

Mum sounds quite upset as she says, "He got a call. All leave's been cancelled, and he's reporting to base tomorrow.

Your dad's dropping him off at the station in the morning. I'm sorry, babe, I know you were enjoying spending time with him but well, it's his life I suppose."

"Yes, it is."

She jumps up and Squirrel growls and jumps onto my dad's lap, and I watch as he strokes her soft head and looks a little sad. I know my dad adores Lucas and has enjoyed his company. It makes us all miss Beau even more because there's always a huge aching chasm when we realise he's not here and the fear that one day we may get a call telling us he's never coming home. It's hard to live with and I say gently, "I'm sorry, dad, it must bring a few bad memories to the surface."

"It does." He smiles and says ruefully, "It's why I left and why I promised your mother I'd do it for her. It wasn't fair on her waiting to see if I made it home and was lucky again. It always felt like I was running on borrowed time, and I made the decision to do something about that. You know, I think I had more than five lives granted to me, and I knew something had to give."

I'm shocked when he looks up and the emotion in his eyes takes me back a little as he whispers, "I'm sorry, princess."

"What for?"

"For interfering in your life. For making things uncomfortable for that boy you seem keen on and for encouraging Lucas and inviting him here."

"So, you did plan this."

He shakes his head. "No, not really. Todd did ask me, and I was happy to offer Lucas a bed for the night. But I could have had your back a little more because the last thing I want for you is life as a military wife."

"But…" I'm lost for words, and he sighs, tickling Squirrel on her tummy as she growls in contentment.

"It's just, well, I love Lucas like a son, and he is good for you. In every way but one. His occupation. I was kind of hoping he would change direction, maybe reconsider his options and provide you with a life I want for you. Someone to care for you and make you happy. It's all I've ever wanted for you, but he is young and thinks he's invincible and wants to conquer the world. In fact, he wants it all, and that includes you by his side. Well, I'm not that happy with his plans as it happens, so I just want you to know I'll back off. Leave you to make your own choices and if that involves moving to Scotland to be with Lucas, then fine. If it involves running off with the local lothario, I'll have to suck it up. You see, as your mother pointed out, you're over twenty-one and an adult. My role has changed, and I no longer have the right to tell you what to do. So, what I suppose I'm saying is, that I'll back you up whatever you decide."

The tears build once again as my father does what I've always wanted and puts my feelings first for once. I can tell it's hard for him and so I head his way and tuck myself under his arm on the other side of Squirrel and hug him hard. "I love you, dad."

He drops a light kiss on the top of my head and says gruffly. "Love you back, princess."

Mum heads into the room with a tray of hot chocolate and smiles. "Room for one more?"

As she sets the tray down on the little coffee table and takes her position on dad's other side, I feel at peace. The small Christmas tree twinkles in the corner, the fire is hot and the company the best I could ever wish for. The chair that is empty on the other side of the room will hopefully soon be filled with the large muscle-bound body of my brother when he gets leave but for now, he's with us in our hearts as we snuggle up and appreciate the love of a good family.

CHAPTER 37

A gentle tap on my door wakes me and at first, I think I must be dreaming because it's still so dark outside. Glancing at the bedside clock, I see it's 6.30 and groan. Morning already.

Another tap makes me wake up fast and grabbing my warm dressing gown, I head to the door and open it cautiously and my heart skips a beat when I see Lucas looking wretched standing outside.

"I'm sorry, Dolly." He whispers, "Did your father tell you what happened?"

Drawing him into my room, I sit beside him on the bed and say sadly, "He did, and I'm the one who's sorry. It must be hard, especially so close to Christmas."

"Not really. I can live without Christmas. It's you I can't live without."

Wow, two bold statements in one sentence and yet who the hell can live without Christmas? It doesn't make sense and I say incredulously, "I can't believe you said that."

"I thought you knew."

"No, I didn't. I mean, honestly, Lucas, you've shocked me a little because surely everyone loves Christmas."

His low rumble of laughter startles me, and he takes my hand and squeezes it gently. "You always did make me laugh, even when it was the last thing I felt like doing. That's why you're so good for me, baby."

He sighs and wraps his arm around me and says regretfully, "I would love to stay. To persuade you a life with me is the best thing for both of us. To make plans for a life in Scotland – at the beginning, anyway, and to make you fall in love with me – again."

He laughs softly. "But it appears that I've run out of time, and it wouldn't be fair to drag you away from your family and, well, your new life in Dream Valley."

"What are you saying?"

Despite everything, I'm sorry to see him go and I'm afraid for him. I do love Lucas; I always have, but I'm just not sure I love him enough.

He drops a light kiss on the top of my head and whispers, "I want us to freeze this moment in time and visit it at a later date. I know you're not ready to commit to me. I was selfish, thinking I could ride in here and pick up where we left off. I could tell you were struggling, and I feel sad about that. So, let's just leave it here. Know that I love you, want to be with you and will give you space to work out if you want me too. Will you write to me though, accept my calls and be there as a friend? I need you in my life, Dolly, in whatever way you'll let me."

"Of course I will." There's an edge to my voice filled with emotion as my heart breaks all over again. I do love him and the thought I may never see him again is too hard to bear and as the tears fall, he lifts my face to his and smiles. "Don't cry, baby, if it's meant to work out, it will. If you find someone else, I'll survive. Live your best life, Dolly Macmillan. I demand it. If that's with the elf, then I'll be happy knowing someone is looking out for you and taking care of my girl. If he hurts you, tell me and it will be the last thing he does."

I sniff and laugh through my tears with a mixture of relief, fear and pain that he's leaving. Sniffing, I whisper, "Stay safe, Lucas, and make sure you come back to me."

"Always, baby. I intend on living a long and healthy life and maybe one day you will live it with me."

He looks at his watch and groans. "I should go. The train leaves in forty minutes and your dad's waiting." He makes to stand, but I can't let his hand go and the tears fall as I prepare to say goodbye to him all over again.

"Lucas, I…" I can't help crying and he says regretfully, "Be happy, and I'll be back before you know it. I'll write to you."

He drops my hand and leaves without looking back and just by the slight edge to his voice, I know he needs to harden his heart and can't let emotion in. It's how they cope; my dad was always the same and, to a degree, my brother. As I listen to his footsteps thump away from me down the stairs, I bury my face in the pillow and sob my heart out because despite everything, I love Lucas and I always have, but I'm not sure it will ever be enough.

* * *

It doesn't take long for mum to find me and as she drops her hand to my heaving shoulder, I sob, "How did you cope, mum?"

"I learned to. I tried not to think about where he was going and what might happen. I just always believed I'd see him again and he would come back to me. I never allowed doubt to creep in and trusted his training."

"I don't think I'm that strong."

"Strength surprises you sometimes. It helps you deal with

CHRISTMAS IN DREAM VALLEY

it because if you feel bad, how do you think they feel? It's not easy walking away from your life, not knowing if you'll ever return. They deal with it in a different way to us and sometimes we have the rougher end of the stick. It's their life and their job and they love it in a weird way. They are distracted as soon as they meet up with their unit and it's the person at home left with all the worry.

Sniffing, I sit up and draw my knees to my chest. "I think I feel worse because I couldn't give him what he came here for. I feel so bad knowing he's heading off disappointed about that."

"He'll be fine. You don't stay with someone because you feel sorry for them. Life doesn't work out like that, and I think Lucas knows deep down your feelings for him have changed and maybe he's using this to step away from that."

"It doesn't make me feel any better."

"Because you're a kind girl, Dolly, who loves Lucas but not as fiercely as you once did. Don't beat yourself up about not wanting that life or him in that way. It just means that fate has other plans for both of you."

"But I do love him, mum, I always did, but I have learned *not* to love him. He broke my heart, and that's a very hard thing to forgive. For so long I would have given anything for him to walk back into my life, but when he did, I realised he didn't have quite the same impact on me."

"Because you've met someone else and realised the world doesn't begin and end with one man, which tells me you've moved on. Lucas will always be a big part of your past and will undoubtedly feature in your future in some way, but you need this time. This is *your* time, Dolly, to discover who you are and what makes you happy. If Brad makes you happy, enjoy it. If he continues to make you happy like your father does me, then I think you've found a rare gem and should guard it with your life. Just don't look at it too closely, over analyse it and just enjoy the moment and see where it takes you."

She smiles and pulls me close, rubbing my back as if I've woken from a nightmare. Mums are good like that and are there when you need them. At least I count myself lucky that mine is.

* * *

We are eating breakfast when dad returns, and he smiles at me with sympathy as he hangs his coat on the peg behind the door.

"So, we're short of a king."

"Is that all you can think of - your bloody play thingy?"

"I would rather think of this plaything."

Dad winks at me and lifts my mum into his arms and kisses her deeply and watching them makes me smile - as always. Yes, I want that. The deep love and the happy life that my parents have. Maybe I'll get lucky one day and find it here in a place like Dream Valley.

Dad drops her and sits opposite me, and I see the concern in his eyes.

"I'm sorry."

"We've had this conversation, dad and I'm fine. I know you like Lucas and are worried about Brad. You just need to trust me to get it right – for me."

"I know, but it's hard to let go."

"It certainly is."

"You see, Dolly, when I see you, I don't see the incredible woman you've become. I don't see the strong, kind, amazing girl who is much better than I'll ever be. I see my little girl and I suppose I always will and that brings out a protective streak in me that can be hard to deal with—for you. I'll try to tone it down, give you room to breathe, but I can't promise I will ever stop looking out for you. Putting your needs before anyone and doing my best to ward off any attacks on your heart because I may have given up fighting for a living, but I will never stop fighting for you."

"I know." Those annoying tears well up again and even mum brushes a tear from her eye and I move around the table and press a light kiss on my father's cheek and whisper, "I love you too, dad and love how much you love us all."

"For god's sake." Mum sniffs as dad raises his eyes at her choice of words and winks at me.

"It's only seven thirty, and I feel drained already. We've got a full day ahead of us and I'm an emotional wreck. Let's talk about something jolly. It is Christmas, after all. So, what are your plans today, Dolly, an evening ice skating under the stars in Riverton perhaps, or a nice cosy date in that weird balls pub in front of an open fire, with a particular local to cheer your sad heart up?"

Thinking of my plans, I want to tell them it involves feeding the homeless, but I can't, so I just smile and say, "The pub sounds nice, and so does the ice skating. Brad did mention Riverton when he dropped me off last night, so maybe I'll take him up on his offer."

As long as that's all he's offering." Dad shakes his head. "I still can't step around his reputation. It's always there like a big red flag, goading me into battle like an angry bull."

He sighs. "I know I have to trust you, Dolly, but it's hard when all I want to do is torch his stupid bed on wheels and warn him off with a threat and a prayer."

"Oh, Scott, you're so dramatic all the time." Mum raises her eyes. "Come on, eat up your breakfast and let's get the day started. I have shopping to finish off and food to organise. I've even got a festive special planned for, For Christ's Sake and need to glam up for the camera."

She turns to me and smiles. "Don't be late for Harriet

either, Dolly. At least you have a job to take your mind off – well, Lucas."

"Yes, I should get going."

I make to jump up and she fixes me with a hard look. "Not until you eat a full breakfast. It's the most important meal of the day and I will not compromise on that."

As she turns, my dad pours us both a mug of tea and winks. "I'm not the only protective one around here."

As I sip my drink, I feel a lot better and, taking a deep breath, try to focus on what's happening now. I'll deal with my feelings later when they've had time to adjust to what just happened. I know I will see Lucas again and he will be fine. I must believe that because the other alternative is devastating.

CHAPTER 38

Luckily, it's a very busy day in Valley Gifts. We don't even have time for many chocolates today as the steady stream of customers keep us busy wrapping, serving and replenishing the stock.

It's just what I needed, and the customers are in good spirits and there is much laughter and good humour and as the Christmas music plays out from the speakers, I finally feel as if Christmas is working its magic and sweeping away my problems.

We only have time to grab a sandwich from the Cosy Kettle, and they are as busy as we are. It appears the residents of Dream Valley like to support their local businesses, which makes for a thriving community. In fact, as towns go, this one is special, from the community spirit to the effort gone into making it look magical. Christmas trees sparkle in the shop windows and fairy lights wrap around the wooden pillars of the shops that sit high on verandas like something out of a wild west town. Pots of trees are standing outside welcoming shop doorways, decorated with fairy lights and red bows, making it look like a Christmas card.

All we need is snow and the magic will be complete and even the icy chill no longer affects me. Dream Valley is a place where you always feel warm inside and I have fallen deeply in love with it.

As soon as the last customer leaves, Harriet turns the sign from 'open' to 'closed' and exhales with relief. "I think it's an early night for me. What about you, Dolly? Do you have any plans?"

A gentle tap on the door answers her question, as we see Brad peering inside.

She laughs softly as she opens the door. "Sorry, we're closed." She grins and Brad laughs. "About time. I've been waiting to whisk your slave off for a much-needed meal in the presence of the best company in Dream Valley."

"In your opinion."

I grab my coat and roll my eyes at Harriet. "Wish me luck, it looks as if I'm in for a busy evening."

"Enjoy."

Her laughter follows us outside and I smile at the amusement in Brad's eyes as he dips his head and whispers, "You always look like a big white fluffy marshmallow in your fuzzy coat and hat. Just so you know, I happen to love marshmallows."

The look he gives me makes my heart flutter and my toes curl because his attention is a very powerful weapon and despite everything, I'm falling fast for a man who just won't back down.

We retreat to the warmth of his camper van and as we buckle up, I sigh with relief. "It's good to sit down."

"Are you sure you're up for this, Dolly? I don't want to wear you out for Christmas."

"I doubt it and actually, I'm looking forward to it. I've never worked in a shelter before. I know dad spends time there, not yours of course, but similar wherever we've been. I'm interested in meeting the people who rely on it."

"They're amazing." He laughs. "Well, maybe not all of them. Some are a little surly and don't like to talk. It's understandable really when many think the world is against them."

"It must be hard. I couldn't imagine not having a place to go. We are very lucky, aren't we?"

To my surprise, he reaches over and squeezes my glove encased hand. "I think we are."

As we drive towards the bigger town, I feel wrapped in a warm glow. Things may have changed between Lucas and me but I know we will always share that special memory that only a first love can give. Maybe I'll share a few new ones with Brad and maybe I'm destined to meet someone else entirely, but for the first time in a very long time, I feel just content to see what fate has in store. I just want to enjoy spending time with a man who makes me smile and makes my heart flutter, in a special place that I have fallen a little bit in love with already.

* * *

Sadie is pleased to see us when we step inside the door, and I can see why. There's quite a line forming around the room as many people surge in from the cold, hoping for a bowl of something warm to keep the chill off. Many aren't wearing nearly enough and the clothing they have on isn't fit for a harsh winter and I feel bad for them.

Christmas carols play out, creating a jolly atmosphere and a decorated tree stands proudly in the corner. Tinsel hangs from the ceiling and many people sit in their seats, enjoying some food that will help them survive.

Brad calls out to several people and as they answer him, I can tell they're regulars. I love this side of him. The happy, caring man who loves spending time here. The genuine warmth he gives these men and women and the fact he treats them like any other person he meets in Dream Valley. It reminds me that we're all human beings and some have just fallen on hard times. It could happen to any of us, and I count myself lucky that I have a good family behind me, who will always care for me and make sure I'm ok.

Brad leans in and whispers, "If you help Sadie serve up the food behind the counter, I'll clear away and make sure they have everything they need."

I nod and take up my position and Sadie smiles gratefully. "Thanks love. If you serve the soup, I'll take care of the stew."

As we work, it feels good to help in a small way. Most don't make eye contact, but those who do look at me with curiosity and a guarded interest. Many don't speak, some do and as I chatter away, the time passes in a flash and before I know it, the line has stopped, and Sadie smiles her thanks. "That was a busy one."

As we start to tidy away the near empty pots and place them in the dishwasher, I ask, "Is it always this busy?"

"In the winter months, always. It can get pretty busy in here and sometimes they don't leave."

"Do they stay here all night?"

"Yes, I can't turn them out into the cold, so many crash here for the night and are at least guaranteed a hot drink and some biscuits, not to mention breakfast in the morning. They're not silly."

"Do you have help?"

"Yes, there's a steady stream of volunteers, like Brad."

Our gazes fall on the man himself as he laughs and jokes with a group of men on a nearby table and Sadie laughs, "Not many are as pleasant to look at. He's a popular guy here and not just with the ladies. He has an easy way about him they like. He never judges and just treats them like any other guy he meets at the local pub. He's a rare gem."

Looking at Brad laughing out loud at something one of the men is saying, my heart does a little dance inside. Yes, I'm beginning to realise just how special Brad Hudson is, and he is someone I could fall for in a very big way if I let my heart free to decide.

As Sadie prepares a fresh batch of soup, I clean the dishes and put them away and I look up when I hear a loud, "Coming through."

Sadie shouts, "You can take them to the back room, line up and no pushing in."

"What's happening?" I stare in surprise as a group of volunteers stagger in with armfuls of bags and Sadie smiles. "Fresh supplies. The Salvation Army brings bags of clothes, toiletries, blankets and shoes. They're all donated and are very welcome. Sometimes a hairdresser stops in on their way home, or the local dentists spares a few hours when they close. Doctors too and people who just love to help, all flock inside to spare a bit of their time. Especially in winter, it's a more desperate time."

I watch as the room empties as they follow the Samaritans in an orderly fashion and Brad joins us and says cheerily, "I could murder a cup of tea."

Sadie nods. "Coming right up. What about you, Dolly?"

"Great, thanks."

As Sadie pours us a mug of tea from the urn, Brad says with concern. "It looks as if it's a busy one tonight. Do you need us to stay?"

"It's fine." She blushes a little. "Matty said he'd stop by and help. Most of the hard work is done already and some of the volunteers in the back room have promised me a few extra hours tonight."

"Then we're off the hook." Brad turns to me and grins.

"So, delightful Dolly, let me reward you with a slap-up meal at the local pizzeria, followed by a night skating under the stars."

"Have you been talking to my mum?"

"Why?"

"Oh nothing, she just mentioned we should go skating, that's all."

"Then let me make her wish come true."

Sadie laughs and shouts, "Don't go breaking anything and I'm not just talking about legs or arms."

Brad laughs. "Dolly is safe with me, Sadie. I'm a changed man."

He reaches for my hand and as we head out into the frosty air, I am surrounded by a glow I could get used to.

CHAPTER 39

I'm not the best ice skater in the world and neither is Brad, but somehow we manage to make it around the ice under the clear starlit sky. Dinner was heavenly in a sweet local pizzeria, and it felt good sitting opposite a man who is good company and made me laugh for most of the meal. In fact, this evening has been just what I needed after the emotional morning I had, emotional few days actually and as we skate hand in hand under the beaming moon, I feel all my troubles melt into the ice.

We snatch a couple of hot chocolates when we've had enough and as we stand watching the other skaters, with our hands wrapped around the steaming mugs of pure heaven, I tell Brad what happened with Lucas, and he looks concerned.

"I'm sorry, how are you feeling now?"

"I'm ok." I smile. "I will always love Lucas. He's a big part of my life even now, but I know I wasn't meant to follow him to Scotland. Somehow, I've changed, and I want different things now. I'll always be his friend, but I just couldn't commit to anything more, no matter how much I wanted to."

"You wanted to."

His face falls and I say quickly, "I wanted to make him happy. I hated seeing the pain in his eyes that I knew was because of me. I couldn't jump in his arms and say I forgave him because I've moved on and that's what made me sad. He deserves someone who wants him so badly they will do anything to be close to him. To follow him wherever he goes and be there when he returns. A better person than me."

"Yes, he does."

I giggle as Brad nudges me and shakes his head. "Honestly, Dolly, you're a cruel woman. The poor guy. I feel bad for him."

"No, you don't."

He turns and suddenly looks a lot more serious. "No, I don't."

I stare up at him, sensing something is about to change and as the world spins around us, literally, he leans forward and brushes his lips lightly against mine. I hold my breath, but before he can finish the job, somebody crashes into us from behind and he falls against me, reaching out to steady us both. The hot chocolate splashes onto the ground beside us, narrowly missing my white coat, and as I fall into Brad Hudson's arms, fate has delivered a very big kick of encouragement.

Staring into my eyes, Brad doesn't need words to tell me what he's thinking and neither do I apparently because as we lean towards each other in unison, this kiss is a long time coming and reaffirms something I've known all along. I am falling in love with the most unsuitable man in Dream Valley and there is absolutely nothing I can do about that.

I feel warm inside and surrounded by a delicious glow as I kiss Brad under the sparkling stars, my feet barely registering the frosty ground. His arms wrap around me, pulling me close and as kisses go, this one was long anticipated. It feels right, as if I'm coming home and there is not one shred of doubt in my heart that this moment was destiny playing her trump card. Brad and Dolly, a match made in hell. A bad plan on paper, but the perfect twist of fate. And as we kiss and our relationship shifts in a more exciting direction, I push away any doubts and any guilt I may have and enjoy the sweetest moment that was always coming, whether I liked it or not.

Pulling back after a very long time, Brad stares into my eyes and smiles. "I always loved marshmallows. They taste so sweet and melt in your mouth."

"Idiot." I swat him on the arm, and he smiles. "Seriously though, are you sure about this? I'm not exactly the dream."

"You're *my* dream, Brad. Let's just see what happens next, no strings attached."

He nods. "I may like strings. I may not want casual."

He sighs. "You know, Dolly, for the first time in my life, I want more than casual. I want a girlfriend. Does that shock you because it shocks the hell out of me?"

Blinking against the moonlight and the tears that are never far away, I say with a slight quiver in my voice. "No, Brad. That doesn't shock me at all."

Leaning forward, I press my lips against his and love how good they feel. I could get used to having him beside me, but can I be his girlfriend? I already know my answer. However, he doesn't need to know that yet.

* * *

WE HEAD HOME in a haze of expectation, nursing a warm inner glow that only the first flush of love gives you. Brad is perfect for me, and I'm surprised that nobody can see but us it seems.

On the way home, we spoke about the play and Brad

assured me he would daft Jake to fill-in, and I wonder what he'll think about that.

I feel slightly nervous as we park outside the vicarage, and are met by a rather stern looking father.

Brad sighs, "Here we go."

"I'm sorry." I feel so much pity for him because my dad isn't one to back down, despite what he said to me privately and as Brad jumps down and says a polite, "Good evening, sir, before coming around to open my door like a true gentleman, I brace myself for a different kind of battle.

"Come inside."

Dad jerks his head towards the door, and I take Brad's hand, both to spite my father and offer Brad some much needed solidarity.

"Come on, we may as well get this over with."

As we follow him inside, I prepare myself for even more embarrassment and wonder if this will ever end.

Mum looks up and smiles a welcome. "Hey, guys. Good night?"

"Yes, thank you, Mrs Mac…"

"Tina, Brad, just call me Tina."

She hands him a mug of coffee that she miraculously pulls from the pot and whispers, "I would put a shot of brandy in it for a bit of courage, but Scott hates people who drink and drive."

"Thanks, Tina."

She smiles and as I take my own coffee, we head into the living room and settle down beside an extremely welcome fire. Squirrel growls a little as we shift her along and then huffs as she snuggles in beside my leg and I tease her ears absentmindedly as I wait for the fireworks.

Mum and dad join us and it's now extremely hot in here, as the small room struggles to cope with us all, and the fire projects much more heat than is needed right now.

"So, Brad."

"Yes, sir."

I nudge him to let him know I'm right beside him and my father says, "It appears we are one character down in our play. Any ideas?"

"I do as it happens."

My father leans forward. "Go on."

"I thought my brother Jake could fill-in."

"He won't mind?"

"No, sir. We were always starring in the local panto as boys. Mum made us but we secretly enjoyed it, so I'm sure he'll do his bit."

"I'll leave that with you then."

My dad leans back and looks at him thoughtfully.

"I have a few rules."

"Dad, please." I hold my breath as Brad shifts nervously beside me and then I stare in horror as my father lifts a piece of paper from the table beside him and peers down at it as my mum groans. "For god's sake, Scott, do we have to do this now?"

"Now is the perfect time."

"Mum, please, tell him." I beg my mother and she shrugs. "Just get it over with sweetheart, he'll be happy then."

Brad shifts beside me, and I close my eyes and count to ten because could this be any more embarrassing.

"So, these rules, agree to them and I'll back off."

"What do you have in mind?"

If anything, Brad just sounds interested and my dad says sternly, "Rule number one, sell the bed on wheels and get a nice dependable four by four. Something safe and secure that won't fold in an accident. Something that won't get the tongues wagging of Dream Valley when you take my daughter out at night."

"Dad!" I stare at him in horror because Brad loves his

camper van. It's something he needs to travel, but to his credit, Brad nods. "I'll start looking."

"Brad, no." I shake my head and he shrugs. "It's fine, Dolly, I need a car, anyway. That thing guzzles diesel, and it's a waste of money."

Dad nods in approval. "Rule number two, you fill-in this form with fifty words or less what the word 'no' means to you."

"He's not at school, dad."

"Let him finish, sweetie, and then we can all go to bed, um I mean, Brad can, um, leave and go to his bed, I mean…"

"We get the drift, Tina." Dad rolls his eyes and says loudly, "Rule number three, details of how you will treat my daughter. Why we should entrust her to your care and promises you can give to keep her safe. Two hundred words."

I groan and wish this was over already, but Brad just nods. "It will be a pleasure."

Dad nods and says, "Rule number four, never bring my daughter home drunk and never offer her drugs of any kind. That is non-negotiable and will be the last thing you do if this rule is broken."

"You have my word, sir."

If Brad thinks this is a whole lot of inappropriate, he is doing his best to disguise it, and I fall a little deeper somehow.

"Rule number five. Who besides God should you fear the most? Answer that question now."

The look my dad gives Brad would cause a heart attack in most men, but Brad just says firmly, "You, sir"

"Good, then you know my intentions should you ever break my girl's heart because know one thing, that is rule number six and the one you should pay closest attention to. That whatever you do to my daughter, I will do to you." The look in dad's eyes is ferocious as Brad says in a slightly higher voice than before. "Understood, sir."

Hoping it doesn't look as if we've been kissing already, I pray to God as dad's boss to rein him in somehow because how is this happening?

Dad appears to be warming to his subject and carries on with a darker look, if that's possible. "Fifty words on the role of women in the home."

"Yes, sir."

Brad is trying to remain upbeat but is fading fast and dad continues, "Favourite singer?"

"Um, Ed Sheeran."

Dad raises his eyes and Brad says faintly, "Although I love the classics, like, um, Elvis Presley."

Dad flicks a look at my mum who rolls her eyes, and he barks, "And…"

"Dolly Parton, sir."

Now they are just making fun of him, and I open my mouth to speak, and dad says quickly, "References."

"Excuse me." Brad is now in complete shock as my father taps the page and says with determination, "I want three references from the women you've dated. Reasons why it didn't work out and their parent's phone numbers. I need to know your religious history and any countries you've visited in the past five years. Plans for the future and goals in life. I need it all on my doorstep when I wake in the morning, and I need you to show up at 7am for your training."

"Training, sir?" I think Brad has whiplash and who could blame him as dad nods. "I won't have any man spending time with my daughter, who doesn't work hard for a living. 7am we go on an hour long run, followed by log chopping duty in the garden. Then you can assist me on my rounds while trying to convince me to trust you with my daughter. Do you have a problem with that?"

He stares at Brad with a long thoughtful look and Brad says gruffly, "No, sir. 7 am it is."

Dad just nods and stands, offering Brad his hand.

"Then we must shake on that. Just so you know, this is on a trial basis only and could last several years if you don't shape up. Just know I am never going to like you, Brad Hudson, but don't take it personally. I feel the same about any man in Dolly's life. Just prove me wrong, that's all I ask."

"Is that it, Scott? For God's sake, the poor boy's terrified."

Mum flashes Brad a sympathetic smile and says with a sigh. "Come on, babe, I need to go to bed."

"Then allow me to show you out first, Brad."

Dad nods towards the door and thrusts the paper in Brad's hand and he follows him out looking a little shell shocked. As soon as the door closes, I look at mum and groan. "Did that just happen?"

"Oh, you know what he's like, sweetie, he'll never change. That's his way of accepting the situation and giving you his seal of approval. You've just got to love that man."

As *that* man heads back into the room, his lips twitch as he shares an amused look with my mother. "I think that went well."

"If you say so, babe. Now come on, it's been one hell of a day and I'm keen to see the back of it."

Sighing, I leave them to turn out the lights and tend the fire and as I head to my room, I think about what a difference a day makes. The last time I was here, I was sobbing as if my heart would break and now, I'm filled with hope for something that has been denied to me for quite some time. A new beginning, perhaps, a new love to warm my heart. If he can pass the test, he's no doubt heading home to agonise over. That person could be Brad and I suppose the moment I first met him, I always hoped it would be.

CHAPTER 40

It's Christmas Eve and the small church has almost reached capacity. As we watch from the side-lines, Brad groans. "Why is it so busy? Who are these people?"

Jake sounds tortured. "You told me there would only be a few of them, not most of Dream Valley and half of Riverton. I'll never live this down."

"*You'll* never live this down. At least you get to be the gallant king who saves Christmas. I'm the bad guy who is humiliated into an Elf. I will never live this down."

"You think I will." I sigh as I look down at my rather indecent costume that it appears mum ordered in error from an adult's only site and Brad chuckles beside me. "The sight of you in that costume is the only reason I'm going through with this at all. There is a God, and he has a wicked taste in clothes."

Elbowing him in the ribs, I die a little inside. My 'costume' barely covers my embarrassment and I absolutely refuse to bend over. The magic tape holding it in place had better live up to the job, otherwise I'm liable to wipe out the elderly population of Dream Valley in one extremely embarrassing wardrobe malfunction.

Mum is no better. Her Mrs Christmas costume appears to have been included with mine in a buy one, get one free and she is lucky to be dressed in a floor-length robe with her hair covered. At least until she transforms from Mary into Mrs Christmas.

"I bet this is your fault, Jake." Brad grumbles beside me as we watch even more people crowding through the church door, looking desperately for somewhere to sit.

"Why do you say that?"

"Because you're the famous inventor of the hottest game this Christmas and now, by default, a local celebrity. That's always guaranteed to bring in the crowds with their phones set to record in the hope of an exclusive."

"Talking of which, have you heard?"

"What?"

Brad's voice is terse, but my ears prick up as Jake says in a low voice, "Mum told me that Rock Cottage is to have visitors in the new year."

"Why is that news? Rock Cottage always has visitors, it's one of those luxury cottages that people pay a small fortune to rent."

"Yes, and somebody famous has rented it, apparently and is arriving early in the new year."

"Who?"

Glad that I'm in the right place to offer up a silent prayer to God to send Chris Hemsworth my way, Jake says in a whisper, "Bill Monroe."

"What, the Bill Monroe from Emergency Room?"

"Yes, apparently he's taking a sabbatical from the series and is heading somewhere remote to write a screenplay. He's chosen Rock Cottage as that place and the locals are getting very excited."

CHRISTMAS IN DREAM VALLEY

"So, your celebrity crown is about to be stolen by a bigger one than you. I suppose it was good while it lasted."

"Happy to give it up."

Jake chuckles. "I'm not so sure it's because of me. Word is spreading about the vicar and his wife and their alternative services. Sorry, Dolly, I know they're your parents, but the townsfolk love a good laugh, especially at someone else's expense."

"It's fine." I sigh. "It's always been the same and I think they do it on purpose to draw in the crowds. They don't care why they come, just that they do, and it gives dad a whole new crowd to preach to and add to the upkeep of the church. I wish they wouldn't involve me in their theatrics, though. Beau had the right idea when he enlisted in the army. Anything's better than this.

I shiver and Brad wraps his arm around me and pulls me close and it feels so good. In fact, ever since he was kind of accepted by my father, things have been good between us. The fact he was driven to the point of exhaustion when dad took him off for 'training' only made him more determined to prove himself. It appears that Brad Hudson has a very well disguised competitive edge and I think he enjoyed the challenge.

In between rehearsing for the play and working in the shop, not to mention our evening visits to the shelter and helping out at the hospital with the wrapping, I am looking forward to Christmas even more this year.

Brad asked if I would help at the Shelter in the morning and I wonder how we can keep that one from our families because Christmas Day is one of our busiest and my father always likes me to help out. Plus, we have been invited to Christmas dinner at Valley House, so I'm not sure if we will fit everything in.

But first we must endure public humiliation and ridicule

in the name of Christ and support my family in their hour of need. The fact my mother has rigged up cameras to record the whole embarrassing incident as a live stream to 'For Christ's Sake' doesn't make me feel any better at all.

* * *

My father settles the crowd down who are anticipating an alternative take on the nativity and I steel myself for public ridicule.

As the service starts and he plays to his captive audience, we are soon carried along on a wave of festive foolery, mixed with a message that tells us all why we're doing this at all.

Despite how I feel about this, I love seeing the awe on the children's faces as they stare at me with a mixture of envy and disbelief. The little girls love a fairy and so I play up to them and smile and laugh as I go through the motions, desperately trying to block out the keen interest on their father's faces for a very different reason.

Mum, as usual, excels herself and puts one hundred and ten percent into it. Her delivery was as if Dolly Parton was here herself as she speaks with a strange country and western twang and sings her heart out when required. Dad is no better. He loves this in a weird way. I wonder what his friends in the army would think if they could see him now and sometimes I think he's suffering from some kind of post-traumatic stress episode that has turned him this way.

Then there's Brad who has risen to the occasion like a true hero. Diving into his role with his usual good nature and acting as the evil inn keeper with conviction. Even Jake gives everything he's got, and I laugh to myself at the tears falling down Florrie's cheeks as he strides around the church in a very important way, as he over acts in a very splendid manner.

As the candles burn on the stone ledges and the scent of pine and cinnamon assault my senses, courtesy of mum's plug in air freshener that she got a good deal on in Costco, I fall in love with Christmas all over again because who wouldn't want to be a part of this?

The congregation join in, despite the weird choice of 'hymns' and as my dad does what he loves and tries to engage his audience in the reason for Christmas in the first place, I feel so blessed to be part of something amazing, with a very angry elf by my side.

* * *

"Well, I think that went well." Mum fans her face with the hymn sheet and stares at the small gathering with relief. The church has emptied and only the Hudsons remain, keeping us company as we dissect the success of our first Christmas 'performance' in Dream Valley.

"I just can't imagine Harrison Bowers ever running a service like that."

Camilla laughs. "He was so old school with his 'church rules' that were upheld in the strictest of ways."

"I thought he was sweet." Sammy Jo looks at Marcus and grins. "His sex talk when we married will live with me to my dying day."

Marcus grins. "If I remember rightly, there was no talk given the fact the students had already passed the exam."

Sammy blushes and whispers in embarrassment, "I pretended, that's all, to avoid an embarrassing lecture from a man of the cloth."

My father laughs out loud. "I always skip the sex talk. I kind of think it's irrelevant these days."

"Probably." Mum shoots him a look that I know the others don't miss and I turn away, wishing they weren't quite so obvious in their devotion to one another in public, and that's a general description where it concerns them.

"Well, I wouldn't have missed it for the world. My two youngest acting in a play, it was just like old times."

Florrie giggles as Jake pulls a face. "It was the *last* time. Honestly, Brad, the things you talk me into."

"You loved it." Brad grins. "Maybe we could take this show on the road. Broadway beckons and I love New York at Christmas."

"I can sign you up for next year, although you may not survive that long if you don't look after my daughter."

Brad swallows hard as his family share amused looks and Dom laughs. "I never thought I'd see the day when Brad had a girlfriend. The end of an era."

"And the beginning of a new one." Brad pulls me close and kisses the top of my head and it feels so good to be all here together.

Mum chips in, "Babe, go and crack open that communion wine. I think we all deserve a Christmas drink before we head home for dinner, bed and a short nap before midnight mass."

"Why don't you come to us for dinner?" Camilla smiles. "We always have gammon on Christmas Eve and a few cocktails. Then we could all come back and join in Midnight Mass together. It will make Christmas so special."

"Camilla, darling, you're an angel. A miracle from heaven and I could kiss you right now."

Mum jumps up and tries to pull down her short red skirt with the fur around the bottom.

"I'll just go and change, and we will meet you back at yours. I'll lend a hand with the preparations."

Dad's eyes light up and he jumps up after her. "We may be awhile though, um, some urgent Christmas Eve business to attend to."

As he follows my mum like a lovesick puppy, I feel extremely cringed out by the whole scene as Brad's brothers grin and share knowing looks and Camilla sighs.

"I wonder if James is free tonight. I could do with some attention myself."

We all share a look and Sammy says gently, "Um, Camilla, I really think there's something you know about James."

"What?" Camilla appears a little worried and her sons look concerned.

Florrie says nervously, "You do know what a Naturist likes to do, don't you?"

"Yes, of course, dear. Alexa told me it's someone who studies the patterns of nature. Naturalists seek to observe the interconnected relationships between plants, birds, trees & ecology so we can understand the past, present & future of our local and global environments."

We stare at her in shock as she shrugs. "I rehearsed it so I would appear intellectual if he asked me the definition. Are you impressed?"

Marcus snorts as Dom rolls his eyes. "James isn't a naturalist mum, he's a naturist. They are very different things."

"What are you talking about, Dom? They sound the same, and I actually think it's a very noble hobby. We should all respect the environment a little more and do our best to help. I'm thinking of going vegan to follow on from my decision to drive an electric car. It's called doing your bit."

"You're certainly doing that; your car battery is always flat which means you don't drive anywhere. The activists would be proud of you."

Marcus sighs and Sammy nudges him and fixes him with a warning look.

She turns to Camilla and says gently, "It's like this. While many of us prefer to spend our days fully clothed, some prefer to live their lives au naturel. In their birthday suits. Nude. Unclothed. They are naturists."

Nobody knows where to look, and only the sound of the wind blowing a gale outside interrupts this tense moment.

"What, no clothes? You've got that wrong, Sammy. James was fully dressed every time I saw him. Goodness, whatever next, you do get some funny ideas."

Sammy says patiently, "He was talking about when he sails, and visits that club he spoke about. I think the term, take your shoes off and leave them on the mat, includes the rest of your clothes."

Camilla just laughs out loud. "You are so funny, Sammy Jo. As if James would be into kinky stuff like that."

"It's not kinky, mum." Dom stifles a grin. "It's just liberating, I suppose."

We all look at him in shock and he says quickly, "So I've heard. Not that I would ever, oh for God's sake."

He shakes his head. "Mum, James takes his clothes off in public and probably expects you to do the same, so if you're not into that sort of thing, I would let him down gently and move onto the next in line."

He stands up and growls, "It's bloody freezing in here and I need a stiff gin and tonic. Who's with me?"

There's a mad scramble as everyone tries to leave a very embarrassing moment behind and Camilla stands, looking slightly bewildered, muttering, "Well, I never. It sounds interesting though."

Her family stops and looks at her in astonishment as she shrugs. "Each to their own. I'll ask Alexa what she thinks when we get back. I may like it. Who knows? You should always keep an open mind and never judge."

As she turns away, she catches my eye and winks, before plastering a blank expression on her face and saying loudly,

"That gin and tonic sounds marvellous. Lead on, Dom, I have some calls to make."

Brad turns and pulls me into his arms as soon as the door closes behind his family and says huskily, "Alone at last. The wicked elf and the sweet angel. You are now my prisoner, and I will corrupt your soul in seconds."

Tapping him on the head with my wand, I giggle. "You are a wicked elf but I kind of love a bad boy, so do your worst."

Maybe it's extremely inappropriate given where we are, but when the angry elf kisses the indecently dressed angel, all my Christmases come at once.

CHAPTER 41

As always, Camilla makes us feel very welcome and I love spending time at Valley House and not because it's so cosy and welcoming, despite its size. It's them. The Hudson family. They laugh and joke and make me feel like one of the family and my parents already adore them, which really helps when it comes to Brad.

We sit in the living room after a glorious supper of roasted gammon, roasted vegetables and baked potatoes, all washed down with the finest of wines and followed by a delicious trifle and a cheese board.

Now we're listening to soft Christmas carols by the light of a twinkling Christmas tree. The fire roars in the huge inglenook fireplace that is decorated by a natural garland, made up of holly, ivy and berries, interspersed with dried oranges decorated with studs of cloves and cinnamon sticks. Candles burn brightly and I love the fact they included Squirrel, who is currently sleeping contentedly on a rug in front of the fire, after being fed titbits by just about every person here through supper.

Camilla smiles and says brightly, "I think we should organise a toast. I'll fetch the champagne and some glasses."

"Any excuse." Dom rolls his eyes and Camilla shrugs. "If you can't crack open the bubbly at Christmas, when can you?"

"Um, New Year, weddings, christenings, substantial birthdays and just about every excuse under the sun in your book."

Dom laughs as Marcus nods in agreement and Jake says to Florrie, "Come on, babe, let's go and get it for mum."

We all watch as he pulls her up and they head off and Camilla smiles at them fondly. "I must say I'm having the best Christmas ever. Since Anthony died, God rest his soul, I wondered if I would ever find that holiday spirit again."

"I never realised dad had any holiday spirit, unless it was the alcoholic kind." Marcus says angrily and my mum smile sympathetically. "I know, hon, it's always up to the women to provide the excitement."

Dad laughs out loud and squeezes her knee. "You do a good job of that, honey."

Rolling my eyes, I throw them a warning look to behave, and Brad says a little nervously, "Um, I may have a reason for celebration."

I don't miss the alarm on my father's face as he looks at me in shock and I say, "It doesn't concern me, dad."

Mum sighs with relief. "Thank God for that. We've only just got over the first hurdle. I want an easy Christmas."

Brad looks around nervously. "We'll wait for the others, but I've been thinking long and hard for quite some time."

"That must have hurt." Dom grins wickedly and Camilla slaps him on the arm.

"Shut up, Dom, and let Brad speak."

She smiles her encouragement as Jake and Florrie head back carrying two bottles of champagne and a silver tray laden with glasses and Florrie gasps, "Please don't make me drop these, I would never forgive myself."

We clear a space on the coffee table, and she sets the tray down with a sigh of relief and noticing everyone looking at Brad expectantly, she says, "What did we miss?"

Clearing his throat, Brad looks at me and I smile. "Go on."

"Well, I just wanted to explain what I've been doing for the past year when I don't come home at night."

"Oh, spare us the details please." Marcus groans and Camilla says, "Oh no, you haven't become a father, have you? I'm not old enough to be a grandmother and I need at least nine months to mentally prepare myself for that."

My father leans forward and fixes Brad with a steady gaze, and I think my mum is holding her breath because she is getting redder by the second.

"I've been volunteering." Brad sighs and smiles, looking relieved to finally get this out in the open.

"It may sound strange to you, but I've been spending time at the homeless shelter in Riverton and helping out."

There are a lot of confused faces around us, and Brad laughs. "To be honest, I love it. The people are great and it's really satisfying. Well, as you know I've wanted to travel for quite some time, and it wasn't for holiday purposes."

This time I fix my dad with a hard stare, and he shrugs as he leans back.

"Well, thanks to dad I can live a comfortable life with my inheritance, so I can afford to take a few risks."

Both Marcus and Dom lean forward at the same time and say, "No!"

"Hear him out, boys, let him speak."

Camilla also looks worried and Brad shrugs. "I won't be using my inheritance. I can't until I marry, anyway, but I've decided to set up a travel agency in Riverton. Dolly said she'd

CHRISTMAS IN DREAM VALLEY

help me, and I've already found a couple of potential retail units."

"Why, Brad, this is all a little out of the blue?"

Camilla is struggling to understand what this all means, and Brad says gently, "I want to set up a non-profit making charity to pay for people who don't get a break, to enjoy a few days away, or even a night in a hotel. To give something back and share the love, after all, isn't that what I'm known for?"

For a moment there's a stunned silence and then Camilla's eyes fill with tears, and she heads across, her arms outstretched. "I'm so proud of you, darling. What a lovely, admirable, incredibly brave thing to do and you have my full support and blessing."

Dom nods. "Mine too. I'll invest."

"Me too." Marcus smiles a rare smile and claps his brother on the back. "I'm proud of you, bro."

Jake jumps up and pulls him in for a hug. "Count me in."

Florrie and Sammy Jo hug him with tears in their eyes and then dad says loudly, "I'm sorry, Brad."

Everyone turns to look at him and I'm surprised at the respect glowing in my father's eyes as he offers Brad his hand.

"I misjudged you and gave you a hard time. I'm sorry for that and it's taught me a valuable lesson."

"Oh, Scott." Mum's eyes are watering and as she brushes the tears away, she hugs Brad hard and says, "I always knew you were a good one. Didn't I, Scott?"

She looks over her shoulder and my dad nods. "She did. She gave me a hard time over it too and like I said, I'm happy to admit I made a mistake, but that rule book stays the same, just so we're clear on that."

Brad laughs and shakes my dad's hand and then looks at me in alarm as my dad pulls him in for a hug.

"Proud of you, son."

Camilla sniffs and Dom says loudly, "Then mum's right, we do need to crack open the champagne and toast Brad, the most unlikely entrepreneur in the family. I mean, good God…" He looks at my father apologetically, but he just shrugs, "He is actually."

Turning to Dom, he nods. "Carry on."

Dom laughs. "You've certainly shocked us this Christmas, first by actually getting a great girl like Dolly to go out with you and more than once, and secondly for shocking us with what you've really been doing. Well, I want to raise a toast to you, Brad, congratulations on growing up at last and I'm certain you will make this a success."

"To Brad." We all raise our glasses to the man who many looked past and thought a fool. Someone who had a lot to prove and took judgement and criticism with good humour. A man who has the biggest heart of anyone I know and never lets life get him down, even under the most stressful conditions and as I raise my own glass to the man I am falling head over heels with, I have everything I want in this room, except for my brother of course but in my heart, I know it won't be long before he joins us.

***

Happy Christmas and in the words of the great Dolly Parton herself…

"The way I see it, if you want the rainbow, you gotta put up with the rain!"

"If you don't like the road you're walking, start paving another one."

"You'll never do a whole lot unless you're brave enough to try."

* * *

If you missed the previous book when Sammy Jo and Florrie came to Dream Valley, you can check it out here.

Coming Home to Dream Valley

If you're keen to see what happens when the new celebrity heads to town, read on for a small taste of what's next.

EPILOGUE

NEW BEGINNINGS IN DREAM VALLEY.

SOMEWHERE FAR AWAY FROM DREAM VALLEY

The rain hasn't stopped all morning and just the gentle drip of the drops collecting in the bucket reminds me I really need a new job and fast.

Sighing, I look out of the window and watch the droplets of water running down the windowpane, matching my mood perfectly.

This is it. My life. Resigned to watching rain fall, one step away from watching paint dry.

"Miss Benson, a word, please."

Startled, I look up as my manager, Mr Henderson, there are no christian names in Pemberley Thompson, frowns down at me.

The fact he has elevated his desk onto some kind of stage in the office means he's always looking down at the workers beneath him. Not that he needs it because he does that with his supercilious expression, anyway.

"Your report is late, and you are staring out of the

CHRISTMAS IN DREAM VALLEY

window as if the answer lies there. Do we have a problem, Miss Benson, because the clock is ticking?"

Forcing myself to smile, in a professional way, of course, I nod. "I'm sorry, Mr Henderson, the report will be on your desk by close of business."

"I take it you mean, close of business today, Miss Benson, because I'm afraid you can't leave until it is. The client is counting on our professionalism in this matter and our reputation is at stake."

"Understood, Mr Henderson."

He turns away and drops behind his desk, keeping his eagle eyes on me as I bend my head to my work, feeling like a modern-day Bob Cratchit. At least that's what it feels like.

I can't recall how many months I've spent at Pemberley Thompson, but I know one thing, I need to leave for my own sanity.

I have been an assistant in a family run solicitors for too long already and aside from Mr Henderson, the only person closest in age to me is Miss Travers, who works the same job as I do. The fact that she's thirty years my senior means we don't have a lot in common and I can see myself in her shoes when she's long since retired. I will *be* Miss Travers unless I do something about it, which brings me back to the reason for my daydream in the first place.

The job application.

I saw it on my way to work this morning as I scrolled through the job adverts on my phone.

Writer requires live-in assistant for six months to assist with admin and housekeeper duties.

The pay is more than I earn here in a year, and it sounds so tempting. I could work for six months and then take six months to find another job. This could be just the break I need, except for one niggling little doubt that just won't go away.

The live-in part.

I mean, I'm not averse to trying new things but to head off to live with a man, at least I think it's a man, in a strange place for six months, screams murdering psychopath. If my mother even knew I was thinking of it, she would have a heart attack and for every reason why I should go, a hundred other reasons why I shouldn't are screaming at me.

Miss Benson.

Mr Henderson barks my name like a sergeant major and I jump as he drives his fist down on the desk.

"I will not tell you again – work!"

Pushing away the job dream, at least until my train journey home, I sigh and turn my attention to the last will and testament of Annalise Turtle.

* * *

ANNALISE TURTLE STAYS with me as I grab my coat and umbrella from the hook by the door. Turn my back on an office that drains the life from my soul every second I spend there and head out onto the busy pavement outside and start the commute home with several thousand other people who are in this rat race with me.

Is this really my life? Annalise Turtle would think me a fool. Despite how arduous my job is, I come across a superstar sometimes and none that shines as brightly as Annalise did when she was alive.

She lived alone in a huge mansion by the looks of things. Her property portfolio is admirable, and her art collection is currently on its way to Christie's. She had it all, bar one thing. A family. There were many admirers, as my mum would say. I like to think of them as lovers.

Picturing her rather hedonistic lifestyle, drifting from Monte Carlo one month to jetting off to the Caribbean the next, with a different companion each time, makes me long for a life like that. I bet she never watched rain drip down the windowpane. She would probably run outside and dance in it. Yes, Annalise Turtle had the right idea and the fact she amassed her great fortune by marriage doesn't even seem to matter to me. A steady stream of ex-husbands. The longest lasting just two years and the shortest a few weeks. A gold digger of the most successful kind, who finally enjoyed her wealth alongside young men with the same idea as she had. But she was shrewd and never married them. Preferring to play the field instead and make the most of her hard-earned fortune.

No, Annalise Turtle wasn't content with normal, ordinary or boring. She wanted it all and I should take a leaf out of her crowded little black book and do something unconventional for the first time in my life before I turn thirty.

I'm going to apply for that job as soon as I get home.

Pre-order now

THANK YOU FOR READING.

I hope you enjoyed this story and are interested to learn what happens next.

Check it out here

If you missed Cruising in Love where Sammy Jo and Florrie meet the Hudson brothers, you can check it out here.
Cruising in Love

After a happy ever disaster Florence heads off on her honeymoon cruise with her bridesmaid.

Hoping to enjoy two weeks of relaxation on an all-expenses-paid trip of a lifetime she was hoping to recharge and reflect on the cruel blow fate dealt her.

Her bridesmaid has other ideas and before she knows it, they are signed up to the ship's cruising in love programme where single passengers are paired up in a bid to find their shipmate.

Seven dates in seven days with a love match at the end and another week to get to know one another.

Will it be love at first sight or an endless round of disastrous dates with nowhere to hide?

A light-hearted romance about starting again and discovering that everything happens for a very good reason.

Thank you for reading Christmas in Dream Valley.
If you liked it, I would love if you could leave me a review, as I must do all my own advertising.

This is the best way to encourage new readers and I appreciate every review I can get. Please also recommend it to your friends as word of mouth is the best form of advertising. It won't take longer than two minutes of your time, as you only need write one sentence if you want to.

Have you checked out my website? Subscribe to keep updated with any offers or new releases.

sjcrabb.com

When you visit my website, you may be surprised because I don't just write Romantic comedy.

I also write under the pen names M J Hardy & Harper Adams. I send out a monthly newsletter with details of all my releases and any special offers but aside from that, you don't hear from me very often.

If you like social media, please follow me on mine where I am a lot more active and will always answer you if you reach out to me.

Why not take a look and see for yourself and read Lily's Lockdown, a little scene I wrote to remember the madness when the world stopped and took a deep breath?

Lily's Lockdown

More books by S J Crabb

<u>The Diary of Madison Brown</u>
My Perfect Life at Cornish Cottage
My Christmas Boyfriend
Jetsetters
More from Life
A Special Kind of Advent
Fooling in love
Will You
Holly Island
Aunt Daisy's Letter
The Wedding at the Castle of Dreams
My Christmas Romance
Escape to Happy Ever After
Cruising in Love
Coming Home to Dream Valley
Christmas in Dream Valley
New Beginnings in Dream Valley

sjcrabb.com

KEEP IN TOUCH

You can also follow me on social media below.

Facebook

Instagram

Twitter

Website

Bookbub

Amazon

Printed in Great Britain
by Amazon